"Mr. Darling, meet your shop assistant."

Words failed him. Rational thought failed him.

Those magnificent violet eyes speared him as the sheriff helped her stand so that he could free her wrists.

"*You* are Nicole O'Malley?"

"In the flesh." The perfect lips thinned with displeasure, then winced as she gingerly rubbed the skin where the rope had chafed.

Quinn winced along with her. He pinched the bridge of his nose. *Way to make a great first impression, Darling.* Then he recalled her culpability in the situation.

"Why did you attack me?" he demanded.

"I thought you were an intruder. Why did you sneak in here after hours?"

"I didn't sneak. This is my store. Besides, the door was unlocked."

The sheriff snapped his knife closed and slid it into his pocket. "I think I'll leave you two to get better acquainted." His smile was rueful as he passed Quinn. "Welcome to Gatlinburg."

Karen Kirst was born and raised in East Tennessee near the Great Smoky Mountains. A lifelong lover of books, it wasn't until after college that she had the grand idea to write one herself. Now she divides her time between being a wife, homeschooling mom and romance writer. Her favorite pastimes are reading, visiting tearooms and watching romantic comedies.

Books by Karen Kirst

Love Inspired Historical

Smoky Mountain Matches Series

The Reluctant Outlaw
The Bridal Swap
His Mountain Miss
The Husband Hunt
Married by Christmas
From Boss to Bridegroom

KAREN KIRST

From Boss to Bridegroom

◆ **HARLEQUIN**® LOVE INSPIRED® HISTORICAL

Recycling programs
for this product may
not exist in your area.

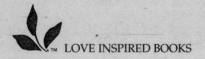 LOVE INSPIRED BOOKS

ISBN-13: 978-0-373-28308-8

From Boss to Bridegroom

www.Harlequin.com

Printed in U.S.A.

I will praise Thee; for I am fearfully and
wonderfully made: marvellous are Thy works;
and that my soul knoweth right well.
—*Psalms* 139:14

To Meredith Black—many thanks for your encouragement and sound advice.
I'm so grateful the Lord brought you into our lives.
Love you, dear friend!

Chapter One

June 1882
Gatlinburg, Tennessee

There was an intruder in the mercantile.

In her haste, Nicole O'Malley had forgotten to lock the rear entrance, and now she was alone.

While not common in this area, robberies weren't unheard of. In fact, this very store had been targeted two years ago, and her oldest sister, Juliana, kidnapped by outlaws.

A shudder ripped through her as stealthy, faltering steps echoed down the long hallway that led past the private quarters, storeroom and office to where she'd been dusting shelves in the front area of the store. Whoever had dared enter after hours was up to no good.

Alarm pooling in her belly, Nicole seized a large enamel pot from the nearest shelf and wedged herself into the narrow space between the high shelving unit and door frame. She lifted it high over her head.

Her sister had been fortunate. She'd escaped unharmed.

Would Nicole face a worse fate?

What if he had a gun? What if he shot her on sight?

That's why I have to be faster than him. Seize the element of surprise.

The footsteps neared. Paused somewhere in the vicinity of the office immediately on the other side of the doorway. Her hands curved around the pot handles until they bit into her palms. Heartbeat roaring in her ears, her arms began to tremble from the strain. The safe containing the money was in the office. If he went in there, she could try and sneak out the front entrance.

But he didn't enter the office. Instead, he stalked through the doorway. Halted inches away, hands on lean hips as he surveyed the interior. By now things like his scent—peppermint of all things—and impressive height were registering.

The intruder seemed to be cataloging the goods. What was his plan? Steal the valuables and sell them for profit?

He started to pivot in her direction, and she caught a glimpse of sleek jawline above a starched white collar. Nicole's throat closed up. She would *not* be taken hostage like Juliana. If he had time to draw his weapon, she was done for. *It's now or never.*

She swung with all her might. The impact of the heavy cookware against his head knocked him forward. He grunted, hands going up as if to defend himself from another blow.

Go. Now. The pot hit the just-swept floorboards with a dull thud. She dashed into the shadowed hallway, desperation powering her rubbery legs. A low growl cracked the air. He scrambled into the hallway after her. Without warning, strong arms stole around her waist, halting her forward movement and digging into her stomach. She was shoved face-first against the wall. His large body followed, heaving chest pinning her.

"Who? Why?" he panted against her ear, hot breath fogging her neck.

"Let me go, you ill-bred ruffian!" Raising her foot, she slammed her heel down, grinding it into his boot.

He gasped, jerked, and Nicole slipped sideways out of his grasp.

"Oh, no, you don't."

He captured her before she could put any sort of distance between them, this time seizing her arms in a painful grip. Ignoring her struggles and seething threats of retribution, the intruder propelled her into the store, snatched a silk tie from the rack on the counter and tied her wrists behind her back. Anger pulsed at her temples. "You won't get away with this," she said.

He spun her to face him, pushed her into the lone chair and, shoving aside her skirts, bound her calves to the chair legs. Insides quivering with indignation, she did everything she could to make things difficult for him. She wiggled. Strained against the ties.

When she delivered another threat, he straightened to his full height, folded his arms and glared down at her, his honey-colored eyes glittering with ill humor. "If you don't want me to gag that pretty little mouth of yours, I suggest you shut it."

A lock of jet-black hair flopped over his left eyebrow, and he shoved it back, wincing when he came into contact with what was probably a good-size knot on his head.

"I don't know what your story is, lady, but you had better hope it's a good one. You'll be telling it to the sheriff here shortly."

Her frazzled mind belatedly homed in on his accent. It wasn't the slow, easy drawl typical of East Tennessee. His words were clipped. Fast. Northern?

Dread clawed upward into her throat, nearly choking

her. *Please don't let this be who I think it is.* Nicole did a quick inventory of his appearance—quality brown leather boots peeked from beneath perfectly creased blue trousers. His navy vest and white shirt had been crafted from sturdy material. He didn't dress like a ruffian. Didn't look like one, either, with the clean shave, neat haircut and carved features. Power and authority cloaked him.

"Did you say sheriff?"

"Sure did." He jabbed a finger in the air above her nose and quirked a mocking brow. "Stay put."

Outrage flamed in her cheeks. "Wait. I can explain—"

But he was already undoing the knob lock. "Save it."

The door clicked shut behind him.

Nicole listened helplessly to the retreating footsteps of Clawson's new owner—and her new boss. She hung her head in defeat. She was never, ever going to live this down.

Quinn Darling made his way down the boardwalk, head throbbing with each step. That was a fine welcome to his brand-new life. He'd wanted change, a simpler existence than he'd led among Boston's elite. Nothing simple about being assaulted by a madwoman the second he arrived.

Gatlinburg had the appearance of a peaceful place. Majestic mountains cradled the town, green slopes cast in waning golden-orange sunlight. Businesses lined either side of Main Street, and a white church boasting stained-glass windows sat at the far end, surrounded by rolling fields and scattered tree groves.

Spotting the lone horse outside a building marked Jail, Quinn picked up his pace. His muscles ached from days of travel; his belly was protesting the long hours since lunch and his headache—compliments of *her*—had quadrupled in size. He wanted the female out of his possession so that he could unload his personal belongings and explore the store that belonged to him.

"Excuse me," he addressed the rugged, fair-headed man behind the desk. "Are you the sheriff?"

Eying Quinn, the man stood, hands perching on his gun belt. "Shane Timmons. How can I help you?"

"The name's Quinn Darling. I purchased the mercantile from Emmett Moore."

The caution in the lawman's eyes receded a little. "We've been expecting you, Mr. Darling."

"Yes, well, I've only just arrived. You can imagine my surprise when I discovered a trespasser in my store. I'd appreciate it if you'd come and fetch her."

"Her?" His lips twitched. "What does this trespasser look like?"

"Deadly." His fingers once again prodded the tender knot at the base of his skull. She knew how to put up a fight, all right. When the sheriff, who looked to be in his mid-to-late thirties, appeared to be fighting an expression of amusement, Quinn continued, "Beautiful, but in a fatal, black-widow sort of way."

"Huh." Unhooking his Stetson from the chair back, Timmons nodded to the door. "Let's go take a look."

They crossed the nearly deserted street. The few remaining stragglers openly stared. "Do you have a lot of crime here?"

The lawman shot him an enigmatic look. "Depends."

"On what exactly?"

"On what you'd describe as a lot."

Hardly a helpful answer. Emmett Moore had assured him Gatlinburg was an ideal place to set down roots, find a God-fearing wife and pursue a new and different lifestyle—one where friendships weren't based on business connections or social standing or amount of accumulated wealth. He hadn't said a word about crime being an issue.

Too late now. Quinn kept his silence as they approached the entrance.

When they entered the darkened area, his captive jerked her head up, expressive eyes wide and accusing. Sheriff Timmons took one look at her, shook his head and strode to the nearest window, yanking the thick curtain open with a snap. Soft evening light spilled into the space, giving Quinn a much clearer view of the woman in the chair.

He sucked in a breath. If he hadn't just tussled with the little wildcat, he might've been duped into thinking her a complete innocent. Maybe it was the bride-white dress. Or the youthful perfection of her skin, like finest alabaster, in direct contrast to the thick mane of glossy raven curls spilling from their pins and framing her delicate face. Her eyes were an unusual color a man wouldn't soon forget—lavender ringed with deep violet—accentuated by a fringe of thick, inky lashes and topped with sweeping, elegant brows. Her dainty, bow-shaped mouth added to the illusion of innocence.

Timmons somberly bent to unknot the silk ties at her legs. Her lashes swept down and hot color surged in her cheeks. Quinn studiously avoided looking at the layers of snowy-white petticoats. In the heat of the struggle, his focus had been on restraining his assailant, not whether or not his actions were that of a gentleman.

"You might want to interrogate her before you release her. This one's unpredictable." In addition to the knot on his head, his toes would likely sport a nasty bruise, thanks to her.

"No need. This here isn't a petty thief." Shane paused, amusement twinkling in his blue eyes. "Mr. Darling, meet your shop assistant."

Words failed him. Rational thought failed him.

Those magnificent violet eyes speared him as the sheriff helped her stand so that he could free her wrists.

"*You* are Nicole O'Malley?"

"In the flesh." The perfect lips thinned with displeasure, then winced as she gingerly rubbed the skin where the ties had chafed.

Quinn winced along with her. He pinched the bridge of his nose. *Way to make a great first impression, Darling.* Then he recalled her culpability in the situation.

"Why did you attack me?" he demanded.

"I thought you were an intruder. Why did you sneak in here after hours?"

"I didn't sneak. This is my store. Besides, the door was unlocked."

"I think I'll leave you two to get better acquainted." The sheriff's smile was rueful as he passed Quinn. "Welcome to Gatlinburg."

Placing the ties atop a wooden counter worn smooth from years of transactions, she attempted to divest the material of the wrinkles with the press of her hands. He attempted to ignore the contrast of jet curls against milky skin.

"You're three days late," she said.

"An unavoidable delay." Irritation sharpened his words. None of his previous employees had dared question him. But after this regrettable first meeting, he supposed he owed her an explanation. "My wagon suffered a broken axle. I assume Emmett and his wife have already left?"

"You assume correctly."

"That is unfortunate. For both our sakes."

She finally gifted him with her attention. "How so?"

"Because that leaves you to give me the grand tour."

Her hands stilled atop the lengths of silk. "I have no say in the matter, do I?"

"You *are* in my employ." He did nothing to mask the challenge in his tone. Had Nicole O'Malley spoken to Emmett Moore this way? Or was it just him and the fact he'd tied her up invoking this attitude?

Her stiff spine stiffened a fraction more. Her glare could've frozen the rain-swollen river out back. "You manhandled me."

Now would be a good time to point out he'd merely been reacting to the threat he'd perceived in her. His mother had reared him to be a gentleman, however, and so he refrained. "I apologize."

She considered him for a long moment, dipping her head as if she were a duchess and he a lowly estate servant. "I suppose I owe you an apology, as well."

Quinn bit the inside of his cheek to keep from retorting. He wasn't at his best right this minute…travel weary, hungry and hurting. Tomorrow would mark a new beginning between them. For now, he merely wanted to see his store.

Abandoning the ties, Miss O'Malley gestured to the long counter topped with glass display cases. "As you can see, we keep the more expensive items under lock and key. Silver, crystal, jewelry." Pivoting neatly, she gestured to the shelving units running the length of the walls on either side of the hallway door. The bottom half consisted of closed cabinets and drawers, while the top half was all open shelves. "And here we have a vast assortment of goods."

Quinn walked slowly past her, his attention on the haphazard collection of canned foods, boxes of wafers and cookies, tableware and linens. Mantel clocks and kerosene lamps perched on the top ledge. When he reached the end, he opened the nearest drawer and frowned at the mess of paper scraps and writing instruments. "Why isn't the merchandise more organized?"

"Order and neatness weren't among Emmett's strengths."

Posture proud and regal-like, she folded her hands amongst her lace-scalloped skirts. While she'd spoken without censure and her expression revealed not a hint of disdain, he sensed Miss O'Malley didn't approve of the former owner's management.

"It's been this way for as long as I can remember," she added. "The arrangement may not make sense, but the customers know where to find everything."

Quinn approached, stopping closer than necessary simply to gauge her reaction. She didn't retreat. Her lips tightened in disapproval or dislike, he couldn't tell which.

"Show me more."

Again, the royal-like dip of her head. Adjectives scrolled through his mind and, as was his custom upon meeting new people, he began a mental list of attributes. *Reserved. Prickly. Beautiful.* Too bad that last one didn't appear to extend beyond the surface.

Moving between the two counters, she led him down three side-by-side aisles crammed with a variety of goods—tools, animal traps, ready-made clothing, toys, books and paper products, barrels packed with pickles, flour, sugar and crackers and more. A woodstove occupied the far back corner, surrounded by several chairs and a spittoon. A checker set perched atop an upturned barrel.

"What is this?"

"This is where our male customers gather."

Dark tobacco stains marred the floorboards, indicating not everyone had good aim. The upscale Boston establishments his family had frequented would never have allowed such a thing. "How often?"

"Whenever we're open."

Quinn blinked, searched her face for a sign she was merely jesting. There was none. "Do you mean they gather here every day?"

"Every single one."

"Are we talking an hour or two in the afternoons?"

"No, they pretty much hang around from dawn to dusk."

"Let me get this straight—these men sit here for countless hours, disrupting the flow of foot traffic and taking up valuable space that could be used to house more items? And that was acceptable to the Moores?"

"It's the way things have always been done. Besides, they're harmless."

She refolded a calico shirt on a display table piled with neat stacks of ready-made clothing that likely didn't bear the Darling name. While his family's garment factories currently supplied the Northern states, his father had plans to expand in the future. There was no question of the venture failing. Anything Edward Darling put his hand to succeeded.

Clawson's Mercantile in the Tennessee mountains was far removed from Boston and the Darling empire, however. His father had nothing to do with it. Whether it failed or flourished was entirely up to Quinn. For the first time in his adult life, he had something entirely his own. This store was his chance to prove to himself that he was capable.

"Not everyone lives close by. Some customers travel an entire day to get here. This is where they catch up on local happenings and reconnect with old friends."

If Quinn had arrived before Emmett's departure, he could've discussed this and much more with him. The delay had cost him. He ran a finger along the cold metal stove that wouldn't be lit for many months.

"Simply because something has gone on for a long time doesn't mean it can't be changed." *Never be afraid of change, son. Be bold but prudent.* Quinn may have earned a business degree from Harvard, but his practical knowledge he'd gleaned from working side by side with his father. He gestured to the chairs. "These are going away."

She looked at him as though he'd suggested they set up a piano in the corner and hire saloon girls to sing for the customers. "Where will the men meet together?"

"I saw a café across the street. Let the owner of that establishment deal with them."

"You can't do this."

"The last I checked, my name was on the deed. I can and I will."

"Have you ever managed a store before?"

Not accustomed to having his competence called into question, he retorted, "Until recent weeks, I was second in command of the Darling empire—a garment production business that supplies much of the Northeast. I believe I can manage to operate a small country store."

Her smirk poked holes in his calm demeanor, allowing tendrils of irritation to curl into his chest. He inhaled deeply, the odd mixture of scents around him—leather, the vinegar-laced smell of pickled fish, the fruity tang of plug tobacco—reminding him of why he was here. For change. A simpler life. A chance to carve his own way in the world, to prove to himself he could succeed apart from everything his father had built.

One prickly shop assistant would not mar this experience for him.

She brushed past him, snowy skirts whispering as she rounded the last aisle and pointed to the low cushioned benches beneath the windows flanking the front door. "This is where the ladies socialize. I suppose you want to be rid of these, too."

Wonderful. More people gossiping instead of shopping.

"I don't object to customers resting for a few moments. The benches stay. For now."

Her displeasure was written across her features.

"How long have you worked here, Miss O'Malley?"

"Since January."

Six months. Enough time for her to become accustomed to conducting business in accordance with Emmett Moore's policies. No doubt she wouldn't welcome his views. She would simply have to accept that he was in charge. If she couldn't adapt to his approach to the business, she could always quit.

Spinning on her heel, she led the way as they retraced their steps. When they reached the row of candy-filled glass containers, he lifted one of the lids and snagged two peppermint sticks. After popping one in his mouth, he offered the other to her.

Her serious gaze shifted between the candy and his face. "No, thank you."

"Free of charge, of course." He waved it beneath her nose, interested to see if she'd accept.

"Sugar is bad for your teeth."

He removed the minty stick from his mouth and grinned. "I've been partial to sweets since boyhood. Does it look like my teeth have suffered?"

Startled by the question, she gave them a cursory glance. "Uh, they appear to be in fine condition."

"See? No harm in indulging yourself every now and then." He extended the candy once more.

She was loath to take it, that much was clear. She did, though, in order to appease him. The graze of her fingertips across his palm arrowed into his chest, and the urge to capture her hand in his caught him unawares.

"Thank you," she murmured.

Deliberately stepping away, he didn't draw attention to

the fact she didn't immediately sample the treat and, instead, held it awkwardly at her side. Turning back to survey the store that was nothing like he'd imagined, he said, "I suggest you prepare yourself, Miss O'Malley. There will be changes ahead."

"You should prepare yourself, as well, Mr. Darling." Retrieving a bead-encrusted reticule from a drawer, she deposited the peppermint inside. "The response to your changes may not be what you expect or desire."

Chapter Two

The moment she spotted her new boss conversing with her cousin Caleb, Nicole's already nervous stomach squeezed into a hard knot beneath her sternum. Pace slowing, she toyed with the idea of feigning illness. Humiliation surged. She'd replayed last evening's events a thousand times and it never got any better.

"Mornin', Miss Nicole," old Martin Walton called from the rear door of the barbershop. "You're lookin' as fresh as a flower today. When are you gonna find a man and settle down?"

"When I find one as worthy as you, which we both know is highly unlikely."

He grinned, revealing crooked teeth, and went back to sweeping. "You might be surprised."

With a wave, she continued on her way. It was a familiar conversation. He was kind, harmless, his teasing lacking bite. The sight of his stooped frame in the barbershop never failed to strike her as out of place, though. In her mind, the shop would always belong to Tom Leighton, a close friend of their family. Tom had abruptly left Gatlinburg back in April, and her younger sister, Jane, had yet to recover.

Nicole envied Tom. He'd escaped this town, something she yearned to do, had been set to do when a shortcut through the woods six months ago altered her life. Her plan of opening her own dress shop in Knoxville had had to be postponed, at least until she figured things out. *If* she ever figured them out.

As she made her way along the riverbank, a gentle, honeysuckle-scented breeze caressed her cheeks. Down below, the greenish water gurgled lazily along, a family of brown-tufted ducks skimming the opaque surface. The mercantile's springhouse sprawled at the water's edge. Constructed of river rock and kept cool by the rushing water, it was the perfect place to store perishable items such as the milk and cheese supplied by her Uncle Sam's dairy. Caleb made deliveries several times a week.

"Nicki."

Her cousin knew perfectly well she despised the shortened version of her name and yet insisted on using it. "Morning, Caleb."

Briefly greeting his horses, Midnight and Chance, she used the wagon bed as a barrier between her and the two men. They were surprisingly similar in coloring…inkyblack hair, brown eyes and sun-kissed skin. But where Caleb was scruffy, his hair slightly mussed, Quinn Darling was as neat as a pin. His clothing bore the mark of wealth, his bearing that of privilege. He looked rested this morning, hair slicked off his face and lean cheeks freshly shaved.

She wondered if his head was paining him. Not that she planned on putting voice to a question that would call forth the embarrassing incident.

Arms folded, wearing a grin that stretched from ear to ear, Caleb hooked a thumb at the man beside him. "Quinn told me about your meeting last night."

Her heart sank. Quinn's eyes—a shade lighter than Caleb's—crinkled with mischief. How dare he smile at her after deliberately relating embarrassing details?

"Nicole was a knowledgeable tour guide."

What all had he told him? Quinn's intent regard smacked of smug arrogance. Her palms itched to slap it right off. The man knew absolutely nothing about her!

"Nicki is nothing if not professional," Caleb said.

Ha! If he could only read her thoughts right this moment...

Pushing off the wagon bed, Caleb held his hand out to Quinn. "It's a pleasure doing business with you. I've got to get home and check on my wife."

"Oh, is she ill?" Concern pulled his brows together.

"Not in the normal sense of the word." A proud grin flashed. "She's expecting our first child this fall. She tends to overdo it."

"Rebecca's aware of her limitations," Nicole pointed out. "You're being overprotective."

"One day you'll have a husband who dotes on you, Nicki. I guarantee you'll relish every minute of it."

Nicole squeezed the reticule in her hands until the beading bit into her palms. Acutely aware of Quinn's scrutiny, she tipped her chin up. "You're speaking fairy tales, cousin."

"I don't think so. Remember what I said about making plans for your life?" He winked, the scarred flesh around his eye stretching.

How could she forget? The recent conversation plagued her in the oddest moments. Their extensive family had been gathered at his parents' home. When she'd expressed her firm intentions to wait for marriage and children until she'd achieved success with her seamstress shop, a venture that could take years, he'd loudly announced his expectation that her plans would fall apart. *In their hearts humans plan their course, but the Lord establishes their steps.* The verse he'd quoted refused to leave her, raising questions she wasn't brave enough to face.

"Goodbye, Caleb."

He tipped his hat and grinned. "I'll tell Becca you said hello." Swinging up onto the seat, he released the brake and set the wagon in motion.

All too soon, she and Quinn were left to stare at each other. He did a slow inspection. Confidence in sadly low amounts that morning, she'd dressed in one of her favorite outfits, a lavender dress adorned with deep purple ribbons.

"You look to have suffered no ill effects from our confrontation," he said.

His features portrayed nothing of his thoughts, not appreciation or distaste. Nothing, which left her feeling unbalanced. Hefting a round of paper-wrapped cheese beneath one arm, he held out the other for her. "Shall we go inside?"

Loath to touch him, Nicole adopted a similarly bland expression and forced her bare fingers to his forearm. The heat and strength of corded muscle bled through his shirt's fine material. Shock shimmered through her as the totally inappropriate urge to explore his physique surged. Close contact with men was limited to her uncle and cousins, and much of the time she succeeded in keeping them at arm's length. This touch, though impersonal, ricocheted through her defenses and opened up a yawning cavern of inconvenient awareness.

I don't need anyone. She'd been telling herself that since the moment she realized she was different and no matter how hard she tried, she would never measure up to her sisters.

She focused on the narrow steps. "What exactly did you tell Caleb?"

"You have no cause to worry, Miss O'Malley. Despite what you might think, I am a man of discretion. It would not be in either of our best interests if the details of our… misunderstanding were to be revealed. Especially in my case, considering I'm a newcomer and in need of earning the locals' trust and respect if I am to be successful in this venture."

The tension she'd experienced since first spotting her cousin eased somewhat. Neither she nor Quinn planned to speak of the incident. And Shane Timmons was not what one would call a gossip. Like herself, the sheriff was a loner, a private man not given to conversation. No one would learn of the incident from him. And perhaps, given enough time, she'd manage to look her boss in the eye and not remember their initial encounter

"Will I be meeting any more O'Malley family members?"

"I come from a large family, so it's unavoidable."

She felt his appraising side glance. "How large?"

"Caleb is the youngest of three. Josh is the eldest, and Nathan is the middle son. All three are married. Their parents, my uncle Sam and aunt Mary, have a farm close to town."

"What about you? Any brothers or sisters?"

"Four sisters. Two older, two younger." Might as well prepare him. "All possessed of beauty, grace, generosity of spirit and keen intelligence. My sisters are not only admired by the locals, they are upheld as the epitome of what a female should be."

At the top of the stairs, she snatched her hand free and waited for him to open the door. Hand resting on the knob, he studied her. "You excluded yourself in the description. Are you not upheld as the epitome of female desirability?"

Nicole swallowed the familiar bitterness, aware it was unbecoming and futile. She'd stopped questioning God a long time ago. "You will come to discover that I am nothing like my sisters, Mr. Darling."

He opened his mouth to speak again, thought better of it and wordlessly opened the door, allowing her to enter first. Glancing into the private quarters on her left, she noticed Ruthanne had left the cheerful red-checked curtains behind, no doubt for Quinn Darling's benefit.

For what must be the umpteenth time since learning of their plans to move east, Nicole wished Emmett and Ruthanne could've remained here. While absentminded and a bit disorganized, Emmett had been a kind and understanding boss. The practical knowledge she'd gained in her employment here would benefit her in the running of her own shop. In a different town, where no one knew her or her family.

He must've noticed the direction of her gaze, for he gestured to the pile of trunks shoved beneath the window. "The space is hardly large enough to accommodate one person. Not sure how the Moores were able to make it work as long as they did. Are you aware of any land parcels or homes for sale? I would like to pursue a permanent residence as soon as possible."

Continuing into the long, windowless office, she slipped her reticule from her wrist and stored it in the top left desk drawer. "Maybe you should hold off until you're sure you want to stay. Gatlinburg can't possibly compare to Boston."

"That's the reason I chose it."

"Why Tennessee? Why this store? You aren't related to Emmett or Ruthanne."

"Not family, but they are friends of my father." Setting the cheese atop the paper-littered desk, he folded his arms and leaned forward at the waist. "Can you keep a secret, Miss O'Malley?"

His lithe, powerful body blocked the exit, and, despite not being claustrophobic, she felt his nearness suck the air from the tight space and render her light-headed. She now knew what a cornered animal felt like.

"I'm not a gossip, Mr. Darling."

"Somehow I sensed that about you." He edged even closer, lowered his voice to a confidential whisper. "The reason I came here was to avoid the authorities. You see, I—I killed a man. Shot him point-blank. It was self-defense, but I don't have evidence to back my claim. You won't tell anyone, will you? I hear prison food is deplorable. And I doubt the beds are comfortable."

"I—" Completely breathless now, Nicole pressed a trembling hand to her throat. For a couple of seconds, she actually believed him. Then she noticed the upward tug at the corner of his sculpted mouth, the muted sparkle at the back of his eyes.

He was making fun of her, the suave, worldly-wise Northerner toying with the naive mountain girl. Well, she received enough mockery from the local thickheaded males. She wasn't about to put up with it from Quinn Darling, boss or no boss.

Chin up, she stepped forward. "Let me pass."

His brows shot to his hairline. Turning sideways, he did as she asked. She turned in the direction of the rear exit.

"Where are you going?"

At his curious, bordering-on-nervous tone, Nicole smiled to herself as she strode down the hallway. "To pay Sheriff Timmons a visit. I'm afraid I can't keep your secret, Mr. Darling. I refuse to work for a cold-blooded murderer."

Catching up to her, he snagged her arm. "Wait."

Memories of what had occurred in this hallway less than twenty-four hours ago overtook her—him imprisoning her against the wall, her pitiful efforts to fight back. She shook them off with effort. *What's wrong with me? Why am I allowing him to get to me?*

"It was a joke, Miss O'Malley." His smile begged forgiveness, the look in his eyes expectant, confident of her reaction. "You will find being outrageous is one of my many faults. I blame it on having a gullible younger sister."

The man's charm and good looks might've proved a lethal combination were she not dead set on a course free of romantic entanglements. "Since I only just met you yesterday, and that meeting left much to be desired, you'll understand my need to consult with Shane on this, see if there are any wanted posters bearing your likeness."

His smile remained, but unease flickered in his expression. "You can't be serious."

"What would you do in my position?" she asked innocently, enjoying seeing him squirm.

"I cannot have a rumor such as that running rampant in this community."

"It's no fun being made to feel a fool, is it, Mr. Darling?"

His gaze scoured her face, searching intently, the tension ebbing from his stance.

"Life is short, Miss O'Malley," he murmured silkily, tapping her lightly on the nose. "You should learn to take it less seriously. And the next time you are tempted to lay the blame of our unfortunate first meeting at my feet, keep in mind that it was *you* who ambushed *me*."

Nicole floundered for an appropriate response. He baited her, and yet *she* was the one who needed to loosen up? She wanted nothing more than to ram that arrogant condescension down his throat.

Pounding on the front door startled them both. Fishing a polished pocket watch from his navy vest, he frowned. "We don't open for another half hour. Is this a usual occurrence?"

"No. Suppliers making deliveries use the rear entrance."

"I had better go see what our early visitor wants."

Curious, Nicole trailed behind him. She didn't at first recognize the hulking form through the glass. His long strides eating up the space, Quinn flipped the lock to admit the older man.

"Good morning, sir. Please, come in. How can I be of assistance?"

"Who are you?" he snapped from the other side of the door. "Where's Mr. Moore?"

That voice. She knew it from somewhere.

"The Moores have moved to Virginia, and I am the new proprietor of this mercantile. The name's Quinn Darling. It is a pleasure to welcome you, Mr.—"

The man entered. Snatching the battered hat off his head and mopping his unruly silver hair out of his eyes, he shot her a dismissive glance. "Carl Simmerly."

The face combined with the name weakened her knees, and she braced her hands against the counter for support. He had come back.

Out of the corner of his eye, Quinn noticed his assistant's brittle armor had shattered. Hunched over the counter, she watched the stranger with wide, flustered eyes, the swirl of violet stark against moon-white skin. Interesting.

"I wanna post this notice." Mr. Simmerly thrust a wrinkled paper into Quinn's hands.

Quickly scanning the scrawled writing, his concern grew. This man was searching for his missing children, a fifteen-year-old girl and seventeen-year-old boy. "Your children have been missing a long time."

The bulky man's lined jaw worked. "Going on six months now. I'm desperate to find them."

A quiet gasp came from Miss O'Malley's direction. Averting her face, she fiddled with the roll of brown paper used to wrap purchases.

Quinn motioned to the board where news postings were hung. "Of course. I'll post this right away."

"My place is on the outskirts of the next town, Pigeon Forge, so I can't get here as often as I'd like. I plan to return next Saturday to see if anyone has come forward with information."

"You have my prayers, Mr. Simmerly."

His mouth tightened in a way that made Quinn think he didn't appreciate the sentiment. As a fairly new Christian and filled with enthusiasm concerning his relationship with his Creator, he couldn't fathom anyone not wanting divine assistance.

With a curt nod, Carl Simmerly stuffed his hat on his head and bustled out the door, the bell's ring loud in the wake of his departure.

"Can I see that?"

Pivoting, Quinn handed her the posting, observing her features as she read the descriptions. Her glossy curls had been tamed into submission, and the lavender confection she was wearing the perfect foil for her skin. Dressed as she was, his assistant could've easily fit on the streets of Boston or the upscale mansions his family and friends' families owned. She certainly wasn't what he'd expected a simple mountain girl to be like.

Miss O'Malley's lower lip trembled. She bit down hard on it. The action momentarily paralyzed him.

There was no denying she was an exquisite creature, her

loveliness without rival, and as the eldest heir in the promi-
nent Darling family, he'd known his share of beauties. But
she was not the uncomplicated, sweet-natured woman he
craved in a wife. He'd had enough of difficult women.

"I'll put this with the others," she said at last, moving to
an area on the wall where different notices had been nailed.

Leaving her to scan the notices, Quinn tugged open the
scratchy wool curtains. Beyond the glass, several horses
and riders traveled down sun-washed Main Street. Excitement peppered with trepidation balled in his gut. How
would his first day go? He may have held the second in
command position at Darling Industries, but he had no
firsthand experience with patrons. *Lord, please give me
guidance and wisdom.*

"Have you seen Mr. Simmerly before?"

Heading for the counter, she paused to straighten a stack
of catalogs. "A couple of times around town. Why do you
ask?"

"His presence seemed to distress you."

Without looking at him, she continued between the
counters and, stopping before a row of aprons, chose a
black one and slipped it over her head. She deftly tied
the strings behind her waist. "You're imagining things.
That knock on the head must've hindered your senses,
Mr. Darling."

He didn't believe that for one moment, but as they were
set to open shortly, he let the matter drop. Snatching a
lemon drop from the glass containers, he leaned a hip
against the shelving unit and sucked on the sugary treat.
"Mr. and Miss are too formal for my taste. Do you have
any objections to the use of given names?"

"You want me to call you Quinn—" her lips parted "—in
front of the customers?"

"Or Darling, if you'd prefer."

At her incredulous expression, a chuckle slipped between his lips. The woman had absolutely no sense of humor. Teasing her was going to make this venture that much more enjoyable.

Chapter Three

"Such a pretty fabric." Nicole folded the yards of green paisley within the confines of the paper length and tied it up with string. "You've chosen well, Mrs. Kirkpatrick. Will you be making a dress for yourself?"

The elderly lady nodded, gray eyes optimistic behind thick spectacles. "I'm not as gifted with a needle as you are," she said, eyeing Nicole's lavender shirtwaist enhanced with delicate black stitching and buttons. "But hopefully the dress will look decent once I'm finished."

Making note of her purchase in the ledger, Nicole slid the package across the counter and smiled. The sweet widow was one of her favorite customers. "I can't wait to see the finished product, Mrs. Kirkpatrick. And thank you for your patience."

Hugging her purchase to her chest, Mrs. Kirkpatrick slid a dubious glance at the other length of the counter, to where Quinn was supposedly helping James Canton. Judging by James's disgusted expression and the way Quinn pinched the bridge of his nose in frustration, he wasn't helping much.

"Maybe you should lend him a hand."

Nicole considered this. He'd made it clear managing a country store was well within his capabilities, hadn't he?

When the group of elderly gentlemen in the far corner erupted into laughter, and her boss winced as if in physical pain, she gave in to the pulse of compassion. He'd obviously changed his mind about evicting the checker players. She could afford to help him out.

"I suppose you're right. Have a good evening."

"See you in church tomorrow morning." She bustled toward the exit.

Quinn was glaring at the cages on the counter and the squawking chickens inside. "Need some assistance?"

Despite a long and trying first day, he looked decidedly unruffled save for the hint of uncertainty in his aristocratic features. He was good under pressure, she'd give him that.

"I would appreciate it."

To James, she said, "Are you buying these chickens or selling?"

"Selling." He looked relieved to be dealing with someone who knew what they were doing.

Hefting the oversize ledger onto the counter beside the cages, she flipped through the pages until she found his name. Quinn watched as she inserted the value of his chickens into the first column.

"Will you be purchasing anything today?"

"A pound of sugar is all."

"I'll get that for you." To Quinn, she said, "Normally we'd put these chickens outside on the boardwalk for customers to see, but since we're closing in thirty minutes, we'll store them in the barn out back. Would you mind taking them out there while I finish up this transaction?"

"Not at all." He reached for the cages. His smile had a grim turn to it. "I apologize for your wait, Mr. Canton.

Please tell your boy to help himself to a bag of penny candy free of charge."

James's brows went up at that. At his young son's hopeful grin, he nodded his acquiescence. "Much obliged, Mr. Darling."

Quinn walked out, cages held away from his body as if the chickens were diseased. Fighting the urge to roll her eyes, Nicole readied the sugar and waited patiently for the little boy to decide which candy he wanted. After father and son left, she assisted two other customers, then went to flip the sign over. The trio in the corner shuffled out. Quickly sliding the lock into place, she retrieved her basket from beneath the office desk and rushed to fill it. A wedge of cheese, a tin of peaches, a sack of dried pinto beans. She frowned at the nearly empty produce bins. It was too early in the year for most fruits and vegetables. A delicious-looking batch of asparagus had come in that morning but was too expensive for her budget.

The rear door opened. Nicole dashed into the office and returned her basket to its spot. Pulling the palm-size ledger from the desk drawer, she was inserting the items she'd just taken and the cost of each when her boss stepped into the doorway.

Half sitting on the desk so that his muscled thigh nearly brushed her arm, he smiled ruefully down at her. "You were amazing today, Nicole. In his letters, Emmett indicated how valuable you were to this business. Now that I've watched you in action, I can see he was right."

She stared at him. His masculine appeal, his succinct accent pronouncing her name, rendered her mute. Quinn was sophistication personified, yet there was a rugged strength beneath the fine appearance and expensive clothing.

"You were efficient," he went on. "Civil to the customers, in some cases anticipating their needs." His lower leg swung back and forth, stirring her skirts. "That is something you won't find in Boston's finer establishments."

Irritated that he affected her at all, she laid her pencil down and arched a single brow. "I'm surprised you'd find anything to impress you in our crude little backwoods store."

His leg ceased its motion. "I'm curious. Do you find it difficult to accept compliments in general or is it me that is the problem?"

Nicole's jaw sagged a little at his bluntness. "Do you always speak exactly what's on your mind, Mr. Darling?"

"It's Quinn, remember? And I asked you first."

Replacing the ledger, she pushed to her feet. "I don't have time for witty banter, Quinn." She winced at the informality. "I have floors to sweep, merchandise to straighten and work awaiting me when I get home." Once her errand had been completed, of course.

When she made to move past him, his fingers closed over her wrist. "What sort of work?"

"If you must know, I'm a seamstress. I have dress orders to fill. Trousers that need adjusting."

A line appeared between his brows. "Go home. I will tend to the cleaning."

Heat spread outward from his touch, delaying her response. "Y-you don't have to do that."

"I know, but you did the lion's share of the work today because I hadn't a clue what I was doing. I was sorely out of my element. Which brings me to my request."

He was readily admitting his shortcomings? "What sort of request?"

Laughing, he said, "Do not look at me as if I am about to suggest something improper."

Smoothing her features, Nicole extracted her arm from his hold. "What then?"

"You obviously know what you're doing around here. I had planned to arrive in time for Emmett to show me the ropes, but since I wasn't able to, I wonder if you would be willing to tutor me."

The prospect of spending even a minute more than necessary in Quinn's company did not appeal to her in the slightest. Despite the humble nature of his request, his self-important air remained intact—no doubt a result of living a privileged, entitled life typical of the wealthy. Worse than that, he seemed to gain a great deal of pleasure from provoking her. Something she could do without.

But how was she to refuse him? If he didn't learn to run the store, hectic, chaotic days like today would become the norm.

"Fine. I'll do it."

"Wonderful. Do you have time tomorrow after church?"

Nicole thought of the sewing projects she really needed to complete. "I will give you two hours. No more."

His blinding grin served to enhance his good looks, if that were even possible. "You are a jewel."

Quinn couldn't stop staring at the jarring sight of his prickly, reserved assistant cradling a slumbering infant in her arms. The church service had drawn to a close, and folks were gathering their things and making their way along the aisles to the exit, stopping to exchange pleasantries here and there. Nicole was standing against the right wall near the piano. Sunlight streamed through the stained-glass window behind her, bathing her in an ethereal glow. That wasn't what had arrested his attention, however. It was the way she was looking at that baby.

Gone was the cool detachment, the wariness that typically marked her delicate features, and in its place was a vulnerability, a tenderness that made Quinn feel as if he were intruding on a private moment. He'd only just met her, but he knew instinctively she would not be pleased to know her inner emotions were on display.

A heavy hand clapped onto his shoulder, and he turned to see Shane Timmons. He looked slightly less dangerous this morning, blond hair brushed off his forehead and hard cheeks free of scruff.

"Afternoon, Sheriff."

Memories of their last interaction pushed to the forefront of his mind. He imagined the sheriff had had a good, long laugh over his and Nicole's misunderstanding.

"Call me Shane." He removed his hand. "How are you settling in? Did you get things cleared up with Nicole?" Subtle humor lit his assessing blue gaze.

"I suspect it will take some time to settle in. And for her to forgive me for trussing her up like a common thief."

Nodding, Shane's attention swiveled to the object of their conversation. She was still standing apart from the people he assumed were her family members. A lone buoy in a swirling sea of humanity. Was that her doing or theirs? *Why do I care?*

"Nicole is…" Shane trailed off, rubbed his chin in thought.

"Prickly? Difficult? Completely lacking a sense of humor?"

His brow quirked. "I was gonna say hard to get to know. She strikes me as one of those women who'd be worth the effort, though."

Quinn ran his fingers along the spine of his brand-new Bible. He wasn't sure he agreed with the other man's assessment. "Sometimes a man gets burned for his trouble."

Before Shane could respond, the reverend joined them

and welcomed Quinn to town. When there was a break in the conversation, Quinn made his excuses and worked his way through the pews to Nicole's side.

As if sensing his approach, she lifted her head, shoulders tensing when she spotted him. Her countenance transformed into something statue-like. Emotionless. Her eyes were a deep, bruised purple in her pale face, perhaps an effect of the jet-black material of the formfitting, cap-sleeved blouse she'd paired with full purple-and-black-striped skirts. A small black hat perched atop her upswept curls.

Quinn considered tweaking the single rogue tendril caressing her cheek simply to see her reaction. "I didn't figure you for the maternal type," he said in the way of greeting.

He instantly regretted the comment, could see in her pained expression that his observation stung. Before he could backtrack, she leveled a frosty glare at him. "I'm not. That doesn't mean I can't enjoy other people's children, however."

He turned his attention to the light-haired infant resting comfortably in her arms. "What is his name?"

"*Her* name is Victoria," she responded in a softer tone. "She's my cousin Josh's daughter."

Reaching out, Quinn lightly skimmed the downy soft hair. "She's family, then."

Subtly returning his attention to Nicole, he watched her watch the baby, intrigued when her guard slipped again and she went soft before his eyes. If she ever were to look at a man like that…

A tall man with a goatee, accompanied by a sophisticated young woman with hair the color of chocolate and intelligent green eyes, rounded the pew.

"We should get this little princess home before she wakes up and demands to be fed."

Nicole carefully transferred the infant to her father's arms, tucking the blanket about her small body. "Josh, have you met Quinn Darling?"

Measuring blue eyes slid to his. He nodded a greeting. "Pleased to meet you. This is my wife, Kate."

"A pleasure to meet you," Quinn shook her proffered hand. "That is one beautiful baby."

"Thank you. We think so, too." The smile Kate directed at her husband was at once peaceful and adoring.

At the look passing between husband and wife, Quinn experienced a twinge of jealousy. Thoughts of settling down and starting a family of his own had been plaguing him of late. Since accepting Christ six months ago, he'd begun to pray for a wife of God's choosing. He wanted what his parents had—a loving partnership based on trust and true companionship—a rare occurrence in his high-society world where many marriages resembled business transactions.

"You're the owner of the furniture store?" He addressed Josh.

"That's right. Kate runs her photography business out of the same space if you're ever in need of a photo."

"No plans to hang one of myself on the wall, but I'll keep it in mind for when my family visits. I peeked at your inventory through the window. Impressive selection."

Nicole's expression challenged him. "He's crafted every single item in that shop by hand. The locals prefer his furniture to those available through mail-order catalogs."

Hugging his daughter to his chest, Josh shifted uncomfortably. "Obviously, I can't supply every item those large companies offer."

Quinn aimed a wide grin at his assistant, letting her

know the dig didn't sting. "In business, competition is un-avoidable. It isn't always a bad thing."

Her gaze slid away from his, but not before he caught the flare of displeasure.

Kate tugged on Josh's sleeve. "We should go."

"I'm sure I'll see you around," the other man said to Quinn.

As soon as the couple headed for the exit, a pair of flame-haired, green-eyed twins flanked Nicole. "Aren't you going to introduce us?" This from the one in green.

With a resigned sigh, Nicole said, "Quinn Darling, meet my younger sisters, Jane and Jessica."

"I'm Jessica." The one who had spoken grinned cheekily, jammed a finger in the other twin's direction. "She's Jane."

"How do you do." Jane, dressed in head-to-toe blue, spoke in a more demure fashion.

"Pleased to meet you both," he said, unsure if he'd ever be able to tell them apart.

"Don't forget me." A petite young woman with a mass of white-blond ringlets crowded in beside the blue twin. She thrust out her hand. "Hi, I'm Megan. I'm the second oldest. That's my husband over there, Lucian Beaumont."

Quinn followed her gaze to a tall, distinguished man with olive skin and dark, wavy hair. Nicole hadn't been kidding when she'd said the O'Malley family was exten-sive.

"We have another sister, Juliana, who lives in Cades Cove with her husband and young son."

Shaking her hand, Quinn studied their faces. While Megan and the twins did not share the same coloring, they had the same cheekbones, nose and chin. Nicole looked nothing like them.

"Do you and Juliana look alike?" He posed the ques-tion to her.

Indefinable emotion darkened her eyes. "No."

Megan shook her head, setting her curls to bouncing. "Juliana and the twins look very much alike. Nicole and I are the odd ones."

The look Nicole shot her bordered on accusing. "You are not the odd one. You all have the same facial structure. I don't look like any of you." To Quinn, she said, "My mother assures me I wasn't found in the vegetable patch. I have my doubts, however."

The twin in green…Jessica, he thought it was, chuckled. "We like to joke that Nicole is a long-lost princess."

"Jessica," her twin warned with a frown.

"What? She certainly acts like it sometimes."

Megan sighed as if she'd heard it all before. "You take after Grandma O'Malley. You have her hair and eyes."

"Too bad she's not alive to validate the fact O'Malley blood runs through my veins."

The sisters fell silent, and Quinn realized he'd stumbled upon a touchy subject.

"Do you have lunch plans, Mr. Darling?" Jane asked.

"No plans." He adjusted the Bible in his hands. "I had thought to dine at Plum's Café, not realizing the establishment was closed on Sundays."

"You must have lunch with us," Jessica piped up.

"Yes, please do." Jane's smile was genuine.

He studied Nicole's expression, frustrated when he couldn't read it. "I'm not sure your sister would approve considering she's now consigned to endure my presence on a daily basis. She's already promised to help me this afternoon."

"We have to eat first. You should sample Jane's cooking," Nicole said soberly. "And Jessica made pie for dessert."

"I have a weakness for sweets."

A single raven brow arched. "I've noticed."

"Then it's settled." Jane clapped her hands together. "You're coming home with us."

Chapter Four

Quinn soaked in the serene beauty of their surroundings, the endless green forests on either side of the lane alive with birds and squirrels and other wildlife. Gardenia blossoms sweetened the humid air.

"I'm glad we chose to walk." The twins had needed time to put the finishing touches on their meal. He looked over at Nicole strolling quietly beside him. He added *content with silence* to the list of her attributes. "Too much inactivity and I get surly."

"We wouldn't want that, would we?"

He laughed outright at her sarcastic tone. "How could I have forgotten you got a taste of my surliness? Although, that was mostly your fault."

"My fault?" she gaped.

"If you hadn't given me the worst headache in history, I wouldn't have had cause to be."

Stopping short, she crossed her arms and glowered. "You weren't the only one with good reason to be upset. Never in my life have I been handled in such a degrading manner."

Memories surged…the roughness with which he'd bound her wrists. His mother would be appalled.

Guilt pricking his conscience, he sobered. "For that, I am truly sorry. My only defense is that I was acting on faulty assumptions. Will you forgive me?"

Some of the starch went out of her. Her lowered eyes tracking the grass-smattered lane beneath her black boots, she nodded. "Maybe you could get someone to take you hiking in the mountains."

He blinked at the sudden change of topic. "Are you volunteering?"

"Me? No. I don't have that kind of free time. Caleb knows the high country like the back of his hand. I'm sure he'd be willing to take you."

From what he'd observed of the couple that morning during church, the man would not willingly leave his expectant wife, not even for a day's outing. Nevertheless, he said, "Maybe I'll speak to him about it."

"What did you do in Boston to stave off the surliness?"

"Are you familiar with the sport of fencing?"

"I have heard of it," she said drily.

He smiled, silently reminding himself not to assume the locals were cut off from the world. They had access to books and newspapers. And he wasn't the only out-of-towner to move here. People from all walks of life had passed through the town, carrying with them stories of other places.

"I took up fencing a few years ago. My good friend Oliver and I practiced several times a week, and we entered competitions on a regular basis. That and swimming helped channel my energy. I enjoy people-watching, too, so I often strolled the city streets."

Not only did he miss the competitions, he missed his outgoing, boisterous friend. As soon as he was settled, he'd extend an invitation. Always up for an adventure, Oliver was one of a handful of people who'd approved of Quinn's plans. Since he wasn't engaged or married, an extended trip to Tennessee wasn't out of the question.

Nicole batted away a fly, nose wrinkling adorably. One look at the raven-haired beauty, and his friend would be instantly smitten. He wondered what his assistant would think of Oliver.

An uncomfortable feeling slid into his chest. The heat was suddenly too much. Shrugging out of his coat, he slung it over his shoulder.

"You never told me why you left a city full of unlimited opportunities to start over in our unremarkable town."

"It's not easy to explain." He began walking again, and she fell into step beside him. "My family has been blessed. My great-grandfather Edward Darling founded Darling Industries, and it's grown into a prosperous empire, for lack of a better word. We provide solid employment for a vast number of people. We're in the position to fund many charitable works. That part of our life I am proud of. However, one doesn't hold that particular position in society without having certain social responsibilities, ones I have grown exceedingly tired of in recent years."

"You were required to entertain them?"

"According to my father, we have to coddle our current business partners and woo new ones in order to maintain our current level of success."

Her gaze abandoned a bird's nest in a nearby tree and fastened onto him. "What do you have against parties?"

He kicked up a shoulder. "I enjoy music and dancing and excellent food. I guess what bothers me is the shallow nature of it all. We weren't vacationing with these people because they were family or close friends. It was for the sole purpose of insuring their continued support. I began to crave genuine relationships."

Quinn thought of his last disappointment—Helene

and the conversation he'd overheard between her and her friends—and how it had confirmed that a life of social climbing, the relentless pursuit of increased wealth, was not for him. "More than that, I needed to prove to myself that I could make it on my own. That I could accomplish something worthwhile apart from Darling Industries."

"How did your parents take the news?"

Kneading the back of his neck, he winced. "I didn't exactly prepare them. I waited until after I had already purchased the store."

Dark brows lifted until hidden beneath the side sweep of her hair. "So it would be too late for them to try and talk you out of it?"

Perceptive went onto the list. "Partly, yes. I also acted quickly in order not to lose the opportunity. My father, especially, was blown away by my decision. Unlike my mother, he hadn't seen the signs of my dissatisfaction. I suspect he thinks I will tire of small-town life and return within six months' time."

Her brow creased, and she would've spoken if a bundle of reddish-brown fur hadn't ambushed her ankles.

He put a hand out. "Careful—"

"It's all right. He's a friend of mine." Humor laced her voice as she bent and scooped up the wriggling dog.

Quinn watched, fascinated, as Nicole's reserve melted away. Unmindful of her outfit, she snuggled the animal close to her chest, laughter as light as tinkling glass hovering in the still air as the dog attempted to lick her face. Without the armor in place, her radiance shone like rays piercing the clouds, her loveliness making his heart thump and his stomach twist uncomfortably.

Who was the real Nicole O'Malley? The lethal attacker with the killer aim? The distant duchess capable of giving a man frostbite with a single glare? Or the warm, alluring woman with soft eyes and a smile that promised dreams-come-true?

Quinn drew closer and, after letting the dog sniff his fingers, buried them in the thick fur. His scrutiny wasn't on the dog, however. It was on Nicole's face, waiting for—and dreading?—the inevitable change.

"What's his name?"

"Cinnamon."

He'd noticed her extra attention to Caleb's horses yesterday morning. "You have a soft spot for animals and babies."

"That's because they don't judge." Twisting slightly, she glanced at the wide clearing that had opened up on their left and extended as far as the eye could see. "He belongs to my aunt and uncle." In the distance, blue-toned mountains were framed against cerulean sky. A two-story cabin sat right in the center, surrounded by a large barn and outbuildings. Another, smaller cabin was tucked against the far left tree line. "Caleb and Rebecca live in the small one, and Uncle Sam and Aunt Mary have the large house. Rebecca's younger sister, Amy, stays there with them. Josh and his wife, Kate, have a cabin behind the main house. Their property adjoins ours."

"Family members that are also neighbors. That's convenient."

The guardedness rushed back, and he wondered at it.

"It can be." With a brief kiss to Cinnamon's head, she set him on the ground and watched pensively as he raced across the grass, diverted by a flitting butterfly.

At the decided lack of enthusiasm, he made to question her, but she headed him off. "We shouldn't linger. Jane will worry the food might get cold."

Quinn fell into step beside her, glad of the interruption. Her personal life was none of his business. In fact, he should probably limit spending time with her outside of the store. Maintaining a civil working relationship was paramount to success. Failure was not an outcome he was willing to explore.

Nicole watched as Quinn effortlessly charmed her mother and sisters. Seated diagonally from her at the head of the table, he answered their incessant questions with practiced ease, completely at home in their humble cabin in spite of the air of old-money clinging to him.

The black pin-striped suit coat, which he'd slipped into once again before entering their home, molded to the wide span of his shoulders like a second skin. *He must have a personal tailor.* He'd slipped the buttons free before easing his lean body into the scuffed wooden chair, giving her a glimpse of the silver-filigreed vest and crisp white shirt underneath hugging his torso.

Had he been born a charmer? Or had his skills been honed by his high-society life? Either way, he annoyed her.

She skewered a potato with more force than necessary, and it disintegrated into mush. Quinn's vigilant liquid eyes focused on her. One brow lifted in silent question. Nicole mimicked his expression. The slow, impertinent smile that followed made her insides jittery. Not familiar with this particular reaction, she frowned at him, which only served to widen his smile.

Lowering her gaze, she concentrated on sipping the fragrant tea without spilling it.

"Won't you miss living in Boston?" Across from Nicole, Jessica eyed their guest with open admiration.

Laying down his fork, he fiddled with the teacup's handle. "I will miss my family. And my favorite Czech bakery. They sell the most delicious *kolaches*, pastries filled with cheese or fruit." His expression turned wistful. "I'm at peace with my decision, however. I look forward to experiencing life in a rural, close-knit community."

Nicole hid a smirk with her napkin. He'd soon learn small-town life wasn't all lemon drops and roses.

Jessica looked at Nicole. "Our sister has talked about leaving Gatlinburg behind and starting fresh in the big city for years."

Nicole restrained herself from kicking her under the table. It wasn't that her dream was private—everyone in town was aware of her plans. But Quinn was her boss. Now that he knew she intended to leave town, he could possibly decide to find an early replacement. A tremor of unease wound its way through her. She desperately needed the income.

Quinn was looking at her with a strange mix of surprise and disappointment. "Is this true, Nicole?"

Before she could formulate an answer, Jane leaned forward in her chair, auburn hair brilliant in the afternoon light streaming through the windows. "Tell him your plans."

"I told you I was a seamstress."

"Yes…I recall the conversation."

"My goal is to open a boutique of my own in Knoxville."

"When?" He sat motionless, good humor draining away.

"She was supposed to go in March," Jessica piped up. "She refuses to tell us why she had to postpone."

"I—"

Their mother aimed a reprimanding glance at her youngest daughter. "That is Nicole's business, young lady. Don't pester her."

"Yes, ma'am."

Nicole attempted to gather her wits. No one could discover the true reason for the delay. "I—I will have the necessary funds eventually."

Still unsmiling, Quinn sighed. "Emmett did not mention your plans. Your expertise will be missed."

"I promise to give you ample notice of my departure."

As if sensing her turmoil, he said, "I want you for as many days as I can have you."

Nicole's lips parted. Jessica giggled.

Red slashed his cheekbones as it sank in how his words had sounded, and he looked uncharacteristically uncertain. "I meant—"

"I know what you meant." Dropping her napkin on the table, she stood abruptly and gathered her plate and silverware. "If we're going to have time to look over the ledgers today I suggest we go. I have alterations to do later."

"But you haven't eaten dessert," Jane protested.

Their mother rose, as well, smiling broadly at their guest. "I'll send some with you. I'm sure you will want to take a break at some point."

Nicole stumbled, nearly dumping her dish. Sure, she'd seen that speculative gleam in her mother's eyes before, but in regards to her sisters. Not *her*. Surely she didn't think she and Quinn would make a good match!

Setting her dishes in the dry sink, she pitched her voice low. "Please tell me you aren't entertaining romantic notions about me and my boss."

Alice patted Nicole's arm. "Would that be so bad? He seems like a fine young man."

Remembering his arrogance as he'd loftily informed her of impending changes, she swallowed a retort. Fine young man? Huh. "I'm not interested in him or anyone else. I have plans, remember?"

"Have you consulted God about those plans?" It wasn't a

harsh question. Concern and understanding were reflected in her lined face.

"I know you'd rather I stay here and, like Megan, settle down and maybe start a family. That's not me. And, since God made me, He knows I wouldn't be happy living a conventional life"

Nicole wasn't about to admit that lately she'd been experiencing rogue thoughts…like what it might be like to have a man adore her the way Lucian did Megan. Or what it would feel like to hold her very own baby in her arms. Josh and Kate's little girl, Victoria, had worked her way into her heart with zero effort. Simply holding her, absorbing her innocence and sweetness, had altered her view of parenthood.

"Well, it can't hurt to have a friend, can it?" Her mother sliced up two generous portions of pear pie.

Nicole didn't want Quinn Darling for a friend. The debonair Northerner wasn't exactly comfortable to be around. On top of that, he was the last person she'd feel inclined to share confidences with.

When the dessert was carefully placed in a small basket, Nicole endured a motherly hug. "I'm not sure what time I'll be home. Don't expect me before supper, okay?"

Hopefully she could hurry along this session with Quinn. There was an errand she couldn't put off.

Nicole pressed against the lichen-coated tree trunk, listening, waiting, heartbeat loud in her ears as she stared at the run-down shack tucked between three trees of varying size. In the lush canopy far above her head, birds were constantly in motion, the flap of their wings competing with rustling leaves and swaying limbs. A tickle on her pinkie caught her attention. Brushing off a tiny black ant, she checked the dense woods behind her. No one. Good.

Gripping the basket she'd snuck out of the mercantile following her blessedly brief tutoring session with Quinn, she picked her way over exposed roots and the damp, mossy forest floor. The midsummer sun rarely breached the leafy banner, and last autumn's fallen leaves had yet to fully decompose. The air was dense, fragrant and slightly moist. Trickling stream water pulsed beneath all other forest sounds.

At the shack door, she rapped her knuckles against the brittle wood in a distinct pattern. A few seconds passed before the door scraped open and a young man with pleasant features, albeit strained and pale, stared back at her. His dishwater-blond hair hung limp across his forehead.

"Nicole."

Shuffling a step back with the aid of his cane, he admitted her.

"How are you, Patrick?"

"Nothing has changed since the last time you asked. That was what? Two days ago?" His attempt at a smile failed, pain clouding his gray eyes.

She wished for the hundredth time he'd gotten proper care for his injured leg, wished he'd agreed to let her summon the doctor. It hadn't healed properly, hence the ongoing pain.

Patrick's younger sister, Lillian, greeted her with her customary hug. Nicole returned the embrace without a trace of awkwardness. She'd grown accustomed to the sweet-natured girl's affection.

Lillian released her. "You look especially pretty today. How was the church service?"

"I'll tell you all about it in a moment." She lifted the basket. "First, I brought you some things."

"You always do." Patrick had lowered himself onto the ladder-back chair in the dim corner. Her ongoing charity bothered him a great deal. He was aware, as they all were, that he and his sister couldn't survive without it.

"She knows we'll pay her back someday." Lillian carried it to the tiny, lopsided table shoved against the wall beside the door and eagerly lifted the checkered material. Her wavy flaxen hair, caught in a neat ponytail and tied with a strip of leather, hung to her waist and shone in the lamplight. Several hours remained before dusk fell, but the single window let in precious little natural light.

Moving to sit on one of two narrow beds, Nicole pondered their reaction to her news. The ancient bed frame creaked under her weight, and the mattress was pathetically thin. The ticking would need to be replaced soon. How was she supposed to accomplish that without arousing suspicion? Sometimes, the weight of this secret was almost too much to bear.

Lillian exclaimed over the paper and pencils. The fifteen-year-old was too thin, as was her brother, her skin as pale as the paper in her hands due to spending most daylight hours in this ruin they called home. Neither could detract from her fair beauty, however. Big, cornflower-blue eyes shone in a face that seemed perpetually filled with hope.

Patrick didn't share his sister's optimistic outlook. His worries, his deep-seated concern for his sister, cloaked him in perpetual strain. Bouncing the cane between his fingers, he stared hard at Nicole. "You look more pensive than usual. What's bothering you?"

After six months of almost daily visits, they treated her as an older sibling. She considered them friends of the dearest kind, friends she'd never dreamed she'd find in her hometown. Patrick and Lillian didn't care what her last name was. They didn't know her family or that she paled in comparison to her sisters—Juliana, beautiful and courageous; Megan, the romantic dreamer who brought joy to children's lives; sweet-tempered Jane, whose generosity of spirit bordered on legendary; and high-spirited Jessica, the twin who could bake her way out of any fix.

No, they liked her for her. A heady experience, it was the reason she'd do anything to protect them.

"Something happened yesterday before we opened the store."

While she'd told them about her new boss, she'd left out the details of their first meeting. Patrick scowled. "It was him, wasn't it? Our stand-in father was in town again."

"I didn't recognize him at first, but he introduced himself to Quinn." Clasping her hands tightly on her lap, Nicole suppressed a shudder. "He had a sign with your names and descriptions, and he asked Quinn to post it on the board."

White lines bracketed Patrick's mouth as he gripped the cane. "Did he?"

"No. I asked to see it and, when he wasn't looking, I slipped it in my pocket."

Lillian sank onto the mattress beside Nicole, fingers worrying a tear in the coarse blanket. "You could get in trouble if he finds out."

"I don't like this," Patrick said.

Nicole couldn't feel bad about what she'd done, not knowing how risky hanging that sign would've been.

"Don't worry. Quinn's so busy plotting modifications to the store, he won't even notice."

"Even if you did post it," Lillian said, "I don't think we'd have anything to worry about. It's not like we go anywhere where people would see us or ask our names."

Their forced solitude, their bleak existence, was like a gaping wound that refused to heal. No matter where she was or what she was doing, she couldn't *not* think about them here with no one but each other to talk to. Nicole *hated* that they were being punished when they were innocent of any wrongdoing. "I was hoping he'd have given up by now," she admitted.

"Carl won't do that," Patrick said, defeat weighing him down. "He wants the necklace."

She'd seen the ruby-and-diamond necklace that once belonged to their late mother. While she wasn't an expert on jewelry, it appeared to be of great value. And because Carl had been married to their mother, he surely thought of it as his property.

"He will also go to any lengths to punish us for disappearing with it."

She stared at his injured leg. Carl had done that to him. If he got his hands on Patrick a second time, there was no telling what he'd do.

"Let me involve Shane Timmons," Nicole entreated, not for the first time. "He's a fair man. He'll help you. And you'll finally be able to resume a normal life."

Patrick dropped the hand he'd placed over his face and jutted his chin in that stubborn way of his. "As a sheriff, he's duty-bound to follow the law. We're still minors. He'd be forced to reunite us with Carl."

"He's not our father," Lillian piped up.

"Doesn't matter. He's our legal guardian."

Knowing where the argument was headed, Nicole stood and sighed. "I have to get home."

"We'll see you tomorrow?" Lillian pushed to her feet, her countenance resigned.

"Of course." Pausing with her hand on the door latch, she looked at Patrick. "Please think on what I said."

"It's no use, Nicole. Your way will lead to trouble. If Carl finds us, he will finish the job he started. I won't be

able to protect Lillian. You don't want that on your conscience, do you?"

Soundlessly letting herself out, Nicole sagged against
the door and closed her eyes. Without her, there would
be no one to help them. No one to keep their secret. As
long as Patrick and Lillian needed her, she was stuck in
Gatlinburg.

Chapter Five

The siblings' predicament still weighing heavily on her mind the next morning, Nicole wasn't prepared for the sight of her boss hefting chairs along the back hallway. He was dressed as impeccably as usual, black hair neatly combed, and beneath the rolled-up sleeves thick forearms lightly sprinkled with dark hair were visible. Sturdy shoulders bore the weight effortlessly.

"Duchess. You came." A brash grin curving his lips, he stopped in front of her, his tall frame blocking her way. Beneath the scent of peppermint wafted soap and spice and man. "I thought after yesterday's session you might've given up on me."

Nicole pursed her lips together to stop the forming compliment. Quinn was in possession of a keen mind. It hadn't taken him long to catch on to the trade credit system. She wasn't about to boost his already healthy self-confidence, however.

"Why did you call me that?"

"Duchess?" His honey eyes twinkled. "It fits you."

Was he implying she acted like a snob? That she thought others were beneath her? Because that was so far off the mark—

"As much as I'd like to stand here and chat with you," he said, adjusting his grip on the chairs, "we've a mountain-size job ahead of us. I need for you to make up a sign letting customers know we'll close today at noon and reopen tomorrow at the same time."

"Why would we do that?"

"After you left, I spent several hours examining the current arrangement and deciding how best to rearrange the merchandise. I've hired a couple of men to help us implement my plan."

Flustered, the significance of the chairs finally sank in. "Are you going to put those back once we've finished?"

"No. I told you my store will not be a gathering place." His brows shot up. "Do you know how difficult it's going to be to get those tobacco stains off the floor?"

Nicole was on the verge of warning him of the consequences when she stopped herself. Quinn Darling had overseen a vast clothing conglomerate. He thought running a country store was small potatoes, so why would he heed her advice?

"I'll go make that sign."

Pressing against the wall to avoid brushing against him, she waited for him to pass. Instead, he set the chairs down and folded his arms across his chest. The movement brought him too close in the narrow hallway. The fact they were completely alone in the building wasn't lost on her.

Not that she feared him. Despite Quinn's singular ability to get under her skin and lodge there like a stubborn splinter, she felt completely safe in his company. Safe was not the same as relaxed, though. Whenever he was nearby, her skin felt too tight. Her pulse raced. Her entire being came alive, senses soaking up every detail—everything from the heat blazing off his skin to his short, clean nails to the throb of his heartbeat in the hollow of his throat. Talk about disturbing.

"Something on your mind, Duchess?"

She lifted her chin. "Don't call me that."

"I can see the disapproving light in your eyes. Tell me what's on your mind."

Somewhere outside, a horse whinnied and male voices could be heard.

"Most people don't appreciate change. Evicting the checker players isn't going to go over well. The same goes for rearranging the goods. While I can see the wisdom of such a plan, I'm not sure the customers will respond positively."

"Hmm." His probing gaze roamed her face, making her feel exposed. "I understand your point of view. However, I'm of the opinion that, while change may not be welcome in the beginning, it doesn't take long for people to adjust."

The rear bell rang, signaling a delivery. With another of his devastating grins, he moved out of her space and retrieved the chairs. "I'll get that."

As he strode away from her, Nicole found that she could breathe easier. Think more clearly.

"Can't say I didn't warn you," she muttered, heading to the office to do his bidding.

If she was a duchess, what did that make him? King?

She spent the bulk of the morning answering the same questions over and over. Why were they closing? Why wasn't the checker game set out? And her personal favorite, for which she had no answer—what was that pesky Northerner thinking?

About five minutes before noon, as the last customer was leaving, Quinn waved three young men through the entrance.

"You're right on time." Shaking their hands in turn, he

glanced over at Nicole. "You're already acquainted with Miss O'Malley."

Clamping down on the familiar dread fixing her boots to the floorboards, Nicole forced her gaze to Kenneth Jones. Blond, blue-eyed and as solid as an elk, he'd been a thorn in her side ever since she'd turned down his invitation to the harvest dance last year. Kenneth did not take rejection well.

"Yes, sir. We grew up together." Kenneth adopted a respectful air, but his eyes gleamed with anticipation. No doubt he saw this as the perfect opportunity to harass her—no O'Malley family members in sight.

His friends, red-haired, freckled Timothy Wallington and lanky Pete Ryan wore matching predatory smiles. In this trio, Kenneth was the leader. They behaved in accordance with his whims.

Reminding herself she wasn't in any real danger, she wiped her damp palms against her apron and squared her shoulders. Hateful words couldn't inflict lasting pain. Not from someone who wasn't important to her.

Quinn beckoned the men to the counter where his sketches were lined up and explained exactly how he wanted things to proceed. His directions were clear and concise.

She listened with reluctant admiration. Here was a man who knew what he wanted and how to get it. A force to be reckoned with. With his wealth and influence, he'd be used to people obeying him without question.

"Kenneth, I'd like for you to remove the tools from that middle shelf." He pointed to the long interior wall. "Once you've done that, Nicole can clean them and then organize the ready-made clothing there so that it is alongside the fabric bolts."

Quinn looked at her, brows raised. "All right with you?"

Aware of Kenneth's leer, she jerked a nod. So they'd be working side by side. She could handle whatever he dished out.

With Pete and Timothy assigned to the middle aisles, Quinn retreated behind the counter to address the shelving units and drawers there.

"I'll go and get the water," she told him, retrieving the pail from a hook near the aprons.

Already comparing the shelves to his sketch, Quinn nodded absentmindedly.

A beefy hand snatched the handle from hers. "I'll help you." Propelling her along the hall, Kenneth said in a voice that carried, "The stairs are steep. Wouldn't want you to trip and break something."

"I don't need your help," she said through gritted teeth.

At the door, the pretense fell away. "You've always been a snob, you know that? Thinking you're better than everybody else. Too good for our humble town. One day you'll regret looking down your nose at me, little witch."

She inwardly grimaced at the taunt that had originated on the school grounds. "It was a silly harvest dance, Kenneth. Forget about it."

His nostrils flared, lips flattening into a sneer. "I will as soon as you've learned your lesson." Turning on his heel, he tossed over his shoulder, "Get your own water."

Hurrying out into the searing midday heat, Nicole descended the stairs on unsteady legs, angry at herself for letting a bully like Kenneth intimidate her. One word to any of her cousins was all it would take to be rid of him. But whining to them felt wrong. She was no longer a child. If she planned to make it on her own in the city, she'd have to deal with problems herself. There'd be no well-meaning protectors to the rescue.

Scooping water out of the rain barrel, she went back inside and, studiously avoiding all four males in the room, gathered soap and rags while waiting for Kenneth to unload the shelves. He ignored her for the most part, but his dislike was made plain in the dark looks cast her way. Working in the aisle behind them, Pete and Timothy's low conversation was interspersed with laughter that sounded mischievous to her ears. Were they laughing at her? Plotting something?

On edge the entire afternoon, she trained her attention on the tasks Quinn gave her. It wasn't until she and Kenneth had moved to the china display that things went awry.

She was carefully removing a stack of dinner plates when Kenneth's hand shot out and, seizing her wrist, yanked so that she tipped the lot of them. The crash reverberated in the silent store. Stunned disbelief held her frozen.

An expression of false concern settled across his features. "Uh-oh. That's going to be expensive to replace. Mr. Darling, I'm afraid your assistant got careless with the merchandise."

Straightening from his crouch at the opposite end of the room, Quinn's frown carved deep grooves on either side of his mouth. He came and surveyed the shards littering the floorboards. Beyond his shoulder, Pete and Timothy elbowed each other.

A resigned sigh escaped him as his gaze prodded Nicole's. "Clean up this mess. And from now on, ask for help with the heavy stuff. Kenneth will be happy to help, I'm sure."

"Anytime." Kenneth's smile held a hint of cruelty. Quinn couldn't see it, because he was looking at her with something akin to disappointment.

Indignation seared her, burned into her cheeks. If she

confessed the truth, Kenneth would only deny it. Her trust-worthiness would be called into question.

Subduing the urge to stomp her feet, she croaked, "It won't happen again."

"Will she have to pay for the damage, Mr. Darling?"

Quinn's brow furrowed. "That won't be necessary this time."

This time. An unspoken warning to not make the same mistake again.

When he'd returned to his work, she shot her nemesis a scorching glare. "How could you do that?" she demanded.

"I didn't." His upper lip curled. "You did."

Leaving her to clean up alone, Kenneth went and pretended to help his friends. Nicole took out her frustration on the broom. Being blamed for something that wasn't her fault left a bad taste in her mouth. Anger and humiliation warred for supremacy.

She could hardly bear to look at Quinn. Irrationally, she blamed him for not seeing through Kenneth's act.

The remainder of the afternoon and early evening crawled by. Just as escape looked likely, Quinn waylaid her in the office. The trio had left ten minutes ago, and she was eager to get away from her boss's assessing glances.

"It's late, Quinn. I'm exhausted and hungry." *I need time to recover before doing it all again tomorrow morning. No telling what my enemy has planned for me.*

"This won't take but a minute." He leaned against the door frame, hands in his pockets and ankles crossed.

"If this is about the dishes, I—"

"No." His expression turned thoughtful. "I detected something…off between you and Kenneth. Do you two have a history? Because if you're uncomfortable working with him, I can send him on his way in the morning."

"If you're asking if we've ever courted, the answer is no," she spluttered. "Absolutely not."

"Then what's the problem?"

Here was her chance to explain everything. To absolve herself and be rid of Kenneth and his buddies. But she was, above all, a private person. Exposing her problems to her boss didn't hold an ounce of appeal.

"No problem." Pushing an errant curl behind her ear, she rubbed a sore spot in her lower back. "If there are no more questions, I really do have to go."

Quinn didn't appear convinced. Still, he moved sideways to let her pass. As she was edging through the doorway and he was centimeters away, he said softly, "Good night, Duchess."

Nicole stiffened at the brush of his minty breath across her cheek.

She didn't like nicknames on principle. Caleb did it to tease her—good-natured, brotherly ribbing that nevertheless irked her. Kenneth's intent was to demean her. What was Quinn Darling's motive? And why did a little thrill zip up her spine?

Risking a glance at this close range, she didn't detect a trace of cruelty in those light brown eyes, merely lazy curiosity.

She was an enigma to him, was she? Well, he was wasting his time trying to figure her out. She wasn't about to divulge her secrets to the likes of him.

The locals weren't adjusting to Quinn's implemented changes as quickly as he'd hoped. Ever since they'd reopened three days ago, the customers had doggedly avoided him. Some went so far as to denounce his decisions to his face, unsatisfied with his explanations.

No amount of pleasantness or willingness to help had put a dent in their wariness.

Leaning against the shelving unit, he eyed the five-deep line of customers waiting for Nicole's assistance.

He caught the familiar elderly lady's eye and thanked the Lord he had a memory for names. His smile didn't come as easily as it had that morning. "I can help you over here, Mrs. Kirkpatrick."

Crinkling her nose, she shook her head, gaze skittering away.

The rejection stung. He, Quinn Darling, heir to the Darling fortune and a man whose very presence deemed a social gathering a success, could not convince the lady to let him wait on her. Weariness pressed behind his forehead, turning the slight headache he'd nursed since Nicole whopped him with that pot into a full-blown hammering against his skull.

He pinched the bridge of his nose. Shoving off the counter, he strode to his assistant's side. "I'll fill orders for you. What have you got?"

Her face a polite mask, Nicole's pencil hovered above the ledger and pointed at the row of red metal spice bins on the bottom shelf. "I need one ounce of cinnamon, four ounces of cream of tartar and one container of vanilla extract."

"Throw in a pack of chewing gum," the needle-thin man on the opposite side of the counter added.

"Coming right up, sir."

Grinding his teeth, Quinn quickly gathered the items. Up until this moment, he hadn't considered himself a proud man too good for lowly work. He hadn't started out at the top. Edward Darling had thought it important his son experience all facets of the industry. He'd done everything from sweeping factory floors to operating ten looms at once.

Why, then, was being reduced to Nicole O'Malley's go-to boy so difficult to swallow?

Because this is my store. I bought it with my own money, gave up everything I've worked for—upsetting a lot of people in the process—to start over in an unfamiliar place where I know no one.

Neatly folding the paper sacks, he slid them across the counter. "Will there be anything else?"

Lord Jesus, help me not to be prideful. Help me to win these people's trust.

The man squinted at his list. "Nope. That will be all."

Nicole informed him how much credit he had left and moved on to the next customer. Together, they worked through the line until the last person had been served. The clock chiming three o'clock split the weighted silence.

Without a word, Quinn pivoted on his heel and stalked down the hall to the cramped, low-ceilinged quarters. He needed an outlet for his pent-up frustration. Since he couldn't drop everything and go for a swim, going through the motions of making coffee would have to do. He was filling the kettle with water when Nicole peered around the door frame.

"Is it safe to come in?" she said, cringing when he thumped the kettle down with more force than necessary.

"Enter at your own risk." Snatching the tin of coffee grounds from the shelf, he slammed it down.

"Even if I come bearing gifts?" Emerald green skirts skimming the polished floorboards, she approached and slowly lifted her hand. Two peppermint sticks lay on her open palm.

He looked deep into her luminous eyes. "Are you trying to tame my surliness with sweets?"

"I am."

He glimpsed a flicker of compassion, almost imperceptible but there nonetheless, and the loneliness inside him receded a little. Two more attributes went onto the growing list. *Unpredictable. Kindhearted.* The second one was just a hunch and would need to be confirmed.

Quinn accepted the offering only to hold one up to her lips, pressing gently. "I cannot be the only one to indulge."

Startled eyes stared back at him, confirming she wasn't used to his brand of teasing. *You didn't treat the women in Boston like this, though, did you?* a voice prodded. *Something in her manner provokes you to outrageousness.*

When she reached to take hold of the stick, her cool fingers closed over his, the contact unexpectedly comforting. Lowering his hand, he popped the sweet in his mouth and resumed the motions of making coffee.

"They do not trust me," he said, pulling down two blue enamel mugs from the shelf. "They lack confidence in me." He hoped she didn't recognize his underlying hurt.

"I don't think Gatlinburg has seen anyone quite like you."

Pausing in scooping the grounds, he cast her a sidelong look, smiling a little at her attempts to eat the peppermint without becoming a sticky mess. "What do you mean?"

"Have you looked in a mirror lately?" She waved her hand up and down. "You exude power and privilege, wealth most people around here can't even begin to imagine. Your slick ways and your funny accent sets you apart. It's painfully obvious you are out of your element."

"Don't hold back, Duchess," he said drily, "Tell me what you really think."

His ego sure was taking a bruising lately. His father would say it built character.

"That doesn't mean they won't come to trust you eventually. Are you a patient man, Quinn Darling?"

Irrationally, his conversation with Shane Timmons

came to mind. The sheriff was of the opinion that, while hard to get to know, Nicole would be worth the effort. He wasn't sure he agreed. Nicole O'Malley was not even close to what he required in a wife.

She awaited his answer, calm and regal in her high-collared green confection of a dress, raven curls confined in a loose chignon at the base of her swanlike neck. How would she react if he were to sink his fingers in the beguiling mass?

"That all depends," he said on a sigh.

"On what?"

"On what it is I'm waiting for."

She didn't have a response, merely watched him with that stoic expression.

"I have a question for you." He imagined he could see her pulling her armor in close.

"Yes?"

He took his time pouring coffee into the cups. "Why aren't you gloating?"

"Excuse me?"

"You warned me. I didn't listen, and now—" he replaced the kettle on the stove "—they see me as the bad guy. I've been waiting for you to rub it in."

"You'll be waiting a long time."

He held out the mug. She studiously avoided his fingers. Quinn had noticed she took pains not to accidentally touch him. Why was that?

She wasn't shy. What, then? Did he make her uncomfortable? He frowned at the notion.

"You're not the type to point out a man's errors in judgment?"

"I clearly don't need to. It hasn't even been a week and you've already seen the effects of your decisions."

"You think I should open my store to loiterers."

"Folks will eventually get over you moving the merchandise around. The organization makes sense." Against the blue mug, her fingers were long and slender, piano-playing hands, his mother would say. "Prohibiting folks from gathering for harmless fun and conversation, on the other hand, strikes them as callous and unfeeling. They won't forgive you for that."

"It was purely a business decision," he defended.

"The wrong one."

The ringing of the bell echoed through the store, and Nicole left his quarters to go and greet the new arrival. He refused to be disappointed at her departure, even if, for a couple of minutes in her presence, the magnitude of his problems seemed to have receded.

Chapter Six

For the remainder of the afternoon, Quinn didn't attempt to wait on anyone. Instead, he focused on assisting Nicole and interacting with the customers in a nonthreatening way. He mulled over their conversation. She was right— in order to gain their favor, he was going to have to think less like a businessman and more like a member of this community. He was going to have to invite the checker-playing, tobacco-spitting gossip-sharers back.

Around five o'clock, an hour before closing, Kenneth and Timothy swaggered in and headed straight for the counter. Neither man observed him in front of the notice board. Remaining where he was, Quinn switched his attention to Nicole, curious to see if her behavior altered. He didn't buy her denial that no issues existed between her and the cocky blond.

What was she hiding? And why?

In the middle of helping a young mother with a fussy toddler clinging to her hip, Nicole's smile wavered the moment she became aware of the young men's presence. Her shoulders went rigid. When her gaze sought out Quinn across the store, widening when she encountered his steady perusal, his feet carried him straight to her side. Somehow, he sensed she needed him.

"Kenneth. Timothy. What can I do for you?"

"Afternoon, Mr. Darling." With smooth cordiality, Kenneth tapped a battered hat against his leg. "Came in for shaving soap. But Nicole knows what I like. I'll wait for her."

Nicole didn't react, didn't acknowledge their conversation in any way.

"I wouldn't want you to wait needlessly." Quinn moved to the case holding shaving supplies and opened the rear panel. "What brand?"

The flaring of his nostrils was the only sign of his displeasure. "Colgate."

Quinn wrapped up his purchase and took the payment. "Thank you, gentlemen. Have a good afternoon."

"If you have any other jobs around the store, we'd be happy to help out."

"I'll keep that in mind."

Glancing surreptitiously at Nicole, Kenneth tucked his purchase beneath his arm and left with his friend.

Quinn approached, lightly touched her wrist. "Do you mind watching the store for a couple of minutes? I've an errand to see to."

"Of course not."

Out on the boardwalk, the intense midsummer heat immediately closed in. Boston hadn't been nearly this humid. Wouldn't be long before his skin was slick with perspiration and he wished he didn't have to wear so many clothes.

There was no sign of Kenneth. Striding in the direction of the jail, Quinn was relieved to find Shane behind his desk, seemingly free to talk.

The man's features lit with mild surprise and the paper

he'd been perusing hit the desk. "Trouble at the mercantile?"

"No." He gestured to the empty chair. "Do you have a moment? I'd like to ask you a few questions."

"Have a seat. What's on your mind?"

Dropping onto the unforgiving chair, he rested his ankle on his knee. "What can you tell me about Kenneth Jones?"

He thought a moment. "Not much to tell. Like most folks in these mountains, his family farms the land. Decent, hardworking people. Regular churchgoers." He tapped the desk surface. "Why do you ask?"

Quinn explained about the job he'd hired Kenneth to do. The tension he'd picked up on.

"You aren't aware of any romantic links or friendship between him and Nicole?"

Shane huffed a laugh. "Afraid I can't help you there. Keeping up with who courts who in this town is not in the job description."

Pushing to his feet, Quinn stalked to the barred window overlooking the street. While he recognized some of the passersby, he didn't know their names, reputations or their histories. "I'm at a disadvantage here. It's like trying to piece together a puzzle without first seeing the whole picture."

"All I can tell you is Nicole isn't one to frequent festivities. I can't recall her name being linked with anyone. If she attends a church social or dance, it's with her family."

Shoving aside the intense curiosity and twisted pleasure those statements evoked, Quinn turned. "To be clear, my motives for coming here are strictly professional."

The look Shane directed at him silently challenged that statement.

"I'm concerned because she's my assistant," he persisted. "If she has a problem with a customer, I need to know about it."

The tapping on Shane's desk increased. "Have you broached the matter with her?"

"I did. She wasn't forthcoming."

"Meaning, she denied there being a problem, and you don't believe her."

"Yes."

Shane slouched against the chair back. "Your only option then is to keep your eyes and ears open. You can't force her to confide in you."

If only he could. He stuck out his hand. "Appreciate the help."

Standing to his feet, the sheriff shook his hand. "I know how it feels to be the new man in town. Takes time, but eventually folks will open up to you."

Thanking the other man and feeling as if he'd made a trustworthy friend, he returned to the store in time to lock up and flip the sign to closed. When he spotted Nicole hunched over a small book and scribbling furiously, Quinn's gut tightened. He knew exactly what he'd see at her feet.

Acting as if nothing were amiss, he strolled past and headed into the office, suspicion burning his mouth like acid. For several days, he'd watched her surreptitiously place items in a large basket that she endeavored to keep hidden from him. It appeared his assistant was keeping more than one secret.

Was it possible she had been stealing from Emmett? The notion sickened him.

There was no other choice but to confront her.

Quinn stalked around the corner, scowling when she jolted in surprise and trepidation rippled across her features. He clasped his hands tightly behind his back. "May I ask what you are doing?"

"I—" Thick lashes sweeping down, she pointed to the book. "I—I'm entering my purchases. Emmett detracted the cost from my wages."

"I would like to see that." He held out his hand.

Her dark brows collided. "You don't trust me."

"You are my employee, Nicole. I need to be able to trust you. That's why I need to see it."

Her reluctance was plain as she handed him the book. Antagonism radiated from her stiff form. Quinn flipped through the pages, saw what appeared to be lists of ordinary supplies and entries by both Nicole and Emmett.

"New policy. When you make a purchase, I will enter it into this ledger, not you."

Nicole snatched it from his fingers, holding it to her chest like a shield. Deep purple sparks shimmered in her eyes. "Emmett didn't feel the need to supervise me in this."

"I am not Emmett," he snapped, angry at her for inspiring this distrust in the first place. "If you do not feel you can meet my standards, you can cease your employment here."

Again, he sensed fear in her.

"Fine." Hauling the basket up to the counter, she opened the ledger and held it up to his face. "You're the boss. Go ahead. Inspect it."

Despising the position she'd put him in, he checked that the items she'd gathered matched her entries. "You may leave," he murmured, not looking at her. "I will see to the cleanup."

He noticed her hands shaking when they folded over the handle. She didn't speak, just whirled away from him and marched down the hallway, slamming the door behind her.

"What exactly are you hiding, Nicole? And what has you so afraid?"

* * *

"We have a problem."

Humiliation humming through her veins, Nicole plunked the supplies one by one on the tabletop. Candles. Soap. Tea.

"What is it?" Features pinched, Patrick leaned heavily on his cane.

"Not it. Who. Quinn Darling is the problem." Insufferable man. "He practically accused me of stealing."

Lillian, whose neat blue-and-brown paisley blouse and nut-brown skirt Nicole had fashioned herself, clapped a hand over her mouth. "How horrible."

Studying the growing collection of things she'd brought, Patrick's shoulders sagged. "It's because of your frequent purchases, isn't it?" He nodded to the table. "I'm not surprised he's suspicious."

Noting his growing displeasure, Nicole worked to calm herself. "I haven't done anything wrong. He knows that. However, I may have to stagger my visits for a while."

"Of course," Lillian placed a hand on Nicole's arm. "We appreciate everything you do for us. We would never want you to put your job in jeopardy. Because of Patrick's traps, we have sufficient meat. And there's all the fish and crawfish, too."

The pair waited until dusk to do their fishing and bathing. While not ideal, it was the best way to avoid detection.

Patrick retreated to his corner chair, resting the cane across his knees. "Maybe we should move on to a different town. Somewhere farther away from Carl. We've taken advantage of Nicole's generosity long enough."

Both females gasped. Lillian rushed to crouch in front of him. "Patrick, no! I don't want to leave Nicole. She's our family now. Besides, there'd be no one to help us. No place to stay."

The younger girl's impassioned plea squeezed Nicole's

heart. The fact that Lillian valued their friendship as much as she did filled her with an unfamiliar sense of connection, of being valued for who she was, not who her family was. Over the past six months, a bond had developed between her and these down-on-their-luck siblings. She was loath to sever it. But what did that mean for her dream? Did she dare attempt to take them with her?

She'd been supporting them here. There was no reason she couldn't support them in the city once she'd replenished her savings.

Would they want to join her? Out of respect for their feelings, Nicole hadn't shared her plans with them. Patrick, especially, would've refused her assistance if he'd known what she was sacrificing.

"I could find work." At his sister's protest, he said, "Desk work. Something that doesn't require me to stand for long periods."

"Who would take us to this new town? Where would we live?" Launching upward, she paced in the tight space, golden hair bouncing between her shoulder blades. "People would ask questions. What if they guessed our identity? You said yourself that Carl is tenacious. Who knows how many towns he's visited." Seizing Nicole's hands, she exclaimed, "Talk some sense into him, please."

Briefly hugging her friend, Nicole moved to sit on the bed closest to him. "Let's not be hasty. Quinn has absolutely no notion about any of this. He didn't question my reasons for my purchases. It was my behavior that tipped him off. If I hadn't acted like I had something to hide, he wouldn't have suspected anything amiss. I'll be smarter from here on out."

Patrick was quiet for a long stretch. "Lillian, will you bring my satchel to me?"

When she'd done as he asked, he dug in the side pocket

and, extracting a brooch, held it out to Nicole. "This belonged to our grandmother. Carl doesn't know of its existence. I'm not sure how much it's worth, but I want you to take it as partial payment for what we owe you."

The brooch was exquisite, a blue-and-white cameo outlined in silver and with a cluster of diamonds on the top. "I can't possibly—"

When his jaw went taut and his gray eyes grew stormy, she was reminded of her cousins and the lessons they'd taught her about male pride.

She gingerly plucked the brooch from his fingers. "It's beautiful, Patrick. Thank you."

Tucking it in her reticule, she determined to hold on to it for them.

Lillian pointed to the stew bubbling on the ancient stove. "Would you like to have supper with us?"

"I wish I could, but I have chores to tend to at home."

"Maybe another time. Oh, I finished some of the books you lent me." She pressed the volumes into her hand. "I liked *Wuthering Heights* but didn't care for the volume of poetry."

"Neither did I," Patrick groaned. "She's forced me to listen to it every morning the past week."

A smile broke through Nicole's reserve. "Got it. No more poetry. I'll bring replacements soon, Lillian."

Her blue eyes gleamed with interest. "I'm looking forward to it."

Nicole was grateful her friend enjoyed reading as it helped pass the days spent indoors. During her walk home, she found herself unexpectedly turning to God in prayer.

"Father God, I don't come to You often for assistance." Aloud, her voice sounded stilted. Casting about the forest to make sure she was alone, she lowered it to a whisper. "I'm in way over my head. I thought I could handle this one on my own, but I can't. Patrick and Lillian deserve better. They deserve a normal life, a chance at happiness. They are dear friends of mine, and it would mean a lot to me if You would fix this."

A squirrel circled the tree directly in her path, and she froze, keen to observe the animal.

"One more thing," she murmured. "Please help Quinn Darling mind his own business."

Chapter Seven

Friday evening, Nicole arrived at Megan and Lucian's too late to hear her sister entertain the local children with a story. Weaving her way through the sea of parents and children juggling glasses of lemonade and platter-size cookies, she reached Megan's side only to stop short.

"What is *he* doing here?"

Megan, who tended to dress like the characters in the books she was reading, resembled a shepherd girl tonight. Leaning on her curved staff, she searched the room until she'd located the source of Nicole's ire. Quinn stood in front of the parlor fireplace conversing with Cole and Rachel Prescott. "Lucian invited him."

"Why?"

Wasn't putting up with his superior presence all day at the mercantile enough? Must she be forced to watch him attempt to charm his way into folks' good graces during her off hours, too?

Things had been strained between them since the confrontation. She couldn't dismiss the accusation in his eyes, the humiliation she'd endured while he'd checked the contents of her basket against the ledger input.

"Lucian thought it might be nice for people to get to know Quinn in a casual setting."

"How thoughtful."

At the sarcasm rolling off her tongue, Megan turned to study her. "Why does his presence bother you?"

"Haven't you heard the phrase familiarity breeds contempt? I'm with the man way too much as it is."

"Hmm." Speculation swirled in her sea-blue eyes. "I don't think I've seen you this flustered over a man before. You've always maintained your composure, no matter how handsome the guy and with no thought to the courage it took for him to approach you."

She thought of Kenneth's invitation to the harvest dance. Caught off guard by his sudden appearance in her barn, she'd refused his request without hesitation. Had she been too harsh? Would he still be angry and revengeful if she'd taken pains to let him down gently?

Nicole schooled her countenance. If she didn't squelch the matchmaking light in her sister's eyes, there'd be trouble of the most embarrassing kind. "I am not flustered. *Irritated* would be a better word. Quinn Darling irritates me. But I didn't come here to discuss my boss." Holding up the slim volumes she'd borrowed for Lillian, she nodded toward the wide entrance. "I'm finished with these. Mind if I borrow more?"

"I told you already, you may take as many as you'd like." Megan's cheeks flushed with peach-hued pleasure. "I can't get over your newfound love of books. We finally have something in common."

Nicole grimaced as guilt washed over her.

Megan saw it and, smile fading, clasped her hand. "Nicole, is something besides Quinn bothering you? I've had the sense something has been troubling you for a while. You can confide in me, you know. I won't judge."

"Like you confide in me?" she retorted.

The only reason she knew about Megan's struggle to have a baby was because Rebecca had let it slip. Her own sister had confided in Caleb's wife rather than her. While the knowledge hurt, it didn't surprise her. Nicole wasn't close to any of her sisters.

Freeing her hand, she continued, "We don't have that kind of relationship. Never have. I'm the piece of the O'Malley puzzle that doesn't quite fit."

Megan's sigh was audible above the chatter in the well-appointed room. "You do fit, Nicole. In your own way, you do. You just refuse to see it. And for whatever reason, you refuse to let anyone close. You're the one who throws up obstacles in order to keep the rest of us at arm's length."

Her words sliced deep. Megan was right. She had intentionally created space between herself and her sisters. And even though Nicole acknowledged the truth, recognized her role in the current state of their sisterhood, lifetime habits weren't easily broken. "I'm exhausted. I'm going to return the books and head home."

"Nicole, wait—"

Ignoring the soft protest, she hastened to reach the hallway. The sooner she left Gatlinburg, the sooner she could start fresh in Knoxville. Cultivate better relationships in her new surroundings.

At the far end of the hall across from the stately dining room, the softly lit library was blessedly empty. Scents of leather and paper masked the room's musty hint. Bold maroon wallpaper contrasted nicely with the dark wood furniture and gleaming floors. While she wouldn't choose to read in here, it would be a nice place to curl up with her needles and fabrics.

Thoughts in turmoil, she traversed the narrow space between the red-striped camelback sofa and floor-to-ceiling shelves on the wall behind it, absently skimming her fingers over the spines. Hitting upon the empty slots where her latest picks belonged, she slid them in and began hunting for stories that would please both siblings.

She was perched near the top of the rolling ladder, scanning the upper shelves, when an accented voice from the doorway startled her.

"I did not figure you for a reader."

Upper body swaying dangerously, Nicole dropped the book in order to seize the ladder with both hands. She scowled at the dapper figure striding toward her. "How did you figure that? Was it something in my eyes? The way I speak, perhaps? Do I not sound intelligent to your Northern ears?"

Quinn scooped up the book and, stretching his left arm behind her legs, gripped the opposite ladder edge. His face was upturned, brown eyes fastened onto her face and a slight pucker in his brow. "I observe people. Call it a hobby, if you will." He lifted the book to her. "I guess I was wrong this time."

The press of his muscular arm against the back of her knees rendered them practically useless. Oh, why must physical contact with him cause these strange bodily reactions?

"Are you attempting to trap me up here?"

Sparks of mischief kindled in his eyes. "I was preventing you from falling. Wouldn't want you to break something and be unable to perform your assistant duties."

"I wouldn't be in danger of falling if you would keep your distance."

One black eyebrow arching at her, he removed his hand but remained where he stood. Nicole carefully made her way to the bottom and retreated to the single window on the opposite side of the room, occupying herself with the view of the sweeping side yard bathed in the pastel orange and pink swirls of sunset. *Go away, Quinn.*

He didn't take the hint. Following her, his lean body boxed her in, not invading her space but close enough for her to sense the heat coming off him, smell his spicy—and no doubt expensive—cologne. A cushiony chair blocked her escape.

"What do you want?" Sighing, she turned to face him, realizing too late her mistake. Inches separated them. She found herself fascinated by the ripple of hard muscle beneath the fine white cotton shirt, the strong, golden column of his throat above the charcoal coat collar, his carved chin that was at once charming and obnoxious.

He was wearing a serious my-dog-just-died expression. "You want the truth?"

Not really. "Um—"

"I followed you because I wanted to apologize for the way I acted the other evening. I overreacted, and I'm sorry. You've given me no reason not to trust you."

"Oh."

"I couldn't help but notice, too, that you seemed upset while talking to your sister. I came to make sure you were all right."

Nicole found herself tongue-tied. Quinn was worried about her? The knowledge didn't irritate her as it should. In fact, his concern caused a sticky-sweet warmth to build up inside.

"I'm fine."

"Why don't I believe that?" He cocked his head to one side, his astute gaze laying bare her inner secrets. "I've had plenty of time to observe you in the company of your sisters, and there exists a barrier between you. I've noticed you tend to keep everyone at a distance. I wonder—"

"Stop." The warmth dried up, leaving her empty and

wanting. Angry, too. "Stop acting as if you know everything there is to know about me, Quinn Darling. You've
twice accused me of being a thief, and now you're analyz-
ing my family relationships?" She poked his chest, and he
blinked in surprise. "You think you're so high and mighty
because you're a member of the prestigious Darling family,
heir to a vast fortune and lifelong resident of the great city
of Boston. You think that because we talk slower and live
in log cabins and wear calico and overalls that we're dull,
illiterate provincials. Let me tell you something—your
Harvard diploma doesn't give you the right to come here
and judge us when it's clear you know nothing."

Pushing past him, she left the house without saying
goodbye to Megan and without the books she'd promised
Lillian. If she didn't get far away, she would be tempted
to strangle her boss. The foreign notion evoked a bubble
of hysterical laughter.

Admit it, a voice prodded, *you're angry because he
echoed Megan's assertions. You're upset that he can see
the truth about you. You're worried that, like everyone else
in this town, he'll look too closely and find you lacking.*

Quinn hadn't been able to get their exchange—and Nicole's obvious distress—out of his head. He'd tossed and
turned all night, plagued not only by worries about how
to secure the townspeople's confidence, but about her, as
well.

Despite her air of competency, Quinn's perceptive nature had homed in on the vulnerability she worked val-
iantly to mask. His standoffish assistant had stirred his
protective instincts to life, and he couldn't think of anyone who'd welcome his protection less.

A few feet below where Quinn stood on the riverbank,
Caleb locked the springhouse door and maneuvered the

steep incline with ease. Whipping off his worn Stetson to run a gloved hand through his black hair, he rested against the wagon bed. "That's the last of it. I'll have another delivery early next week."

Quinn pocketed the key Caleb held out to him. "We may need more cheese. It's popular with my customers, and Mrs. Greene has need of it for her café menu."

"We can provide whatever you need." Glancing in the direction of the bridge spanning the river, Caleb straightened. "Here comes my cousin."

Quinn squinted in the early-morning sunshine streaming through the leaves overhead. From this distance, he couldn't make out her expression. Her bright apricot skirts swished with each long stride, the nipped-in bodice and capped sleeves showing off her lithe figure. As she came nearer, he noticed her hair had been wrestled into a more severe hairstyle than usual, a tight, long twist nestled between her shoulder blades, not one lock out of place. What she couldn't know was the style showcased her most impressive feature—those unusual-hued eyes that appeared to glow with lavender light.

"Morning, Nicki," Caleb drawled with a wicked grin.

"Caleb." She flicked her cousin a narrowed glance before addressing Quinn. "May I have a word with you?"

Her resigned expression filled him with unease. Was she about to quit her position? His insincere challenge the other evening had slipped out, fueled by annoyance. He valued her work and would miss her competence and dedication when she left. "Certainly."

Placing a hand at the small of her back, he guided her farther down the grassy bank. A groundhog scuttled away, seeking refuge near the deep green water's edge, but he gave it only a cursory glance. "What's on your mind?"

Fingers plucking at the pleats on her skirt, she shifted

away from his touch to stand facing him. Her chin went up. "It's my turn to apologize. You're my boss, and I shouldn't have spoken to you the way I did last night."

The tension left his shoulders. "It is true that I'm your boss part of the time. However, when we aren't at the mercantile, we are…" He rummaged through his brain for an appropriate label.

"Acquaintances."

Quinn frowned. That wasn't quite what he'd been going for. "Whatever we agree to call our relationship, you and I are on equal footing. It won't be easy at first, but we will find a way to navigate our interactions."

While her violet gaze was unflinching, he caught a flicker of something akin to trepidation. "I still have a job, then?"

"Yes, of course." He huffed a light laugh. "Nicole, I value honesty. I want you to be frank with me. I can handle whatever you feel the need to say."

Her thick lashes swept down to skim her cheeks. Boot toeing a cluster of dandelions, she nodded.

Behind him, Quinn heard the restless shuffling of Caleb's team. He half turned. "I think your cousin is ready to leave."

"I'll go on in and open up."

Sweeping past him, her sweet-as-a-rose scent enveloped him, and he watched her nimbly ascend the stairs, spine straight and shoulders set, posture fit for a queen. He never would've expected her to apologize, especially to him. One thing was certain—she prized this job and the income that would allow her to one day leave Gatlinburg.

He strode over to Caleb, ignoring his obvious amusement. "Help me out, O'Malley. Share your insight on how to best navigate daily interactions with your cousin."

He tilted his head back and laughed outright. "Not a

chance, my friend. No one gave me a clue how to handle Becca, yet we managed to figure each other out just fine."

"You misunderstand." He held up his palms, "I'm not asking in a romantic capacity. Not at all. My interest is strictly professional."

Better watch it, Darling—wouldn't want to get struck by lightning.

"Whatever you say." Still chuckling, Caleb hauled himself onto the wagon seat and looped the reins in one hand. "I could give you some pointers, but I wouldn't wanna rob you of the fun of figuring her out on your own. If you can. Truth is, I haven't had that much luck."

With a final wave, he released the brake and set the wagon in motion.

"Fun?" he muttered to himself. "You and I have different ideas of fun, my friend."

Climbing the staircase, he left the cheerful birdsong and increasingly familiar hum and splash of the river behind in favor of the cooler, fragrant interior. Heading down the hallway and going straight for the jars of penny candy, his steps slowed as he attempted to make sense of the sight before him. Along the lengthy interior wall, where the ready-made clothing was displayed, Kenneth, Timothy and Pete surrounded Nicole.

Were they deliberately boxing her in?

One hand resting on the first jar's lid, he studied her face. While her eyes were defiant, her lower lip trembled. And her back was pressed against the shelving unit behind her.

Not acceptable.

Reminding himself to keep calm and not jump to conclusions, Quinn skirted the counter.

"Where's your broom, little witch?" Kenneth, whose back was to Quinn, taunted. The other two snickered.

"Was that your black cat I saw on the street?" Still unaware of Quinn's presence, Timothy elbowed his cohort.

Nicole's jaw went taut. "If you aren't here to do business, I suggest you leave. I have more important things to do than entertain you."

"I can think of a few ways you could entertain me."

When Quinn heard the silky innuendo in Kenneth's voice, his blood began to simmer. "May I assist you, gentlemen?"

The two who could see him stiffened, shrugging and shuffling their feet. Kenneth pivoted. "We're just perusing the goods, Mr. Darling. Seeing what might be of interest to us."

Tempted to wipe that smirk off his face, Quinn's fingers closed into fists. "Well, Mr. Jones, you and your friends are preventing my assistant from doing her job."

Placing his hat over his heart, Kenneth dipped his head in a mock bow. "My apologies, sir."

"Let's go, Kenny."

While the other two made for the exit, Kenneth nodded and turned as if to leave, at the last second shoving his face close to Nicole's and whispering something in her ear. Quinn was on the verge of physically removing him when he skirted away, deliberately toppling a stack of shirts onto the floor once he reached the end of the aisle.

"Oops," he said, and grinned over his shoulder.

Face averted, Nicole moved to straighten the mess. Quinn stopped her with a hand on her forearm. "Leave it. I'll take care of it."

Striding after the trio, he heard her call out. "Quinn, wait. What are you going to do?"

Out on the boardwalk, he closed the door firmly behind him, calling out for them to stop. They hadn't gotten far. Across the street, passersby looked their way.

"I will not allow my employee to be mistreated in any way. If you bother Miss O'Malley again, you and your family members will be barred from this establishment." He met each man's eyes squarely. "It would be awfully inconvenient for you to have to travel to Pigeon Forge for your supplies."

"We understand, Mr. Darling." Timothy looked properly chastised, as did Pete. Kenneth, however, wasn't cowed in the slightest. Hooking a hand on Timothy's arm, he towed him away, Pete trailing behind.

Quinn rejoined Nicole inside, hurrying to help her shake out and refold the shirts. "I told you to wait."

She shot him a heated glance. "I can take care of myself, you know."

"I am well aware," he said drily, recalling her full-on assault that first night. Their fingers collided as they both situated a shirt on the stack. "This is my store, however, and I will not stand by and watch you or any of my patrons be treated in that manner."

"While I appreciate your efforts, I doubt it will have any effect."

Covering her hand with his, Quinn stalled her movements. "What did he say to you, Nicole?"

"Something stupid and not worth repeating."

He couldn't help but think about Tilly, his fifteen-year-old sister, and what he'd do if she was in Nicole's position. *Throttle the culprits, that's what.*

Her skin was like ice. Taking her hand in both of his, he tried to transfer his warmth to her. Her head was bent, so he couldn't tell if the contact bothered her.

"You denied there being a problem. Why?"

"He's angry, that's all." She shrugged as if it was no big deal. "I should've just gone to the stupid dance."

Light glinted in her confined locks. "Let me get this

straight. Kenneth is acting like a beast because you didn't agree to attend a dance with him?"

"I'm afraid I've dented his pride."

Beneath the unblemished skin, the bones of her hand were fragile. He released it in order to warm the other. He liked being connected to her, liked that she hadn't pulled away. Perhaps his nearness didn't bother her as much as he'd thought.

"That's not an excuse. He has no right to treat you like that…" The image of shattered china shoved to the forefront of his mind. Gently, he slid his fingers beneath her chin and lifted her face. "He caused you to drop the dishes, didn't he?"

Swallowing hard, she moved her head a fraction of an inch.

"I'm an idiot." Releasing her before he did something rash, like kissing that dainty mouth of hers, he helped her to her feet. "I'm sorry, Duchess. I should've suspected."

"You couldn't have known."

"You're not clumsy or careless. I know that."

She touched his sleeve. "Thank you."

"For what?"

"Sticking up for me."

"Even though you didn't require my help?"

She smiled at him, a genuine smile that transformed her face into something so beautiful and hopeful he didn't dare blink for fear he'd miss it. "I'll let it pass this time."

He knew then that, no matter how loudly and frequently she protested, he'd always rush to lend her aid.

Chapter Eight

Nicole withheld a sigh as Mr. Craig perused the newest selection of hair tonics beneath the glass. He wasn't one to rush the decision. While he hadn't yet found a cure for his baldness, he continued to test the latest concoctions.

Her gaze strayed once more to her boss, whose sinewy, suit-clad body was propped against the counter, arms folded across his chest as he conversed with Reverend Monroe. Late-afternoon light glinted off his dark hair, slicked away from his face in a dashing style. How he managed to appear neat and unruffled no matter how many customers came in or how stuffy the place got she couldn't fathom.

Snatches of their conversation drifted over. When the reverend asked how Quinn was settling in, she was surprised to hear him admit he wasn't having much luck with the locals and that he felt like an outsider. Considering his status in Boston, his troubles here must be particularly difficult to cope with.

"Give it some time," the reverend urged, craggy features sympathetic. "They miss Emmett. He was their confidant, advisor and friend."

Quinn nodded. His attention slipped to her and, embarrassed to be caught staring, she ripped her gaze from his worried one.

"I believe I've made up my mind." Mr. Craig smiled, revealing stained teeth. "I'll take the Imperial Hair Tonic." He pointed to the tall bottle in the middle.

"I'll wrap it up for you."

Ripping off a square of brown paper, she unlocked the case and lifted out the bottle. Quinn strolled up as she was handing the parcel across the counter.

"Appreciate your business, Mr. Craig." Quinn's smile was forced.

Closing the case, she said, "What was the notice Reverend Monroe dropped off?"

He pinched the bridge of his nose, leading her to wonder if he had a headache. "A reminder about the Independence Day picnic."

The calendar displayed on the wall showed the July Fourth holiday fell on a Tuesday. "Are you going?"

The foursome playing cards in the corner burst out laughing at some private joke. Quinn glanced over his shoulder at them, shaking his head as if he couldn't figure out why he was allowing them to waste space in his store. He wasn't thrilled to have them back, but Nicole thought he'd done the right thing. Pushing off from the counter, he came around and, passing her, retrieved a horehound candy from a jar.

She couldn't stop thinking about how his hands had warmed hers.

"I suppose I will."

At his marked lack of enthusiasm, she tried to see things from his perspective. He'd left his home and family, with whom he'd apparently shared a close bond, and he was completely alone in an unfamiliar place where not everyone was happy he'd come. She recalled how, without the slightest hesitation, he'd defended her against Kenneth last weekend.

Dropping the case key in her apron pocket, she said, "Why don't you come with me? There will be food. Games. Music. It's a nice change from the routine."

He hesitated before popping the treat in his mouth, brow creasing as he considered. "I'd like that…if you're certain you wouldn't mind spending your day off with me."

An image of prior town-wide celebrations popped into her head, of enamored couples sharing picnics beneath the shade trees and strolling arm in arm. She shook off the un-settling image of her and Quinn engaging in such behav-ior. They shared a professional relationship. Nothing more.

Unlike other girls her age, she didn't pine for a clinging beau, didn't dream about marriage proposals. Romance was the furthest thing from her mind. So the fact that she'd contemplated—even for a second—such behavior with her boss bothered her no small amount.

"I'm certain."

He followed her into the office, bracing an arm on the door frame. Nicole didn't particularly like sharing this confined space with him because his presence made her twitchy. She became acutely aware of commonplace events—the pull of air into his lungs and subsequent ex-hale, the way his throat worked with each swallow, the movement of his lips as he spoke.

"Will your sisters be there?"

"You're a bit too old for them, don't you think? Jessica and Jane are only sixteen."

His brows shot up. Dropping his arm, he edged closer and propped his hip on the desk. A baffled smile mocked her. "While the twins are loveliness personified, I had not planned on offering for either of them. It was an in-nocent question."

Cheeks burning, she feigned interest in one of the many ledgers laid out on the desk, absently skimming the nearest one. He thought they were lovely, did he? Of course he did. *Please tell me you're not jealous,* an inner voice pleaded. *Quinn Darling can woo whomever he pleases.*

"I know I'm risking getting raked over the coals again for putting my nose where it doesn't belong," he said quietly, "but it's obvious there is tension between you and your sisters. I cannot help but wonder why."

If there had been any hint of lightheartedness in his manner, she would've refused to answer. But he was serious...even concerned. "How would you like it if you were constantly compared to your siblings? If your entire life, you'd been judged and pegged as the odd one in your family?"

A frown cut a groove in his cheek. "Why would you think that about yourself?"

Worrying the edge of her sleeve, Nicole hesitated. Baring her soul to him was a bad idea. The worst. "You wouldn't understand."

"You think I haven't had my share of problems?" he said softly.

"You're the Darling heir. Don't tell me Boston's elite didn't worship the ground you walked on."

A dry half laugh escaped him. "Solely because of the fortune attached to my last name. My winning personality and natural charm wouldn't have gotten me very far if my last name had been Smith or Jones and I'd worked on the docks."

The glimpse of uncertainty in him stunned Nicole. Where was her suave, confident, infuriatingly-sure-of-himself boss? "I imagine it would be difficult to wonder if every person in my life was there because of me or because of the benefits of being my friend."

"You have no idea."

Shadows passed across his face, shadows she felt certain not many people were allowed to see. She'd misjudged him, had taken one look at his well-tailored clothes, slick appearance and cool confidence and assumed he'd led a privileged, problem-free life. But money and status didn't solve the world's problems, did they?

She took a steadying breath. "When I was a kid, my cousins and sisters were my only friends. I didn't think it strange until around age eight. I noticed Juliana, Megan and the twins had friends who weren't family members, boys and girls who *chose* to spend time with them. I wondered why I didn't. Then Kenneth and his buddies started a wild rumor that I was a witch's offspring and had been left on my parents' porch as a baby." Grimacing, she fingered a rogue curl, stretching the strand and releasing it to spring back into place. "Since I didn't look anything like my other sisters, the school kids latched on to it."

"That's ridiculous." He seemed transfixed by her hair, as if he really wanted to test its texture.

Mouth dry, she moistened her lips. "I tried to be more like my sisters but eventually concluded it was a waste of time. I would never measure up. So I stopped trying to please others. Told myself their opinions didn't matter." At his sad expression, she hastened to add, "I don't mind being alone. I have plenty to keep me busy."

Liar, she told herself. *You want what Megan and Juliana have, what the twins share. You crave connection. Closeness. A sense of belonging.*

"Those people don't know what they're missing." Quinn's expression turned thoughtful. "You have a lot to offer, Nicole. I'm positive that if you were to let down your guard, people would respond to you. You're bright and creative. Considerate. Hardworking and driven. You are as worthy of friendship as your sisters."

Nicole floundered for an appropriate response. His gentle praise inspired pleasure and embarrassment in equal amounts. "Sounds like you had those qualities memorized."

"It's a quirk of mine," he said, and smiled sheepishly. "When I meet new people, I make lists about them in my head."

"Lists."

"Strengths and faults."

"I don't want to know the faults you've observed in me during our brief acquaintance."

"Attacking unsuspecting men tops the list."

Refusing to let him see her mortification, she smirked. "You can't place the blame for that entirely at my feet."

The rear entrance bell sounded, cutting off his response. He fished out his pocket watch. "Five thirty. Awfully late for a delivery." He paused in the doorway. "We will continue this conversation later."

She nodded, grateful for the interruption. Now that Quinn was privy to her private struggles, she felt exposed and vulnerable. It was not a comfortable feeling.

The delivery was a large one. The driver had left the larger town of Maryville later than expected. Even with his help, unloading and sorting everything would take several hours. Quinn immediately cleared out the card players, closing the store several minutes early and paid a young boy to take a message to Nicole's mother letting her know she'd be late and he would see her home. He'd promised to treat her to supper at Plum's when they'd finished. Nicole wasn't sure she wished to dine alone with him, however. He couldn't know how an outing like that could be misconstrued. At least at the Independence Day picnic, they'd be surrounded by her family.

had invaded her body, her wet clothing sticking to her
and making the temperature feel colder than it actu-
was. Of course, the ice blocks packed in straw lin-
the rear wall kept the air cool. Quinn whipped out his
ketknife and, kneeling at the floor opening, rinsed it
he river water. Then he located several cheese wheels
carved out wedges for them both. Next, he attacked a
in the far corner.

Coming over to her, his lips compressed as he studied
face. "You should sit down."

All too happy to do as he suggested, she grimaced as
rock wall she leaned against leached more coldness
o her back. While Nicole ate, Quinn dipped out milk
o a tin cup he'd discovered on the shelf.

Lowering himself onto the space beside her, he held
cup out and nodded at the humble snack in her lap. "I
ow it doesn't compare to the café food, but it will hold
until we're rescued."

She took a generous sip of milk. "It's fine. My cooking
ills leave much to be desired," she admitted. "When I'm
my own for meals, this is similar to what I'd fix for my-
f. Needlework is the only thing I excel at."

She tried not to fidget as he studied her outfit with a
ical eye. Since free floor space was limited, he sat close
ugh that their shoulders pressed together.

"You are an excellent seamstress. Tilly would be thrilled
vear your creations."

She found that difficult to believe. His sister had access
he finest clothing money could buy. Unable to contain
curiosity, she said, "What is she like? And your brother.
at's his name?"

Balancing his forearms on his bent knees, he rested
head against the wall and smiled fondly. "Tilly is a
ted, good-natured princess. She's a whiz at the piano

It was nearing eight o'clock when she and Quinn put
the last of the perishables in the springhouse. Her arms
and upper back muscles ached, as did her feet, and hunger gnawed at her. The ham, bread and palm-size portion
of strawberries she'd had for lunch seemed very long ago.

Unable to stand to his full height in the small, squat
building, Quinn hung a slab of dried beef from the low-
slung rafters. "That's the last of it. Are you ready to head
over to the café?"

Nicole shoved the last crock into the corner. Hunger
drove her answer. "More than ready."

"I hope chicken and dumplings is on the menu," he
said, and grinned.

She'd never stopped to think what he did for meals. No
doubt in Boston, he'd had all his meals served to him. "You
don't know how to cook, do you?"

"I can manage decent coffee."

Careful not to bump into the ham hanging nearby, she
straightened. "Did your family employ a French chef to
prepare extravagant meals?"

His low chuckle rippled over her skin, raising goose
bumps that had nothing to do with the river-water-cooled
air. "Justin is from South Carolina, actually. But yes, he
and his assistants do prepare mouthwatering meals for us."

"I suppose you lived in a grand mansion."

"Exceedingly grand." He didn't bother denying it. "Spacious, tastefully appointed rooms, priceless art, vast gardens with pathways and fountains." Cocking his head, he
brought his brows together. "You would have no trouble
fitting in there."

"Because I don't fit here?"

"You don't seem to want to fit here."

"You're right. I don't…hence the plans to leave." Done
with the conversation, Nicole gestured to the door. Out-

side, the sun had dipped beneath the mountain peaks and the gathering shadows made it difficult to see. "I'm going to faint soon if I don't get something to eat."

"Let's get you fed, then."

As he maneuvered a turn in the cramped space overflowing with crocks of milk and sausages, jarred vegetables and fruits and dried meat, the door slammed shut with a bang, enclosing them in darkness. Shocked, neither reacted as the sound of the lock clicking into place and muted male laughter drifted to them.

"Nicole—" Quinn sounded strange "—what just happened?"

"I think…" Battling growing alarm, she blinked to adjust her vision. "Someone's played a dirty trick on us."

Desperation fired through her. She tried to shove past him, forgetting about the narrow opening running smack-dab in the middle of the puncheon floor, rigged to allow the constantly flowing river beneath to cool the interior. Gasping, she threw out her arms to try to regain her balance as icy-cold water seeped into her boots and drenched the bottom of her skirts and undergarments.

Quinn's hands closed over her waist, steadying her. He helped her up. In the darkness, she watched his shadowed outline crouch down, and suddenly his fingers were probing her ankles through the leather boots before skimming up to her calves.

"Are you hurt?"

"No." The gentle touch heated her chilled, wet skin, and the thread of concern lacing his husky voice warmed her insides. "You can stop now, Quinn. I'm fine."

Sighing, he slowly stood.

"We're stuck in here, aren't we?"

"Until someone misses us, yes."

Quinn went and pushed against the door. It didn't budge.

The walls were made of river rock, which for help wasn't likely to do them much good. will worry when you don't return home. She one to search for us."

How long would it take for someone to find if it took until morning?

Another shudder rippled through her. Sh consider the potential for disaster.

"Are pranks such as these commonplace?"

"Commonplace, no. But they aren't unhear times boys get bored."

His eyes gleamed in the darkness. "Is that v lieve the culprits are? Kids looking for a thrill

She bent to wring the excess water from he think there's a good chance it was Kenneth. He d confrontation lightly. Whatever you said to them set him on the idea of retaliation."

"Caleb and his brothers strike me as over types. They haven't defended you against then

A dry laugh escaped. "Kenneth knows be bother me when my cousins are around."

Pushing off the door, Quinn edged nearer you not tell them?"

"Like I said, I can handle whatever he dish

While he didn't answer, she sensed he wa with her response. He slowly surveyed their su "I remember seeing a lamp over here." She clinking as he gingerly explored the springh shelf. He rummaged around until he found flame cast his face in eerie shadow. When lit, he began to search the space.

"What are you looking for?"

"Supper."

Nicole couldn't summon the energy to h

and harp, and she loves horses. Oh, and she has my father wrapped around her little finger. Trevor is eighteen. Athletic. Popular. And keen on proving himself to the world... my father most of all."

"So he's like you."

Swallowing a bite of ham, he chuckled. "Yes, I suppose he is."

"It must be hard on him," she mused, thinking of her own older sisters, "to live in your shadow."

"Trevor and I have a good relationship. He's his own person."

Nicole wondered if that was truly the case or if, like her, his brother kept his true feelings hidden. "You must miss them."

"More than I could've imagined." He sighed. "As soon as I purchase some land and have a house built, I'll invite them for an extended visit. The banker told me about some available property behind the church. I'm going to look at it tomorrow."

"Are you absolutely certain this is where you want to settle? Once the novelty wears off, you might regret leaving Boston."

"This is my dream, Nicole. Like you have a dream, remember?" He nudged her shoulder with his own. "Like me, you'll leave your family behind to start fresh somewhere else. You'll be in a new place, surrounded by strangers and confronted with obstacles you didn't anticipate and aren't prepared for, but because it's your dream, you won't allow those things to distract you from your goal."

"You're right. I won't." Taking a final sip, she handed him the cup. "I have another theory about who could be behind this prank."

"Tell me."

"Not everyone is happy with the new ownership. It could be someone trying to send you a message."

He slowly nodded. "And, unfortunately, you got caught in the cross fire."

Chapter Nine

"Would you smack me if I put my arm around you?"

Nicole looked at him aghast. "Why would you want to do that?"

Quinn had held off asking as long as he could. "Because you haven't stopped shivering since your dunking. I can practically hear your teeth clicking together."

To him, the springhouse was cool, the constant flow of water pulsing moist air through the space. Because of her wet stockings and skirts, the temperature had to feel lower to her.

When she didn't respond for long moments, he tacked on, "If I hadn't left my suit jacket inside, I would offer you that."

"I, uh, suppose it couldn't hurt."

He couldn't help laughing. "Duchess, you do wonders for a man's self-esteem"

Lifting his arm, he settled it around her slender shoulders and tucked her against his side. A wave of protectiveness washed over him, catching him unawares.

"Let's not forget I am your employee." She remained stiff, unyielding, as if his nearness was distasteful. "Pet names are not appropriate."

"I am not likely to forget," he intoned. "Just for fun, what pet name would you give me? Honey? Sugar? Lemon drop?"

"You are impossible."

"So I've been told."

Below her short sleeve, her exposed arm had become chilled. Bringing up his free hand, he lightly rubbed the skin. With a deep shudder, Nicole finally relaxed into him, seeking out and taking advantage of his heat. It felt an awful lot like a victory of some sort...her trusting him.

Now that she was completely within the circle of his arms, Quinn fought a sensation of light-headedness. To ground himself, he focused on the way her silken curls tickled his cheek. Her refreshing floral scent. The contrast of her soft curves to his hard strength. Nicole may exude a frosty exterior, but she didn't feel invincible or untouchable. Maybe it was the memory of her stilted revelation, the childhood pain that had pursued her into adulthood endowing him with this insight.

The longer he held her, the longer he wanted to hold her. His hand growing tired, he settled it atop hers on her lap.

She stiffened. Quinn immediately removed his hand. "Sorry. I didn't mean to make you uncomfortable."

"If they try and force us to marry—"

"Whoa. What?" Pulling away from her, he squinted in the dim light. "Enlighten me as to what you are referring."

"I guess you haven't heard about Caleb and Rebecca's reasons for marrying," she huffed. "Didn't I warn you small-town life isn't rosy-hued perfection?"

"Caleb and Rebecca adore each other."

"It wasn't always that way. They would never have married if she hadn't spent a week nursing him to health with no one but her thirteen-year-old sister for company. Because they were unchaperoned, the town leaders pressured them to marry. To restore their reputations."

Quinn heard the disgust in her voice. "Why would anyone try and force us?"

"If we're stuck here the entire night alone, people will assume the worst."

Reaching up, he massaged his throbbing temples. Questions about his moral character was the last thing he needed. "Unfortunately, this sort of thing doesn't only happen in small towns. I've heard about a couple of instances back home where determined debutantes tricked eligible bachelors into similar situations."

With a shiver, she crossed her arms over her middle. "I don't care what anyone says, I'm not marrying you or anyone else. Nothing is going to stop me from achieving my dream."

Given her sister's intimation that she'd delayed the move to Knoxville, the vehemence of her words surprised him. "If that's the case, why didn't you leave months ago?"

She sucked in a startled breath.

"Are you sure this desperation to leave isn't a simple case of you running from your family?" he prompted. "Your reputation?"

Expression turning frigid, she scooted as far away from him as possible. "My reasons are really none of your business, Quinn. You forget that we're boss and employee. Nothing more."

Shifting around so that he was presented with her back, she hugged her knees to her chest and rested her head atop them.

Quinn buried his fingers in his hair, aware that his assistant was one of the few people on earth with the ability to upset his natural equanimity. The woman was not only unpredictable but as prickly as a porcupine. Any man fool enough to pursue her would wind up with scars to show for his efforts.

I won't have to put up with her insolent attitude forever. It's not that Nicole isn't replaceable. I'll find a suitable candidate to take her spot. Preferably male. Less drama.

As the minutes ticked by, the silence became increasingly awkward. Nicole hadn't made a peep, and he wondered if she was dozing.

When his stomach growled an hour later, he got up to stretch his legs and pound on the door again. The paltry snack hadn't appeased his appetite, and he couldn't stop daydreaming about Mrs. Greene's dumplings. The cold was starting to become bothersome, too. Fortunately for them, it wasn't wintertime. They really would've had a problem on their hands then.

His fist began to sting from the constant pounding.

"You're wasting your time." Nicole's somber voice reached him over the sound of rushing water. "No one can hear you."

Quinn rested his forehead against the door, defeat a sour taste in his mouth. May as well accept they'd be spending the night here. If word got out, his hopes of ever gaining the townspeople's trust and respect would be dashed. Especially if they didn't fulfill expectations and marry.

Even with his back to her, he heard her shivering. A sigh built in his chest.

He pivoted to address the huddled form. "Look, I know you detest me, but I think for both our sakes you should let me hold you again."

Half twisting, Nicole contemplated him with a shocked expression. She visibly swallowed. Reluctantly nodded. Moved to lean against the wall.

Tamping down rogue anticipation, he eased down beside her and gingerly looped his arm around her shoulders once again. She was colder than before. Would this prank end with her falling prey to illness?

When she wrapped both arms about his waist and snuggled into his side, Quinn's heart thumped out a dire warning. *Sure, I'm lonely, but I can't let her touch go to my head.*

She lifted her face to lock gazes with him, and he fought the impulse to toy with her curls.

"You're wrong, you know."

Quinn's brows lifted. "About?"

"I don't detest you."

Laughter erupted. She never failed to surprise him. "Glad to hear it, Duchess. Glad to hear it."

Nicole sighed contentedly and snuggled closer to the warm chest cradling her. What a delicious dream she was having. Self-indulgent and lovely, too lovely to be real. Subconsciously she recognized she shouldn't be enjoying her boss's embrace.

Quinn. The springhouse.

Struggling to lift her heavy, gritty lids, the sensation of floating through the air startled her. She flailed out an arm. When she didn't encounter the stone wall, she panicked.

Quinn's hold tightened. "It's all right. I've got you."

At last her vision cleared, and she blinked up at twinkling, diamond-bright stars in the black sky above. "How did we get out? Wh-why are you carrying me?"

He flicked her a glance, long strides evening out as they topped the riverbank. "You might want to keep your voice down," he murmured. "Unless you want someone to discover we spent half the night together."

"I won't let that happen," a second male voice inserted.

Despite the fog of sleep yet lingering, she knew the owner without having to see his face.

"Caleb? What are you doing here?"

He kept pace with Quinn, and even from this angle she could see the controlled anger in his features.

"When you didn't show, Aunt Alice sent the twins to our place. I came searching for you."

"How did you know where to find us?"

"I've been looking for several hours. The springhouse was my last resort."

Caleb's team entered her line of sight. Without a word, Quinn placed her gently on the wagon bed. The instant he released her, she missed the reassurance of his all-encompassing heat, and it was on the tip of her tongue to call him back.

Her cousin must've handed Quinn a blanket, because he was wrapping it around her, his manner attentive and concerned as if she were a child in need of coddling. She didn't challenge him, however. She was limp with fatigue and cold. And very, very self-conscious.

Caleb left them to take his place on the wagon seat.

When Quinn had finished, he surveyed his work, lines of worry about his eyes. "Are you warm enough?"

"How long was I asleep?" *Did I drool on your shirt? Snore?*

"Several hours."

She shuddered. It must've been torture for him, required to hold her for that length of time. "I didn't realize…"

"Hey." Carefully, he brushed the curls from her temple. "It wasn't a hardship, okay? No reason to fret. I nodded off a time or two myself."

Nicole stared up at him. There were no words to express her emotions. While she was grateful for his attentiveness, this was the first time she'd been that close to a man. Not only in the physical sense. She'd revealed private things, things she hadn't shared with anyone else. Ever.

The experience was so far removed from her reality she was having trouble processing it.

"Time to go," Caleb said over his shoulder. "We can hash this out tomorrow."

Quinn lightly tapped her chin, a trace of a smile gracing his drawn features. "Get some rest, Duchess."

As Caleb guided the team in the opposite direction, she couldn't tear her gaze from Quinn's unmoving form there in the middle of the lane. Something foreign was taking root in her heart, something an awful lot like affection.

She could not allow it to grow, to flourish. When she left Gatlinburg, she would be taking her whole heart with her.

Chapter Ten

Three cups of coffee and his eyes still burned from fatigue. Quinn hadn't slept once he'd climbed wearily to his quarters. He'd lain in his lumpy bed, listening as raindrops pattered against the shingles, his mind full of the night's events.

He wouldn't soon forget how it had felt to cradle a sleeping Nicole in his arms. While he'd told her the truth—he had dozed off and on—much of the time he'd simply reveled in her warmth and softness, fascinated by the serene arrangement of her features. She'd looked younger... untouched by life's troubles.

It had taken all of his self-control and quite a bit of prayer to rein in the drive to kiss her awake. Maintaining his honor had been difficult. Nicole's storybook beauty impacted him. Didn't matter if she was asleep or wide-awake and on the verge of strangling him. But she wasn't interested in romance, or in staying, and giving in to shallow attraction would only complicate matters.

It's not all about her outward appearance, though, is it? I like her sharp mind, her dedication and commitment, her strength.

So she had admirable qualities. That didn't make pursuing her a wise choice. Besides, he couldn't shake the feeling she was hiding something.

"Quinn?" A hand passed in front of his face. "Anyone home?"

"Caleb." Straightening from the notched-log wall beside the mercantile entrance, he grimaced. "A little lost sleep didn't used to bother me."

Black Stetson pulled low over his eyes, the other man surveyed the handful of people hurrying up and down the boardwalk. "Josh warned me to get as much as I can before the baby's born."

Quinn noted the trace of anxiety underlining the wry humor in his voice. "How many more months?"

"Four. Doc thinks the baby will make an appearance in October or early November."

He started in the direction of the jail, and Quinn fell into step beside him. "You must be over the moon."

"I am. Can't help being apprehensive, though. Any number of things could go wrong." Dodging a low-flying wasp, Caleb shot him a sharp glance. "Don't tell Becca I said that."

He held up his hands. "I wouldn't dream of it. She's probably anxious, too, this being her first."

"I'm trying to leave it in the Lord's hands. Trust Him to keep them safe."

"But it's not easy," Quinn supplied, knowing how hard it was not to worry about the store and whether or not he might fail.

Looking out for approaching wagons, Caleb nodded before stepping into the street. "Exactly."

He asked something he'd forgotten to last night. "How did you know to look in the springhouse? The lock was on the door."

"My aunt mentioned there'd been a delivery." His mouth

flattened. "That and the fact I couldn't find you anywhere else. Nicki isn't one to explore the forest or hike the side of a mountain, so I suspected you were close by."

At the door to the jail, Quinn stopped him with a lifted hand. "I want you to know I respect Nicole. I didn't do anything that would cast doubt upon her virtue."

"Let's hope this stays out of the gossip mill. While I thank God Becca and I wound up together, I wouldn't wish a forced marriage on anyone." Gripping the door handle, Caleb waved a greeting at a passing rider. "Especially you two. My cousin is dead set on life in the big city. She'd be miserable and make you miserable in the process."

Entering the jail, Quinn digested the words, glad he'd come to the right conclusion. He could work with Nicole, be her friend, but nothing else.

Shane was at his desk, as usual, gold star winking where it was pinned to his vest. A large mug of coffee occupied his hands atop a stack of wanted signs.

"Morning, gentlemen."

Quinn sat in the lone chair while Caleb dragged another from the corner.

"I heard you had an interesting night," Shane said.

Quinn scowled. "Interesting doesn't really begin to cover it."

One corner of his mouth lifted. "You have a theory about who was behind it?"

"I do."

Sprawling in the chair, Caleb rested his hat on his chest. "Let's hear it."

Quinn hadn't wanted to share in front of Nicole last night. Her cousin was going to be irate when he found out she'd kept Kenneth's behavior from him, and she hadn't been up to a verbal barrage after what she'd been through.

"Did she mention Kenneth Jones invited her to a harvest social last fall?"

Caleb's eyes narrowed dangerously. "No. Why?"

"Apparently he hasn't yet gotten past the fact she spurned his request."

"Talk, Darling."

Quinn outlined Kenneth's behavior, including the incident with the plates. He ended with the warning he'd issued to all three young men.

Caleb got up to pace, fury hovering about his prowling form. "Nicki should've told me. I would've put a stop to it."

"She's an independent woman," Quinn said.

"Too independent, if you ask me," he retorted.

The sheriff scraped his fingertips across the bristles on his jaws, expression thoughtful. "That's quite a warning, Quinn. Are you sure you're willing to follow through?"

"While I understand how such actions might impact my position here, I refuse to stand by and let them harass her."

Caleb slammed his hat on his head and strode for the door.

Shane shot to his feet. "Where are you going?"

"To confront that idiot—where else?"

Quinn stood, as well, gaze bouncing between the two men. "To tell the truth, I wouldn't mind riding along."

"Not a good idea," Shane said, skirting the desk and joining Caleb at the door. "If you go over there itching for a fight, he's only going to deny having anything to do with last night. Give me time to gather evidence."

"He's bullying Nicki," Caleb gritted out, muscle ticking in his cheek.

"I know. I don't like it, either. But we have to keep this thing quiet. I haven't forgotten that awful visit to Rebecca's cabin and you laid up with a bullet hole in your leg."

Caleb's dark gaze locked with Quinn's, even though he

was addressing the lawman. "It wasn't you pressuring us to marry. It was the reverend and Doc."

Bullet wound? He made a mental note to ask Caleb for details later.

"You don't want that for Quinn and Nicole," Shane said. "And that means getting a handle on your anger. Allow me to do my job."

A sigh gusted out of Caleb. "Do it fast."

Snagging his hat from the coatrack, Shane reached around him to grab the door handle. "I'm going over there right now. Join me." Over his shoulder, he said, "You too, Quinn. The more eyes, the better."

"Mornin', Miss Nicole. You look as fresh as a summer flower."

Passing the rear entrance to the barbershop, she mustered up what she hoped was a convincing smile. "Good morning, Martin. Looks like it's going to be a hot one."

He eyed the blue expanse above, the tree branches that hung unmoving in the sweltering air. "I think you're right."

Waving, she continued on her way, curls bobbing against her shoulders. She didn't feel fresh or beautiful. She'd overslept and, without the time to properly arrange her hair, she'd settled for brushing out the tangles and leaving it loose.

Her steps faltered when three figures came into view near the springhouse. Crouched on the bank, Shane combed the grass with outstretched fingers. Caleb stood a few feet away, his hat's brim shadowing his face as he scanned the water's edge. Near the top of the bank, Quinn's head came up at her approach. Murmuring something to the others, he strode quickly to meet her beneath the towering oak tree.

"Nicole." He came near, seemingly distracted by her

hair. Heat flared in his expression, turning his honey-colored eyes to liquid gold. "I like this look."

The feeling of weightlessness she'd experienced in his arms came rushing back. "Mama didn't wake me at the usual time."

He blinked and schooled his expression to professional courtesy. "I forgot to tell you to take the morning off. You could've stayed home and rested."

"The last thing I want is for the culprits to think their prank impacted us."

His brows drew together. "Are you all right? No sniffles? No chills or tight feelings in your chest?"

He was serious. "I'm not going to come down with pneumonia, Quinn. It wasn't that cold."

After a quick glance over his shoulder, he lowered his voice. "Listen, you should know your cousin is not in the greatest of moods."

"Well, he did spend half the night searching for us."

"It's not that. I told him about Kenneth."

"What? Why?" Irritation sharpened her voice. "That wasn't your decision to make."

He set his jaw. "I disagree. When his actions affect your ability to do your job, I get involved. It wasn't just you stuck in that springhouse." He moved his face closer. "And if word gets out, it won't be just you stuck in a sham marriage."

Nicole sucked in a ragged breath. The prospect of becoming Quinn's wife had her tummy doing somersaults. "We are not getting married. I'll skip town first."

"And leave me to deal with the consequences alone? Is the idea of marriage to me that distasteful to you, Duchess?"

The nickname sounded more like an endearment each

time he used it. "Marriage to anyone right now is out of the question."

Caleb's voice intruded. "I want to talk to you, Nicki."

Uh-oh. That stony expression did not bode well.

Quinn wrapped his hand around hers, warm and heavy, earning him a startled glance. What was he doing?

"Actually, that chat will have to be postponed," he said. "I need to go over a few things with my assistant before we open. Business-related things."

Caleb noticed their joined hands and arched a questioning brow. "Is that so?"

Almost instantly, Quinn untangled his fingers to slide them up to the spot above her elbow. "And since I haven't had breakfast, we'll be having our discussion at the café."

He didn't give Caleb a chance to respond. With a brief wave, Quinn guided her around the corner and onto Main, his touch insistent. She shook him off as they walked beneath the café's awning.

Waiting until another couple disappeared inside, she scowled at him. "I don't recall agreeing to have breakfast with you."

"Would you rather I'd left you to be raked over the coals?" A baffled smile lent him a boyish air.

"I can deal with Caleb. I've been doing it my whole life."

"Resistant to help."

"Excuse me?"

"Is it due to standard stubbornness or pride?" He stroked his chin, mischief twinkling in the brown depths. "Or perhaps a need to prove to yourself that you're capable?"

Understanding dawned. "Here's one for your list— insufferable."

Spinning, she yanked open the door and would've entered the café ahead of him were it not for his fingers snaking around her arm. Large body crowding her, he dipped his head down and murmured against her hair, "I have a theory about why you speak freely with me. It's our proximity in age. If I were say, ten years your senior, you would allow me the proper respect."

Tingles of anticipation feathered across her neck, at odds with the urge to punch him. "The same way you treat me with professional courtesy?"

Pulling away, she flounced to an unoccupied table in the far corner, folding her hands tightly beneath the table to keep from snatching up the butter knife.

Quinn followed at a more leisurely pace, smiling at those he passed before easing into the chair opposite her. After they'd ordered—milk, a boiled egg and biscuit for her, coffee and a full breakfast plate for him—he leaned back and rested his hands in his lap.

"I suppose our relationship was doomed from the first moment."

"Relationship?"

"We do have one, Duchess. It's called an employer-employee relationship. And it's gone awry. Certainly nothing like what exists in my father's offices."

Nicole had no trouble picturing Quinn in that environment. His workers must've responded to his charisma and confidence with absolute devotion.

"You sort of inherited me with the purchase," she conceded. "Fortunately, you will get to choose your next one."

Sooner rather than later, she hoped. After their enforced closeness last night, her awareness of him, her sensitivity to his voice and touch, had increased tenfold. She found herself foolishly wishing for that closeness again, no matter that he was her boss. He infuriated her and intentionally provoked her without remorse.

Quinn was right—their interactions were far too personal, and, since she didn't know how to reclaim the proper distance, she was going to have to find a way to survive until she moved away.

Chapter Eleven

Humming a favorite tune, Quinn turned down Nicole's lane feeling more like himself than he had since his arrival three weeks ago. He'd awoken shortly after dawn and, fencing gear in hand, found his way to a remote spot in the woods not far from town and practiced his parrying for several hours. Muscles burning and sweat pouring off him, he'd returned to his quarters for a bath and a shave, after which he'd attended a brief service at the church, where several town leaders spoke and those in attendance sang patriotic songs.

Independence Day was turning out to be one of those perfect summer days, the temperature warm not sizzling and the humidity low, chubby white clouds floating in a sky so blue it hurt to look at it. Bees buzzed and frogs chirruped. The furious flapping of birds' wings rustled tree limbs overhead. The moss-and-magnolia-scented air provided a sweet perfume to rival anything on his store shelves.

Along with every other business in town, the mercantile was closed, and he fully intended to enjoy this rare time of leisure. That he was attending the holiday celebration with the O'Malleys merely enhanced his mood. Alice and the twins put him at ease, welcoming him as if he were part of the family. He was also looking forward to getting to know Nicole's cousins and their wives better.

Neither the failure to discover evidence linking Kenneth to the springhouse ordeal nor the fact he wasn't making much headway with the locals could pierce his good humor.

Passing the enormous barn and a vegetable garden with tidy, orderly rows, he touched a finger to the golden asters flanking the steps before bounding onto the porch of their two-story cabin and rapping lightly on the door.

Jane—or was it Jessica?—greeted him. "Mr. Darling, won't you come in?"

The faint blush and shy smile clued him in. "Thank you, Jane." He entered, his smile widening at her obvious surprise. He made note of her petal-pink blouse for later.

"Nicole will be down in a moment." She indicated the steep, almost ladder-style steps disappearing into the ceiling. "Would you like to join us in the kitchen? Mama is packing our basket."

He followed her through the crowded, narrow dining space and into the homey kitchen. Alice and Jessica—clad in watered-down green—looked up from the counter with sunny smiles. "Quinn—" Alice appeared pleased to see him "—I'm glad you could join us. Nicole overslept this morning, and I'm afraid she's running a bit late."

Concern flared in his chest. He'd been on edge the first day or so after their ordeal, watching for signs of encroaching illness. He couldn't get the shock of her icy skin out of his head, her piteous shudders. *That's not the only thing I can't forget.*

Even now, he recalled with ease how perfectly Nicole had fit in his arms, the wondrous awe of cradling her while she slept, vulnerable and all her usual guards discarded. The silkiness of her hair… *Enough, Darling.*

He cleared his throat. "I hope she isn't coming down with anything."

Alice smiled at his consideration. "I think this is more a case of getting to bed later than usual. My middle daughter tends to become engrossed in her sewing projects and lose track of time."

Quinn would dearly like to see her in such a state. Would she be as impeccably neat as usual, not a hair out of place, or would she be rumpled, raven locks haphazardly tumbling about her shoulders as she lost sense of time and place?

Encouraging himself to keep his thoughts on the right track, his gaze fell on a familiar blue box of chocolate-cream drops perched on the pie safe ledge.

"Nicole favors those, doesn't she? I didn't think she had much of a sweet tooth, but I've noticed she can't get enough of the cream drops."

Jessica and Jane exchanged a doubtful look. Alice's brow screwed up as she placed a bread loaf in the basket. "Nicole doesn't often indulge in sweets."

Jessica went to examine the box, pulling it down from the shelf. "I didn't notice this was even here."

Confused, Quinn said, "Could she have brought them home for you?"

Even as he said it, the feeling in his gut said something wasn't right. Nicole had purchased no less than four boxes in the past two weeks. They weren't expensive, but they weren't cheap, either. She wouldn't have gotten them for the sole purpose of forgetting them on a shelf.

Jane shrugged. "If she did, she didn't say anything."

Alice patted Jessica's shoulder. "Would you be a dear and carry this out to the wagon?"

Jessica hefted the basket, turning down Quinn's offer to help. Untying the faded apron about her ample waist, Alice hung it on a hook beside the back door. "Would you mind if the girls and I went on ahead? I'd like to pick out a prime spot before the crowds descend. There are only so many shade trees to go around."

"We'll catch up to you."

She patted his shoulder in a motherly gesture that had loneliness arching through him. He was surprised by how much he missed his mother's hovering, as he'd called it, the questions that should never be put to a fully grown, adult male. *Did you eat all of your breakfast? Are you getting enough sleep? Are you honestly planning on wearing that particular coat with that shirt?*

Soon, he comforted himself. Soon he would make a decision about the land parcels he'd surveyed last week and get started on a permanent home.

After Alice and the girls left, Quinn wandered around the living area, a space overflowing with couches and furniture. They could do with a little more elbow room, he thought, touching a finger to the painting propped on the mantel.

"That was a gift from Rebecca," Nicole informed him as she reached the bottom of the stairs. "It's my favorite flower."

Turning his back to the cold fireplace, he skimmed her neat-as-a-pin image and was hit with the strange desire to muss her restrained curls. "You look impeccable, as always."

Taking in her lilac ensemble, he never would've guessed she'd been in a rush to get ready. She was as cool and composed as ever. In that moment, he made it his mission to upset that composure at some point today. Nicole O'Malley needed to learn to take life a bit less seriously.

"Thank you." Double-checking the pearl buttons on her bodice, she craned her neck to see past the dining room. Silver earbobs winked at her earlobes. "Are they waiting outside for us?"

"Actually, your mother asked if we'd mind meeting them there. I believe she was anxious to claim a spot."

"Oh."

"Are you regretting volunteering to accompany me?"

"No," she replied too quickly, jerking up her chin. "Are you regretting accepting? Our arrival won't go unnoticed, I assure you. Hazard of small-town life."

Striding forward, he took hold of her elbow and turned her toward the door. "I'm no stranger to gossip, Duchess." Opening the door, he ushered her onto the porch. "Gossip is quite common in my social circles. Today I will be the envy of every man in attendance, young and old, because I have the loveliest lady in Gatlinburg on my arm."

Nicole disengaged her arm and glared at him. "Were you born this way or is it an acquired affliction?"

"To what are you referring, my dear?" Quinn bit back a smile as her color heightened.

"The charm oozing from your pores." She flicked a hand up and down the length of him. "Do they teach that course at Harvard? How to spout ridiculous flattery at will?"

He lost the smile. "Why is it so difficult for you to accept a compliment?"

This aloof, don't-come-near-me attitude masked low self-esteem. Amazing that an accomplished young woman like Nicole could doubt herself.

His serious tone must've unnerved her, for she stormed down the steps ahead of him. "The church is a good twenty-minute walk from here. We should get going."

Sensing her need for space, Quinn purposefully didn't

offer his arm as they walked along the serene, country lane leading to town. The silence between them was companionable, despite her irritation with him. He liked that they could be in the empty mercantile together and not feel the compunction to fill the silence with unnecessary conversation.

By the time they'd reached Main Street and he popped into the store for the lunch basket he'd ordered from Plum's, she no longer looked as if she wanted to strangle him.

She did appear nervous, however.

Locking the front door and pocketing the key, he fell into step beside her. The church property was teeming with people. Food tables had been set up along the side of the clapboard building, the wide, grassy area dotted with blankets and clusters of people setting out picnic baskets. Fiddle music drifted down the street.

Another sigh reached him as they passed the post office, and Quinn cast her a sidelong glance. "You are wishing you hadn't asked me, aren't you? It's all right if you'd rather go and join your family. I'm sure the reverend and his wife would allow me to join them."

Nicole's steps faltered. "It's not that." Thick, black lashes lowered to brush her cheeks. "I, uh, I've never had an escort before."

"To the Independence Day celebration?"

"To *anything.*"

Quinn was hard put not to let his surprise show. The familiar drive to protect her arrowed through him even as an unwise sense of satisfaction took hold.

Passing beneath the branches of the outermost tree in the churchyard, he trained his gaze on the kaleidoscope of smartly dressed people. "Then I am indeed a fortunate man. I will warn you that I am not accustomed to sitting on the sidelines while others have all the fun. As you are my date, I expect you to join me."

Nicole followed his gaze to the lively two-legged race being set up beneath the trees edging the property.

Panic rippled across her features. "Quinn, no."

"Oh, yes." He caught her hand as she made to escape, weaving his fingers through hers and starting in that direction.

She dug in her heels. "I don't participate in silly games."

"I didn't peg you for someone who allowed others' opinions to dictate her actions."

"What's that supposed to mean?"

"Do you honestly care what these people think about you?"

Nicole chewed on her lip, troubled violet gaze sweeping the crowds.

"Come on," he cajoled, tugging on her hand, "you never know. You just might enjoy yourself."

To his surprise and pleasure, she gave in. At the starting line, Quinn got the rope from the man in charge and, binding his ankle to hers, tried not to think about their first meeting and his ungentlemanly actions. The other contestants' competitive smiles held unspoken questions. They were clearly intrigued by his and Nicole's participation, although whether due to her involvement or the nature of their relationship he hadn't a clue.

Quinn counted himself fortunate no one had learned of their time in the springhouse. While he liked Nicole and was certainly aware of her as a woman, he wasn't keen on marrying her. She was prickly and complicated. He preferred sweet and biddable. She was set on becoming a successful businesswoman. His heart's desire was a traditional family.

Of course, searching for a suitable wife among Gatlinburg's residents would have to wait until his house was built and his position in the community more settled. Occasionally spending time with Nicole—as friendly business associates—was perfectly acceptable.

As they hobbled to the starting line, he curled an arm about her petite waist and pressed his mouth to her ear. "Relax, Duchess. Put your arm around me."

She grimaced but did as he suggested. "You think I don't know you're trying to annoy me with the nickname?"

He barked out a laugh. "You make it too easy."

"And what is this exactly?" She waved a hand between them. "Trying to make me miserable?"

"On the contrary. I'm trying to get you to enjoy yourself."

"This isn't my idea of enjoyment."

The pistol shot rang out. Nicole's gasp was whipped away the moment he jolted them forward. Their progress was awkward, stilted, and they nearly landed in a tangled heap half-a-dozen times. Onlookers' cheers spurred them on. Quinn didn't mind that they didn't win. Not when her cheeks were flushed and her eyes sparkled like precious jewels.

Untying the rope, he pointed at her. "Is that a smile attempting to break through?"

"Not quite." She gave him an arch look.

"Guess that means my work isn't finished."

Taking her hand again, he pulled her through the crowd to the rear of the church, where ladies were competing in a skillet toss.

"I'm not doing that."

"What if I offered you a dollar's worth of fabric?"

Her arms, folded across her chest, fell away, and she stared at him with parted lips. "You're serious?"

"I am."

"Make it store credit, and you have a deal."

"Fine."

"Fine."

With a bracing breath, she tugged off her reticule and tossed it at his chest. He fumbled to catch it before it fell to the ground. "Minx."

Watching her march up to the organizer, Quinn couldn't swipe the goofy grin from his face. It remained for the next hour as he persuaded her to take part in musical chairs—which he won—a cakewalk and a sawing contest. They both worked up a sweat on that last one, and by the end he'd accomplished his goal—Nicole laughing freely, inky curls escaping their pins to caress her nape and excitement animating her features.

"I need a drink," she panted, sagging against the solid oak trunk.

Quinn propped an arm on the nearest limb and leaned in, gingerly wrapping one of her curls about his finger. "I will procure you a drink just as soon as you admit you had fun."

A light breeze rustled the green leaves overhead and skimmed their heated skin. Although people milled about the grounds, laughter and children's shrieks and music filling their ears, here beneath this outlying oak it felt as if they were the only ones in attendance. Nicole had gone still. Watchful. Puzzling emotions swirled in her luminous eyes as he explored the texture of her hair.

The air between them thickened, weighted with awareness. He hadn't realized how close their faces were. Her bow-shaped mouth, pink and soft, parted on a sigh. Quinn swallowed hard.

That wasn't an invitation. *Was it?*

His heart picked up speed, pumping hard like it did in the midst of a fencing match.

She's your employee, Darling. Hands off.

It wasn't easy heeding the voice of reason. Not when she was warm and close, her expression open to him like never before.

"I, ah—" he awkwardly disengaged his finger "—suppose we should probably join your family. I've monopolized your time."

She blinked. Color flooded her face. "Yes, that's a good plan."

As they traversed the dandelion-dotted field in silence, careful not to accidentally brush against each other, he wondered how much experience Nicole had had with interested suitors. Probably little to none, if he was her first date.

Quinn wondered if she'd meet someone special in the city, if she'd ever make room in her life for anything other than her sewing. It'd be a pity if she spent the whole of her life alone. Nicole had a lot to offer, even if she wasn't aware of it.

He had never been in love. He'd thought he had something special with Helene Michelson. The daughter of millionaire Donald Michelson, she'd arrived in Boston with her parents eighteen months ago and had made an instant impression on him. Petite, blonde and outgoing, she'd shared his passion for athletic pursuits, eagerly joining him on horseback riding and boating excursions. After months of courting her in earnest, Quinn had begun to consider marriage.

That was before he overheard her talking with her friends. He'd learned she wasn't as interested in being his wife so much as being a Darling. His name—and the status attached to it—had been her desired prize.

The revelation and subsequent breakup had spurred the beginnings of his shift in priorities. He didn't want a superficial life. He craved something substantial. Something real. Lasting. Precious.

Luring Nicole out of her shell was fun, even fascinating at times, but it was a temporary distraction. She didn't meet his requirements. And he certainly didn't meet hers.

Chapter Twelve

What almost happened back there?

Thick grass snagging on her hem as they neared her family's picnic spot, Nicole felt strangely let down, which in turn left her cranky and resentful. Inviting Quinn to join her had been a dumb idea. He took pleasure in pushing her out of her realm of comfort, teasing her all the while, prodding at her defenses until she was open and exposed and then…nothing.

She was a game to him. A shiny, new toy to explore and then discard.

Why am I letting him get to me, anyway? I'm not interested in romance.

Beneath all this pulsed an undercurrent of guilt. Here she was, freely attending a holiday celebration, while Patrick and Lillian were stuck in their meager shack, trapped there until the sun went down. Lillian would take such delight in the music. And Patrick would relish the food. He, especially, needed encouragement. Friends his own age.

This isn't fair, God. I hate what they're having to endure.

When they reached the soaring, wide-limbed sugar maple where her sisters and cousins and extended family members had gathered, Nathan's wife, Sophie, took one look at Nicole and gaped. She elbowed Nathan, who was seated beside her. As a speculative smile creased his face, Nicole fiddled with her earbobs. Was her appearance causing this reaction? Her hair was a mess and she was *perspiring*. In public.

Or was it Quinn's presence beside her?

Hopping up, Sophie made eye contact with Rebecca, who was relaxing against Caleb's shoulder, and Megan.

Sophie reached her first. "Can I talk to you?"

"Um, I guess so."

"If you're ready for lunch, there's a spot beside the twins." Sophie flashed a smile at Quinn. "I won't keep her long, I promise."

Linking arms, the shorter girl led Nicole a short distance away, using a cluster of dogwood trees to block them from view.

Nicole spoke first, attempting to head off the coming inquisition. "That's a new dress. Did you make it?"

Skimming her palms over the paisley skirts, Sophie blushed prettily. "I've been practicing what you taught me. Does it look all right?"

Nicole circled her, tugging here and there to test the stitches, satisfied with the way the cotton draped her form. Before Sophie married Nathan, she'd been a tomboy, content in men's clothing and her honey-blond hair in a haphazard braid. Nicole had gladly aided in her transformation to stylish young lady.

"Your skills have improved. It's beautiful. Your hair looks nice, too."

Sophie beamed, fingers skittering over the sophisticated twist. "Nathan doesn't mind whether I wear it up or down." A dimple flashed. "Actually, that's not true. He prefers it hanging loose so he can run his fingers through it."

Nicole squelched the burst of envy. She absolutely was not jealous. "That would hardly be appropriate for an event such as this."

Megan and Rebecca rounded the dogwoods, and Nicole found herself the center of attention. "What?"

Megan seemed to be bursting with curiosity. "You came with Quinn."

"So?"

"I thought you didn't like him."

Sophie rolled her eyes. "What's not to like? He's handsome, a true gentleman and the way he looks at you…"

"He's my *boss*," Nicole muttered, instinctively clamming up. "I only asked him because he hasn't made many friends here."

Rebecca gasped, jade-colored eyes going wide. "*You* asked *him*?"

"I can't recall a time you ever gave a man the time of day." Megan's white-blond curls shone in the bright sunshine, her porcelain skin enhanced by the aquamarine hue of her formfitting dress. "Come on, sis. Tell us the truth. You fancy him, don't you?"

Nicole could feel the emotion leaching from her face, could feel the ingrained response kicking in. *Stay cool and deny everything*, her mind was insisting.

Her and Quinn's conversation that night in the springhouse came back to her. He'd been adamant in his opinion that others would like to get close to her. Sophie, Megan and Rebecca were family. How many times had they reached out to her, only to be rebuffed? *It's my fault I feel left out, isn't it, God? Not theirs.*

Please help. Sharing my innermost thoughts doesn't come naturally. Of course, I don't have to tell You that.

"To be honest…" She pushed the words past her dry

throat, clasping her hands tightly at her waist. "I can't explain how I feel about Quinn."

The three females surrounding her exchanged glances.

"Try," Megan insisted.

"He is good-looking." At Sophie's nod, Nicole held up a finger. "But he knows it. He's bossy. Smug." She recalled how he'd defended her against Kenneth and his buddies. "He's also protective. Brave. He values honesty. Family."

Rebecca smoothed her rich, copper-streaked brown hair away from her brow. "That's a good start. How does he make you feel?"

"Oh, that's easy. Angry. Frustrated—" she ticked off her fingers "—confused."

"Confused?"

"When he puts his arms around me, I kind of melt into him and I feel safe and warm and yet—" She broke off, not about to admit this unnameable longing he evoked in her.

"Wait. He put his arms around you?" Megan's brows shot to her hairline. "Did he *kiss* you?"

Oops. She wasn't supposed to mention the springhouse.

"*Ew.* No, my boss did not kiss me." Although, hadn't that been on both their minds mere minutes ago? His perfect, slightly arrogant mouth had hovered inches from hers, brown eyes glittering. Her palms went damp.

"Why was he holding you?" Rebecca said.

"I—I was cold. Look, I'm starving. I didn't eat breakfast."

Her sister stopped her exit with a gentle, staying hand. A trembling smile lit up her face. "It means a lot that you shared what's in your heart, sis."

Nicole found herself returning the smile. "It wasn't as horrid as I thought it'd be."

Megan hugged her. "Don't worry, we won't repeat a word."

* * *

Thankfully Quinn didn't ask about their conversation. Nor did he try to goad her into taking part in any more contests. They passed the remainder of the afternoon in the company of her family, her uncle and cousins engaging him in a variety of topics.

It was midafternoon when they began to pack up their things. Nicole assumed she'd accompany her mother and sisters home while Quinn returned to his quarters in the mercantile, but he insisted on walking with her.

"It's the gentlemanly thing to do. It's my duty to see you home."

"It that a Boston rule?"

"It's a Darling rule." He waited patiently for her to take his arm, challenge lurking in his eyes.

The afternoon had been a trying one on many levels. She yearned to be alone with her thoughts, needle and thread in hand and a creation taking shape beneath her stitches. But he was adamant.

Sighing, she took it, keenly aware of the hard muscle beneath her fingertips and the occasional brush of their shoulders as they walked. Strolling along the darkened store fronts, she glanced surreptitiously at his profile.

Had Quinn ever been in love? He'd intimated people admired him solely for his wealth and status, but there was more to him than that. In addition to his good looks, he had a quick wit and dynamic personality. He could be kind and thoughtful when he put his mind to it.

Not that she'd ever tell him that.

"What's brewing in that mysterious mind of yours?" Angling his head, he met her gaze head-on without missing a step.

"I'm wondering how you managed to escape the parson's trap."

"Ah. I thought you didn't consider me suitable husband material."

"I never said that, you know."

"You didn't have to," he said, and chuckled softly.

Her heart skipped a beat, wondering what it would be like to be Quinn's wife. His high-handed attitude would make her crazy within a week…and they'd argue in spectacular fashion…but she'd heard about makeup kisses. And she imagined Quinn was an expert in that area.

"In the eyes of Boston's impressionable young socialites, I'm certain you were considered quite the catch."

They crossed the wooden bridge suspended above the bustling river, their boots thudding against the worn slats. Something in his expression turned pensive, and she wondered at the cause.

"As a matter of fact, I came very close to binding myself to one particular young lady. I suppose I'm fortunate to have discovered her true motives before it was too late."

The hurt in his voice troubled her, and she unconsciously squeezed his arm.

"I'm sorry, Quinn."

"I was sorry for a long time, too."

Nicole strove to comprehend this revelation. So much of the time, he projected a carefree attitude. To know that his heart was as capable of injury as the next person's altered her view of him.

Against her better judgment, she gave in to the burning desire to question him. "What happened?"

He averted his face toward the lush forest on his side of the quiet lane, steps steady and slow and matched to hers.

"You don't have to tell me," she murmured. "I shouldn't have prodded."

"I had begun to suspect I was in love with Helene," he started quietly.

Envy snaked its way around her throat, surprising in its intensity, threatening to choke off her air supply. It was wrong, so wrong to envy this unknown woman who'd ensnared Quinn's affections. *Good thing you don't covet his admiration*, she comforted herself. *That would be unreasonable. And foolhardy.*

"We had a lot in common. I assumed we could have a good life together." His lips flattened. "Turns out I misjudged her. Helene wasn't with me because she cared about me, about the man I am when the superficial is stripped away."

"She was after your fortune?"

"And the prestige that comes from marrying into the Darling family," he said matter-of-factly.

"So Helene wasn't from an affluent family?"

His lip curled. "As a matter of fact, her father was a business associate of ours. Socially speaking, we were on equal footing."

"I don't understand."

"The thing is, Duchess, having money sometimes generates intense greed. People become obsessed with having more. Always more."

They passed beneath a low-hanging branch, startling a pair of mourning doves. She tracked their upward flight.

He'd said he'd come here for a simpler, more meaningful life. Nicole finally understood what drove him.

"I'm sorry," she said again, wishing he hadn't had to endure such treatment.

Her heart fluttered at the appearance of his soft smile. "Don't be. If it weren't for her, I wouldn't have recognized what my life was missing. I certainly wouldn't have wound up in this tiny mountain town."

"Most of Gatlinburg's marriage-minded young ladies come from humble homes. Aren't you worried history will

Chapter Thirteen

Quinn was going to be sick.

Standing on the riverbank the next morning, he surveyed the destruction of property. The springhouse door stood ajar. Crocks had been dragged out and smashed to bits, the earth beneath them soaked with milk. Broken jars shone in the early light, jewel-hued vegetables lying discarded in the grass. Half-submerged cheese wheels littered the water's edge.

What a complete and utter waste.

He didn't hear Nicole's approach until she was right beside him. "Quinn, what happened?"

Having recovered from his irritation with her—he wasn't one to hold a grudge—he flicked her a quick glance, absorbing her serene, ice-blue-bedecked elegance. The shock and disgust swirling in his gut was reflected on her face.

"Someone is trying to send a message. What that might be, I have no inkling."

She clasped her throat. "This is horrible. Can anything be saved?"

"The springhouse is empty. The perpetrator did a thorough job."

repeat itself? Even if you weren't rich, the fact that you own the mercantile makes you a desirable candidate."

His gaze probed hers for long, unsettling moments—surely the yearning sliding through the honeyed depths wasn't directed at *her*—before shifting to the lane winding through the trees. His shrug offset his serious demeanor. "I'm trusting God to lead me to the right woman. That's all I can do."

Ignoring the pinpricks of discomfort his words inspired, she drawled, "Well, if the numerous longing looks cast your way today are anything to go by, you won't lack for options."

"I'm sure I don't know to what you're referring."

At his mock innocence, she rolled her eyes. "You mean you didn't see Harriet Nichols nearly tripping and falling face-first into her potato salad when she passed by you?"

"It would've been impossible not to." He chuckled, shaking his head wryly.

They fell into a companionable silence, with Nicole mentally cataloguing every simpering whisper she'd intercepted while with Quinn. Not one unattached young lady hadn't noted his presence. As soon as the locals figured out that he was all right for a Northerner, he'd be fielding supper invitations left and right.

When her lane came into view, she slipped her hand free and stepped away. Here in the pleasant shade, his hair was a richer hue of black, his skin a shade paler and an undergrowth of bristle visible along his jaws.

Why must she notice these things? And why did he have to be tantalizingly handsome?

"I can make it the rest of the way without incident."

Slipping his hands in his pockets, he smiled, teeth flashing. "Thank you for today."

"In spite of my high-handed escort, I had fun." She smiled. "See you in the morning."

She'd half turned to leave when his words stopped her. "Oh, I meant to ask you. I saw a box of cream drops in your kitchen earlier. Your mother and sisters didn't have a clue who they were for."

The burning intensity in his eyes belied his casual tone. "Why do you care?"

"I noticed how you favor them." He shrugged. "Just wondering who liked them so much."

Lillian adored the dainty chocolates. Couldn't get enough.

A panicky feeling skittered through her, white-hot anger on its heels. "You have no right to interrogate me about my purchases. You don't treat your other customers this way. Don't do it to me."

This anger inflicted pain. She didn't want to be angry at him, not after his revelation and the sense of connectedness it had given her.

Quinn's cool fingers closed over her wrist. He bent close, concern warring with suspicion. "You're overreacting, don't you think? It was a simple question."

Lifting her chin, she glared at him. "Not so simple. Once again, I get the feeling you're accusing me of something underhanded."

"I admit your behavior has led me to wonder if you're hiding something. Are you?"

Ripping free of his grip, she gritted, "Goodbye, Quinn."

He didn't say a word as she stalked away. In fact, it was his utter silence that had her glancing over her shoulder at him. Spying him shoving up his sleeves and examining his arms, she stumbled to a halt.

"What on earth are you doing?"

"Checking for scars." A fierce scowl creased his fea-

tures. "You, Nicole O'Malley, are the prick[...] frustrating—" He rammed his fingers throug[...] "I had better stop before I say something I'll [...] unsaid." With a stiff, formal bow, he said, "U[...] row, Duchess."

Shocked into silence, Nicole watched him st[...] despising the awful way he'd uttered the endea[...] wishing—absurdly—that things could be dif[...] tween them.

The anger humming through his veins was understandable. The defeat riding along with it, on the other hand, wasn't something Quinn was used to handling.

"I have the funds to replace everything, of course." He toed a shard of broken glass. "What bothers me is the malice behind the act. A waste like this is hard to take when there are people in the nation who don't have enough to eat."

"When did you discover it?"

"Just a few minutes ago. Doesn't look like animals have disturbed anything which tells me it's a recent job."

Her hand on his shoulder startled him. Glancing down into her jewel-bright eyes swimming with compassion, he wondered how one woman could evoke such opposing emotions. There were times he didn't know if he wanted to shake her or hug her. Or kiss—

Quinn crushed the thought before it could fully take hold. *Focus on the issue at hand, Darling.*

Frustration broke through his reserve. "I don't understand why someone would do this. I've done everything I can to befriend the townspeople, to garner their trust. And now this…"

"It could be someone who doesn't like the fact you've taken Emmett's place." She removed her hand, a dark frown forming. "Or it could be Kenneth and his friends."

Quinn had seen the trio at the celebration and prayed they would keep their distance, for both their sakes. A public confrontation would've only served to embarrass Nicole and worsen general opinion of him.

"You've worked here for six months. Has anything like this happened during that time?"

"No, but you're forgetting you stood up for me. No one has ever done that."

"I will always stand up for you, Nicole."

His vow had obviously flustered her. When there was no snappy comeback, he sent her inside to put up a sign letting customers know there wouldn't be any dairy today. While she manned the store, he fetched Shane, who was equally disturbed by the senseless crime.

Shane helped him clean up. Quinn thanked the man, then went inside to find the store packed with customers. Nicole, who was dipping out flour for an impatient woman at the counter surrounded by four whining kids, cast him a *help me* look. Six people stood behind the woman. Sending up a prayer, he plastered on a pleasant smile and offered to help the next person in line. Their eagerness to conduct business and be on their way overruled their wariness of him, for he found himself with his own line for the first time since his arrival.

Fighting off a sudden attack of nerves, Quinn disbursed their orders without complication. Not only did he know the location of every item in his store, he was able to calculate trade credit. Being Nicole's helper all these weeks had paid off. When the last person in line smiled her genuine thanks and left satisfied with the service, he briefly closed his eyes. At last. Progress. *Thank you, God.*

The small triumph eased somewhat his upset over the springhouse.

But then Kenneth, Timothy and Pete waltzed in, elbowing each other and laughing, and his mood soured again.

Nicole looked up from her ledger and paled. Quinn immediately went to stand next to her, resting a reassuring hand against the small of her back. "I will not let them hassle you."

"No need to worry about me." Edging sideways, she put distance between them, forcing him to drop his hand. He intercepted a customer's curious stare and understood her reaction.

"Right."

Speculation about their relationship running rampant through town wasn't what either of them needed. Still, he stuck close to her, determined to prevent a repeat of last time. His assistant was a strong, independent woman, but going up against three oversize idiot males wasn't likely to have a good outcome.

Kenneth made eye contact across the store, his arrogant smirk making Quinn's blood boil. The young man was the only one with obvious motive for revenge. A bully like him wouldn't take kindly to being chastised in the midst of Main Street for all to see. As Nicole had suggested, he had reason to retaliate.

There was no way to prove his theory. Shane had promised to return that evening to conduct a second search, but he'd warned Quinn not to get his hopes up.

The men's laughter grated on his nerves. Nicole's composure became increasingly strained as she measured out fabric for a young lady. He could see the tightening about her mouth, the slight trembling in her hands.

Anger spiking, he was about to order them to leave when Megan and Lucian entered. The trio sobered at the sight of Nicole's sister and brother-in-law. While Lucian Beaumont was not related by blood, he was an imposing man both in physical stature and manner, his confidence a product of an upbringing and family situation that mirrored Quinn's.

As the couple approached the counter, Kenneth led his friends out the door.

Quinn was satisfied to see Nicole's stance soften with relief. The knowledge that he'd willingly shelter her from any and all trouble should've bothered him more than it did. He felt the same way toward his sister. Made sense that he'd feel this way about someone in his employ.

He greeted Lucian with genuine warmth.

The dark-haired man pointed at the sign in the window. "What happened to your dairy supply? Caleb been shorting you?"

"Not exactly."

When he'd informed them both, Lucian's countenance grew troubled. "Do you have any suspects?"

"I have my suspicions, but no way of proving them. Yet."

Glancing around at the handful of customers still browsing the aisles, the other man said quietly, "Why don't you join us for supper tonight? We've been meaning to invite you, anyway. It would give us a chance to discuss matters in private."

"I'd like that."

Tucking her hand in her husband's, Megan leaned across the counter. "Come with him, Nicole."

She hesitated in tying up the fabric with a string. "Can't. I have too much to do after work."

Quinn refused to be disappointed. He was in her company all day every day.

"Are you sure?" Megan persisted. "Can't your chores wait an hour or two?"

"No, I'm sorry they can't." Noting her sister's crestfallen expression, she tacked on, "Maybe another time."

The couple stuck around for ten more minutes before taking their leave. The rest of the day passed in a blur and, before he knew it, Shane was back for another search. Quinn left Nicole inside to lock up.

Fifteen minutes into their search, she descended the stairs and walked over to where he was crouched in the grass. She dangled her basket in front of his nose.

"Would you like to examine the contents? I have the ledger listing my purchases in my reticule."

The sheriff gave her a brief, considering glance before returning his attention to the grassy expanse beneath his boots.

"Not this time."

Sighing, she inclined her head in that regal way of hers. "Good evening, then."

Watching her stride away, Quinn gave in to the needling sense that she was hiding something. He stood up and brushed off his pants. "I forgot I have some urgent business to tend to. Would you mind if I left you to it?"

The sheriff nudged the brim of his Stetson farther up his forehead, sharp blue gaze assessing. No doubt he saw right through Quinn's lame excuse.

"Go ahead. I'm almost finished here."

Feeling foolish but intent on discovering Nicole's secrets, he followed her at a distance, praying she wouldn't turn around and spy him. What reason could he possibly give for following her?

When she ducked onto a barely discernible path leading into the heart of the forest, Quinn's gut clenched with dread.

Where was she going? And what would he find at the end of this path?

He wasn't sure he wanted to find out.

Nicole accepted the steaming bowl of fish stew, wondering how she could explain away—again—her lack of appetite once she returned home. Her mother was starting to become suspicious. Like Quinn. Suppressing a wave of irritation, she turned her attention to her friends.

"This is delicious, Lillian."

Cheeks pink, and damp tendrils adhering to her forehead, Lillian perched on the other bed with her bowl. "Tell me about the picnic. Did they have fried chicken?"

Nicole felt perspiration forming on her nape. The interior was stuffy and uncomfortable. It would only get worse as the summer progressed.

"I didn't see any, but I'm sure there was."

Savoring another bite of the surprisingly fragrant stew, she hoped she'd remember to ask the twins to prepare some fried chicken so that she could sneak a few pieces to the girl. In the corner, a quieter-than-usual Patrick trained his attention on his meal.

She lowered her spoon. "I wish you could've been there. There were games and music."

Patrick scowled into his bowl. At Lillian's wistful sigh, Nicole's appetite vanished. Forcing the rest of the contents down, she placed the dish in the bucket.

"I'll take these to the stream and wash them for you."

"No." His head shot up, pale eyes narrowing. "What would someone think if they saw you? We've already had one close call."

Lillian stuck her tongue out at him.

"What happened?" Dismayed, Nicole looked from one to the other.

Patrick dragged his glowering gaze from his sister to answer her. "Lillian was doing her nightly washing in the stream when a couple of elderly hunters came waltzing through the woods. The only thing that saved her is the fact there was a full moon and she didn't have need of a lamp."

"They didn't see me, though, did they?" Lillian didn't appear the least bothered.

But the near miss bothered Nicole. Gaze roaming the cramped shack, the pitiful state of their so-called home, she felt sick inside.

"We have to tell Shane," she blurted. "This nightmare has to end."

Lillian's light brows crumpling, she lowered her bowl to

her lap and stared glumly at her brother. While the younger girl would never complain aloud, Nicole sensed she would willingly go to the sheriff if only Patrick would agree.

As expected, he shook his head. "Can't risk it."

"This has nothing to do with me." Nicole threw her hands up and paced the tiny space. "I have no problem helping you. Believe me, I wouldn't be doing this if I didn't want to help. But it's killing me to see you living like this! You're my only true friends in this town." Tears welled up in her eyes, taking her by surprise. "It's not fair."

Lillian hurried over to wrap her in a hug. "I'm so thankful you found us. You were our answer to prayer."

Astonished by the notion that God would willingly choose to use her to accomplish His ends, Nicole couldn't form a coherent response. She awkwardly patted Lillian's back and blinked away the tears.

Patrick watched them warily. "Crying isn't going to change my mind, you know," he said, setting his bowl aside and using the cane to gain his footing.

"I'm tired of this half life." Lillian pulled out of the hug to face him. "We have to consider bringing someone else in besides Nicole."

"We don't know if we can trust this Sheriff Timmons."

"Nicole trusts him. That's good enough for me." Lillian put up a hand to stall his response. "Promise me you'll think about it."

He heaved a sigh. "Fine."

Somewhat mollified, the blonde's smile returned.

Nicole had her doubts he'd ever agree to her suggestion. "I have to go. Thank you for the meal."

Outside, dusk had fallen. Patrick followed her through the door, his manner uncharacteristically self-conscious. Then he stunned her by giving her a one-armed hug.

Stepping back, he cleared his throat, the tips of his ears

pink. "Thank you for all you've sacrificed for us. I'll never forget it."

"I would do it all again," she admitted. "You and your sister mean the world to me."

Throat working, he gave a half wave and, shuffling inside, gently shut the door.

Bemused, she swung the empty basket to and fro as she traveled the familiar path. The waning light struggled to penetrate the trees. Shadows thickened, spurring her to walk faster.

She hadn't made it very far when, out of the bushes, flashed a tall male form. A firm hand clamped down on her arm. Nicole jumped and would've screamed had she not instantly recognized the distinctive hint of peppermint in the air.

"Quinn!" She was going to throttle him! "What do you think you're doing?"

Quinn towered over her, his hair mussed and tie askew, nostrils flaring. "Who was that young man?"

Fear temporarily eclipsed her ire. He'd seen Patrick. What if he told?

Tempted to retreat, Nicole ordered her feet to stay put. Gone was laid-back Quinn. This was intimidating Quinn, the one she'd glimpsed in the mercantile when Kenneth and his friends had come in. Anger poured off him in tangible waves, every inch of his muscled body primed for battle. He was one enemy she did not want to make.

He invaded her space. "I saw you hug him. Does he live there? Please. *Please* tell me you haven't been so foolish as to carry on a secret assignation with him."

Just like that, her fear disintegrated. Spluttering, she shoved at his solid—and immovable—chest.

"You don't know me *at all* if you can suggest such a

despicable thing." Chin angled upward, she glared at him nose to nose. "Get out of my way, Darling."

Something akin to astonishment flared in the amber depths of his eyes, but he didn't move a muscle.

"That was Darling with a capital *D*, you big oaf."

When she sidestepped to go around him, he smoothly moved to block her exit. "You're not going anywhere until you tell me what's going on."

"Then I guess I'd better get comfortable," she quipped.

"Do not push me, Nicole." His eyes narrowed. "I will have your secrets one way or another."

Chapter Fourteen

The hint of relief on Nicole's features confirmed his decision to follow her. The weight of her secret—he shuddered to think what it might be—had to be a considerable burden. Quinn wondered just how long she'd been hiding this part of her life. And to what end? Forbidden romance?

He couldn't deny the jealousy and inexplicable sense of loss he'd experienced upon seeing her and the stranger embracing. Shoving those useless emotions aside, he held tight to his concern for her well-being.

"Is he who you've been purchasing the supplies for?" He managed a semi-calm tone of voice.

"What I do during my off time is none of your business."

"It's been going on for a while, hasn't it? Since before Emmett left." Her sister's words came back to him. "Have you been supporting him since the beginning? Was that why you took this job?"

She'd gone still, watchful. On alert for a way of escape from his presence and this conversation. In the muted light that reached them here in this remote spot, her violet eyes were deep pools of wariness, her shiny pink lips pressed together in a straight line, and he noted the odd trembling in her slender frame.

His irritation ebbing, he settled his hands on her shoulders, thumbs rubbing a reassuring pattern across the soft blue fabric of her sleeves.

"You can trust me, Nicole."

She gulped. "I'm not so sure about that."

That hurt. "I have never given you reason to doubt my intention to protect you." *Even from yourself.*

Her shoulders slumped as the fight left her. "You aren't going to let this go, are you?"

"I'm afraid not."

"Then I suppose a meeting is in order."

Stepping aside, he followed in her wake. The run-down shack looked worse up close. Surely this was merely a meeting place and not a permanent residence.

She rapped out a series of knocks. A secret code between her and her love interest?

Quinn's chest constricted as they waited. Finally, the door scraped open.

"Back so soon…" The young male voice trailed off as light gray eyes landed on Quinn. He recoiled. "Who's he?"

"May we come inside?" Nicole's manner was resigned.

Her companion lingered in the doorway, weight supported by a cane. He was younger than Quinn had first thought and sickly in appearance, mouth tight with pain and skin nearly translucent.

Reluctantly, the boy admitted them. Quinn worked to keep his features schooled as he entered the tiny space that, from the looks of things, was indeed a home. A pitiful one. Movement in the corner caught his eye. A fine-boned girl latched on to Nicole's arm, eyes wide and hunted as she stared at him.

"Nicole?" she squeaked.

Similar in coloring and appearance to the lad, she was most likely his sister. Perhaps he'd jumped to the wrong conclusion.

"Patrick. Lillian. This is my boss, Quinn Darling," she announced darkly. "He followed me."

Quinn inclined his head in greeting. "Which one of you would like to explain what's going on here?"

Patrick sank heavily onto a chair in the corner, hands hanging on to the cane between his legs. Chin jutted at a stubborn angle, he said, "That depends on what you're planning on doing with the information."

"I can't say until I know what it is you're hiding. And you *are* hiding something, or else you wouldn't be living here." He flicked a hand about him. "My assistant wouldn't be doing your shopping for you and making clandestine deliveries."

"We haven't done anything wrong!" Lillian burst out.

Nicole's glare shooting daggers at Quinn, she addressed Patrick. "Just tell him the truth. He won't let this matter rest until you do. He's stubborn and hardheaded."

He was stubborn? What about her?

"These past six months, Nicole has been instrumental in keeping my sister and I alive and safe."

"Safe?" Quinn repeated. "From who?"

"The man who married our mother and later murdered her."

Nicole clapped a hand over her mouth. "Patrick! Why didn't you tell me?" Rushing over, she knelt before him, fingers gripping his knee. "How did it happen?"

Quinn's gaze narrowed at her open concern for the lad. She very clearly cared for him. How deep did her feelings go?

Patrick ducked his head, hair sliding forward. "They were arguing. He pushed her. Hard. She struck her head."

"She never woke up." Lillian hung back, her legs pressed against the bed opposite, keeping her distance from Quinn.

Scooting out a chair he hoped would bear his weight, Quinn sat down and crossed his arms. "How about we start at the beginning?"

As he listened to the entire story, bits and pieces supplied by all three, his concern for the siblings' welfare deepened and his admiration for his assistant blossomed. He couldn't have imagined her capable of such a noble act. He'd pegged her wrong from the start.

"What are you going to do with this information?" Patrick's knuckles were white on the cane.

"I need to give the matter some thought. One thing's for sure—you cannot remain here. We'll need to find you more appropriate lodgings."

Trepidation tightened the lad's mouth. "If people find out about us—"

"Please don't worry." Quinn stood, noting the darkness and lack of moonlight beyond the window. "I'll do everything in my power to keep you safe." Extending his hand to Nicole, he said, "Your family will be wondering where you are. I'll escort you home."

She hugged both siblings. He couldn't detect anything other than sisterly affection on her part. Nor did Patrick look at Nicole like a man infatuated.

Borrowing a lamp, they entered the woodland path, crickets' chirrups and frogs' chorus echoing through the night. "I have to ask," he said when the suspense became too much to bear. "About you and Patrick…are you…a couple?"

She stumbled over a root. When he steadied her, she shook off his hand. "Of course not. He's younger than me! Besides, I think of him as a brother."

Relief spiraled through him.

"Wait. Do you think *he* thinks—"

"No. I saw no evidence of that."

"I take it you saw something in my behavior that made you jump to that conclusion?"

Quinn chose his words carefully. "Not exactly. You are, however, more open, more demonstrative with them than anyone else."

"They're my friends."

He didn't respond. Didn't disrupt the silence that fell awkwardly between them during the remainder of the long walk to her cabin. His head was too full of discovery.

At the entrance to her lane, Nicole stopped. "You're angry."

He lowered the lamp to the ground. "You're right. I am."

"Well, that's too bad—"

Quinn silenced her with a finger against her lips. "I'm angry because Patrick and Lillian have had to live like fugitives when they've done nothing wrong. I'm angry that you've had to shoulder this burden for so long. They're the reason you've had to postpone the move to Knoxville, aren't they?"

Curling her fingers about his, she pulled them away from her mouth and down to her side but didn't release his hand. "I care about them."

"I know you do." He drank in her upturned features, gaze touching on each point of beauty. Mysterious and alluring like a fine painting, she possessed a hitherto unknown depth he yearned to explore. "I have never admired a person more than I do you in this moment."

Her lips parted. "Quinn."

Ignoring the inner voice yelling at him to stop, to remember who he was and who she was and cease this nonsense *at once*, he cupped the side of her neck. The soft mass of her hair felt like rich mink fur against his skin.

Weaving a little to the side, she braced her hands against his biceps. "I—I feel dizzy."

With his heart thundering in his chest, his fingers closed around her waist and he lowered his head until their breaths mingled and the tips of their noses bumped.

"That's good," he murmured, "because I do, too."

Quinn drew her steadily closer, her voluminous skirts tangling with his pant legs and their boots colliding. When he had her as near as he dared, he fastened his attention on her dainty mouth, aware this wasn't his best idea. Aware but too far gone to heed the voice of caution, which in his case wasn't very loud or insistent.

Besides, he'd given her plenty of opportunity to slap him. Or shove him away. She hadn't, which meant her common sense had gone the way of his.

He carefully brushed his lips against hers. No pressure. Easy. Gentle.

Nicole tightened her hold in response and, with a rush of sweet breath fanning over his mouth, went up on tiptoe to return his kiss.

The world around them ceased to exist. There was only Nicole anchoring him to the earth, her scent enveloping him, her softness a balm for his loneliness, her breath sustaining him.

He deepened the kiss, lips tangling with hers. She followed his lead with endearing eagerness. *Devastating* moved to the top of the list of her traits.

She's innocent, Darling. The reminder had his mind reeling with the implications. *She's leaving. You're staying.*

Nothing could come of this. Nothing but hurt feelings.

This was the best moment in her life.

She had never felt so alive, so *in tune* with another human being.

Quinn saw her as no one else did—she'd hidden nothing about her personality from him—and still he was kissing her, clinging to her the same desperate way she clung to him. He was holding himself back for her sake. Quinn may be many things—cocky, nosy, too handsome for his own good—but for him, her well-being took precedence over everything else. He was her overzealous, self-appointed protector. Who could've guessed the one man who could take her from mildly annoyed to spitting mad in mere seconds could also lavish her with tenderness and make her feel wanted, even cherished, when no one else had?

Please let this continue forever.

Forever?

Forever meant staying in Gatlinburg. Giving up her dream.

She wasn't prepared to give up her dream for anyone. Postpone, yes. Give up completely? For a man who hadn't even asked her to?

Even knowing this, her heart squeezed into a tight ball of regret when Quinn abruptly jerked his mouth from hers. His breathing off-kilter, he stepped out of the embrace and sank his hands deep in his pockets, eyes dark and turbulent.

The hot imprint of where his hands had been on her skin began to cool, and she struggled with the need to resume that contact. Because now that there was air and space between them, the loneliness rushed back in, along with the feeling of *apartness* that had dogged her since childhood, and she hated that feeling even more now that she'd experienced connection. And not with just anyone.

With Quinn.

"I shouldn't have done that." His voice was a throaty rasp.

Clenching her fingers into fists, she pressed them against

her sternum in a vain effort to numb the pain blossoming there. He would not be kissing her again. She wouldn't experience the wonder of his embrace again. It was for the best, but that didn't mean she didn't mourn the loss.

"I shouldn't have taken advantage," he continued with a frown. "I'm your boss."

Sucking in a ragged breath, she did what she had to do to salvage their working relationship. "We're both adults. Why can't we simply put this behind us? Forget it ever happened?"

"I can't say I'll be able to forget—" his gaze went nearly black in the darkness "—but I can be professional from here on out. That is, if you're willing to continue working with me."

"I still need this job."

A door slammed in the distance, followed by Megan's voice. "Nicole? Is that you?"

What was her sister doing here so late? "I'll be right there," she called over her shoulder. Not looking at Quinn, she said, "I have to go."

He bent to pick up the lamp, his face sharp angles and shadows. "Will I see you in the morning?"

"Of course." Did that breezy voice really belong to her? She possessed serious acting skills.

He hesitated as if there was more he wished to say. "Good night, then."

"Good night."

It wasn't easy walking away from him as if he hadn't just irrevocably altered her life.

"Oh, Nicole?"

You can do this. A few seconds more and you can escape.

Pivoting on the dark path, she waited for him to speak.

"Don't worry about your friends. We'll think of a solution to their predicament. Together."

Together. As they'd be hour after hour, day after day. And she was supposed to keep up this pretense—that he was just her boss and she was merely his assistant and nothing whatsoever had changed between them? That Quinn hadn't awakened crazy, wonderful, downright terrifying emotions in her?

She'd been pretending all her life that being the odd sister didn't bother her. She had feigning apathy down to an art. This would be no different.

Chapter Fifteen

Megan was descending the porch steps when Nicole reached the cabin. "Was that Quinn?"

"Yes."

"It's awfully late to be working, isn't it?" Ringlets gleaming in the darkness, she squinted at the distant lane leading to town.

With a noncommittal sound, Nicole changed the subject. "Is there a particular reason you're here?"

"Mama mentioned Jane's been feeling down lately, so I came to try and cheer her up."

"Considering her reason for being sad, do you think you're the right person to do that?"

Nicole wasn't trying to be mean, but the truth was the truth. Jane had been infatuated with Tom Leighton for years. He, however, loved Megan. He'd even proposed to her and had been so devastated over her rejection that he'd eventually left town.

"Jane doesn't blame me for his leaving," she said stiffly. "Personally, I'm not sure if he'll return."

"And even if he did, I don't think the two of them would end up together. Tom sees her as a little sister. "

Sinking on the top step, Megan patted the space beside her. "Is that what you and Quinn are? Just friends?"

Nicole didn't wish to speak of him. Still, if she was to ever enjoy deeper relationships with her sisters, she was going to have to reveal a bit of herself.

Sitting beside Megan, Nicole adjusted her skirts and folded her hands in her lap. Somewhere in the woods behind the barn, an owl hooted.

"He kissed me tonight."

Megan squealed and clapped her hands together.

"He apologized afterward."

That dampened her excitement. "Why? What did he say?"

Nicole found herself pouring out the details. It was nice to share her burden, even if she wasn't seeking answers. There was no future for her and Quinn. Perhaps there'd be someone in the city who'd make her feel this way. Better, even.

"What are you going to do?" Megan said at last.

"Nothing. We're going to put this behind us and focus on maintaining our professional relationship."

"Will that make you happy?" She pivoted, leaned forward at the waist to peer directly at her. "Because I have to say, Quinn strikes me as sort of perfect for you."

"He's not part of my plan. Marriage is something I'll have to wait for until many years down the road. I've worked too hard and too long to make my dream into a reality to simply let it go."

"Plans can change," Megan suggested lightly. "Have you prayed about whether or not your dream lines up with what God wants for your life?"

No, I haven't, she thought guiltily. "God knows my desire. He created me, after all, and blessed me with this ability. Mama's always quoting that verse from Psalms...

'Delight yourself also in the Lord, and He shall give you the desires of your heart.'"

"Have you ever considered He might fulfill your desires in a different way than you've imagined?"

She couldn't fathom any other way of accomplishing her dream. Besides, what possible objection could God have to her moving to Knoxville? He was aware of her discontent.

"Enough about me. Tell me about your trip to New Orleans. When do you leave?"

Each summer, she and Lucian traveled there to visit Lucian's father.

"August fifth." Dipping her head, she concentrated on her clasped hands. "We're planning to visit an orphanage there."

Surprise skittered through Nicole. "Oh? I hadn't realized you were considering adoption."

"Lucian and I have been praying for God to bless our union with children, whether that be through natural means or adoption."

"Well." Unused to private confessions, she scrambled for an appropriate response. This was the first time Megan had revealed her longing for children to her. Watching her fidget with the ruffles on her skirt, Nicole was struck with a surprising thought. Could her big sister find it as difficult to confide in her as Nicole did? After all, this was foreign territory for them both.

"I think it's wonderful," she said, meaning it. "You've always wanted a big family, and you have plenty of space in that monster of a house."

Lifting her head, Megan smiled tremulously, moisture shining in her eyes. "I don't care how I become a mother, I just want a house full of children to love and nurture."

Warmth and a strange but not unwelcome sense of

closeness spread through Nicole. "I hope you get what you want," she said shyly. "And I'm glad you told me."

"Me, too." Then Megan surprised her with a hug. Easing away, she tugged playfully on one of Nicole's loose curls. "We should talk like this more often."

Throat thick with emotion, Nicole nodded. She had Quinn to thank for this step forward. He was the one who'd encouraged her to reach out.

If she was smart, she'd take what she learned from him into her new life.

Quinn was watching Shane exit the mercantile early the following morning when Nicole seized his hand and yanked him into the office, where she all but accosted him.

"What happened to keeping my friends' secret?" she demanded, red splotches on her neck and cheeks and eyes spitting violet-hued fire. "I thought you'd agreed to consult them before involving the sheriff or anyone else."

His instinctive reaction—to glibly comment on how her irritation with him merely served to enhance her beauty—would not achieve the professional atmosphere he'd promised himself he'd provide for her.

"There's no need to get upset. Shane dropped by to tell me he doesn't have any leads regarding the springhouse crime. I stand by my oath to you and your friends. I will not breathe a word to anyone until we figure out the next step together."

"Oh." She turned away from him to sift needlessly through the papers on the desk.

Quinn assessed her neat, stylish appearance, lingering on her upswept hair and the curve of her ear. He was sorely tempted to close the distance between them, wrap his arms around her and plant a kiss against her nape. Soothe her worries with soft whispers.

His pulse picking up speed, he'd taken a half step in her direction before he even realized it. He grimaced. Keeping things strictly platonic was going to be a daily battle.

Trapping his hands in his pockets, he forced himself to remember she was in his employ. As her boss, he had a duty to insure the workplace was safe for her. The last thing he wanted was for her to worry about possible advances from him. He needed for her to focus on her job.

"What are you thinking?" he asked, leaning against the doorpost.

"I have my doubts Patrick will agree to involve Shane." She stacked papers that didn't need straightening. "My numerous attempts have proved futile."

He sensed her frustration. Understandable, considering the effort and sacrifice she'd sunk into their situation. "He hasn't had a dose of the famous Darling charm, though, has he?"

When her lips compressed and she shrugged, he said in a more serious tone, "Patrick knows this is no kind of life for his sister. I'll appeal to his honor as her protector. He'll see reason."

"I hope you're right."

"Don't worry. After work, I'll stop by Plum's and pick up supper for the four of us. We'll figure out a solution tonight."

Her luminous eyes lifting to his—and the faith she was putting in him—was like a gift.

"I'm sorry I jumped to the wrong conclusion. I shouldn't have questioned you."

He had to get out of there before he did something stupid.

Nodding, he backed out the door and into the hallway, gesturing to the storeroom. "Can you check on the front? I've got to see about…something."

Her confused expression stayed with him as he took refuge amongst the shelves. *Better confusion than revulsion, Darling.* Twenty minutes of him pacing and praying passed before he felt ready to rejoin her. The banker, Claude Jenkins, entered just as Quinn reached the counter.

"Quinn." He smiled and waved papers in the air. "Good news. The land purchase contract is ready to sign. Soon you'll be an official Gatlinburg resident."

Several customers glanced up from their shopping to watch the exchange. How would this news affect those locals who hadn't yet accepted him? Would they be more inclined to trust him?

Opening the silver-and-crystal case on the other counter, Nicole shot him an indecipherable look. He didn't have to ask her opinion on the subject. Although she knew what had precipitated his desire for a simpler life, she couldn't understand why he'd want to tie himself to her quaint mountain town.

The thought came to him then that he had the means to replenish her savings. She'd unselfishly used it to help two people who were of no relation to her. Strangers who'd desperately needed someone to care for them and who had no way of repaying her. While he dreaded the thought of her leaving, after last night's embrace and his current battle to keep his distance, perhaps it would be best if she left sooner rather than later.

The banker stood before him, expectant.

"That's wonderful news," Quinn said. "Nicole, will you be all right by yourself for a few minutes?"

"Of course."

He waved the big man through. "Come on back to the office."

When Quinn shut the door, Claude continued to smile his encouragement. "Buying this property is going to go a long way toward cementing your position in our town. Already, I've heard positive comments about you from several patrons who were hesitant at first."

Laying out the paperwork, he pointed to where his signature was needed.

"Progress is a good thing." Sinking into the chair, Quinn took several minutes to peruse the document. Satisfied, he located a pen and added his signature, a little thrill of excitement offsetting the on-edge feeling he'd had since Nicole arrived.

He'd allowed this unwise attraction to distract him from his goals. First and foremost, he had to tend his store and its ongoing success. Secondly, he had to get a permanent home built. The living quarters, though cramped, were adequate, but they weren't home. And his residing in them didn't communicate serious intentions to the townspeople. In their minds, he had the wherewithal to jump ship any moment he pleased.

His thoughts straying to Nicole once again, he reminded himself that once his home was finished, he'd be free to turn his focus to finding a suitable wife.

With the chicken and dumplings consumed, followed by generous helpings of chess pie, Nicole sat back and watched Quinn. He appealed to Patrick's sense of duty to Lillian, calmly and systematically knocking down argument after argument.

She could see that he wasn't simply doing this for her. He genuinely cared for the siblings' future. Their safety. That his privileged upbringing and his vast circle of influential friends hadn't made him into a snobbish boor impressed her.

Face it, Nicole, she told herself, *a lot of things about Quinn Darling impress you.*

Sipping her watered-down lemonade, she pushed memories of his lips molded against hers out of her mind. The memories had crept in hundreds—no, thousands—of times today as they'd dodged and sidestepped each other, extra vigilant to avoid physical contact. More than once, she'd caught him staring at her mouth.

If only this was a surface-deep attraction.

No question Quinn was a striking individual, with his sleek hair and chiseled features, generous lips that could so easily slip into a lazy, confident smile. His stylish clothing, usually made up of safe, businesslike colors like navy and black and charcoal, hugged his body, showcasing his lean, powerful physique. He moved with grace and purpose. No hesitation for the heir to the Darling empire.

Nicole's problem was that, irksome qualities aside, she genuinely liked Quinn. The way his mind worked. His caring nature. His determination and drive, which mirrored her own. He could've complained about his struggles. Instead, he'd admitted he needed her assistance and set about learning how to run the mercantile. And, despite his frustration with the locals' resistance, he'd done everything in his power to win them over, humbling himself in the process.

Liking her boss in this way could not only lead to a very uncomfortable working relationship, it could have her questioning her decision to leave Gatlinburg. That was something she couldn't allow to happen. She had to focus on her dream. Later, once her boutique was open and her reputation established, she could think about marriage.

The acceptance in Patrick's voice caught her attention. "And if I agree to go along with your plan? Where would we stay while the sheriff investigates our situation?"

Quinn turned in his seat to look at her, unaware she hadn't been following their interaction. "You're more familiar with the options than I am. Do you have any suggestions?"

Lillian and Patrick waited, tense and apprehensive.

"As a matter of fact, I do. My sister and her husband, Megan and Lucian Beaumont, live in a spacious, two-story Victorian near town. They have ample rooms available. I'm certain they'd be happy to have you stay with them."

While Lillian's eyes sparked with interest, Patrick looked unsure. More charity, he must be thinking.

"They don't have any children," Nicole added, "and my sister is desperate for someone besides Lucian to lavish her attention on."

Quinn's approving smile made her feel ridiculously giddy. "Would you mind stopping there on your way home? I can accompany you if you'd like."

More time in his company, trying to remain cool and unaffected? No, thanks. She needed a reprieve before her test of endurance started all over again tomorrow morning.

"I thought you were going to pay Shane a visit."

Retrieving his pocket watch, he frowned at the time. "It is getting late. I'll go to the jail first and speak with him, then swing by your cabin so that we can update each other."

"All right." Standing to her feet, she spontaneously hugged Lillian and Patrick, anticipation singing in her veins. Soon, very soon, they'd leave this nightmare behind.

Chapter Sixteen

Muttering under her breath, Nicole glared at the uneven stitch—her tenth in as many minutes—and snipped the thread so that she could start again. It didn't usually take long for a project to dominate her attention and push her worries aside, but she couldn't help reviewing today's events. Plus, she was on edge waiting for Quinn's footsteps on the porch.

The mantel clock chimed eight o'clock. A quick glance out the living room window revealed a typical summer evening, waning light turning the distant mountain sides a deep, purplish blue. A pair of blue jays swooped past.

Where was he?

A sniffle snagged her attention. Curled in the cushioned chair opposite Nicole's spot on the sofa, Jane lowered her book to her lap and swiped at her wet cheeks. Straight auburn hair collected at her nape with a navy blue ribbon, skin dewy and eyes large and shadowed, she looked young and innocent. Not that Nicole would voice such a thought. Jane and Jessica were both eagerly anticipating their seventeenth birthday in September.

"Sad story?" Nicole said.

ve it to me as a form of payment. I couldn't tell him I
d no intention of cashing it in. Will you keep it in the
re safe for them until their stepfather is dealt with?"

Their palms skimmed together, and warmth pooled in
er middle the same instant his gaze went dark and search-
ng. The air sizzled as if humming with mini-lightning
strikes. Then he broke the connection, sucking in a stut-
tering breath, head bent to study the piece of jewelry.

"I'll keep it safe for them," he said, without looking
at her.

"Thank you."

Minutes passed without either of them speaking. Lightning bugs flashed in the gathering darkness, weaving pat-
terns above the rows of vegetables.

When he finally lifted his head, his features were un-
readable but his eyes burned with searing intensity.

"You're an amazing woman, Nicole O'Malley. You deserve to be happy. To realize your dream."

Amazing? No one had ever uttered such words of praise
to her before.

You haven't allowed anyone close enough, a small voice
reminded. *Haven't given anyone a chance to know you.*

What did it mean that she'd dropped her defenses with
Quinn?

"You've proven yourself to be a valuable asset," he con-
nued, "and I believe a pay raise is in order."

She blinked, confused at the subject change. "A pay
ise?"

Emmett hadn't seen fit to increase her wages in the
e she'd worked for him. Where was this coming from?
You're worth it. Besides, you need to replenish the
s for your boutique. This way, you can make the move
noxville sooner."

er insides twisted into painful knots. He sounded al-

"He doesn't love her." Her lower lip trembled. "He
doesn't care that she loves him. Has *always* loved him."

Uh-oh. She wasn't talking about a fictional hero and
heroine, was she? This was about Tom Leighton.

Jessica, whose habit was to bake in the evenings,
must've sensed her twin's angst, for she materialized in
the doorway. Flour dusted her nose.

"He's been gone awhile, Jane," she said softly. "He
didn't tell anyone where he was going or when he was
coming back."

Jane jutted her chin. "I know him. He won't leave his
homestead to fall to ruin."

"He's a barber, not a farmer," Jessica pointed out. "For
all we know, he could've written to Mr. Jenkins to put it
up for sale."

Another fat tear dripped to her chin.

Nicole wished she could think of something comforting
to say. She secretly agreed with Jessica—it wasn't likely
Tom would return. Megan's rejection had hit him hard.
He'd sold his business. He hadn't even returned for his
mother's funeral. There wasn't anything left to draw him
back.

"I thought he'd at least write and let me know he's okay."
Jane looked miserable.

"He should have known you'd worry," Nicole agreed.

Jessica frowned, twisted the towel in her hands. "Do
you want to help me finish up the cake for Mrs. Taggart?"

Jane sighed. Snapping the book closed, she laid it on
the coffee table. "Sure, why not?"

When the girls had left, Nicole stared at the dress she
was making for Rachel Prescott and offered up a prayer
for her sister's broken heart. In time, Jane would realize a
future with Tom was out of the question. The wound would
heal, and she'd find a new love.

Just as Jane would forget about Tom's charms, so would Nicole forget about Quinn's. A new city, combined with all that was required in building a business from scratch, would do the trick.

Ten minutes later, his heavy tread on the steps alerted her to his presence. The twins were still working in the kitchen, and their mother had retired early.

Heart pounding, she set aside the material, careful not to unravel the thread from the needle, and went to admit him.

"Hi," she said.

Holding on to the door, she adopted a nonchalant air and tried not to ogle his slightly disheveled appearance. His suit coat and vest were nowhere to be seen, and the top buttons of his white shirt were undone, revealing smooth, tanned skin. His dark hair was mussed, and a hint of stubble darkened his jaw.

"Hi." He smiled faintly. "Sorry I'm late. Shane had company when I arrived."

"Would you like to come inside?"

He gestured to the rocking chairs on the porch. "It's nice out tonight. Mind if we talk out here?"

She closed the door with a soft click. Quinn waited for her to choose her chair before taking the other one. Gazing at the mountains rising above the treetops, he said, "I hope I never take these views for granted."

"Does your land have a similar one?"

"My land." Turning his head to regard her, he smiled broadly. "I like the sound of that. The house in Boston, the offices and the factories all belong to my father."

"Here the mercantile is solely yours, as is the property."

"Exactly. And to answer your question, yes, it does have a favorable view. I can hardly wait to draw up plans for the house."

"House or mansion?"

His lips twitched. "I will keep it tasteful, ga fear." h

Nicole likely wouldn't see the finished proje s she left. The thought saddened her. Lucian and had insisted on assuming financial support for Patr Lillian, which meant she could pour every cent of come into savings.

"How did the meeting with Shane go?"

"As I'd suspected. Shane's a fair man. He's prom to look into the matter."

"As soon as my sister and Lucian heard about th plight, they offered to take them in. I didn't even have ask."

"Were they upset with you for keeping this secret for so long?"

Recalling the heated lecture she could've done without, she put her foot down to stop the rocking motion and gazed at the shadows gathering in the forest beyond the barn.

He followed suit, his expression going somber. "Nicole you do realize that in hiding Patrick and Lillian, you p your own safety at risk."

Her mouth tightened. "I've already had one set d today, thank you very much. I don't require another sides, I was careful."

"You mistake my intention." His voice came c caress. "I'm not chastising you. I simply wish th felt free to enlist help. A family member or a frie shoulder the burden."

The depth of his concern robbed her of spe ing into her pocket, her fingers closed over brooch. Quinn's brow wrinkled when she him.

"What's this?"

"It belonged to Patrick and Lillian's

most eager to be rid of her. He certainly didn't seem to
care that they'd be residing in different cities and would
probably see each other only once or twice a year.

That house or mansion or whatever of his wouldn't stay
empty for long. He'd find a nice, sweet girl to settle down
with and start a family.

A bereft sensation lodged in her chest, the stark loss of
it freezing the breath in her lungs.

She thought of Jane's heartbreak and assured herself
this wasn't the same. At all. How could it be? She didn't
love him. Sometimes, she didn't even like him!

It was just that Quinn was the only man who'd seen
her for herself, the person she truly was inside when the
O'Malley name, along with her reputation and the cloak
of apathy she used as a shield, was stripped away.

He'd *seen* her and deemed her worthy.

How was she supposed to forget that?

Nicole's sister could hardly contain her excitement as
she led Patrick and Lillian on a tour of the ground floor.
Lucian's gaze trailed his wife, his smile affectionate. The
couple's genuine warmth would go a long way in making the siblings feel comfortable in their temporary home.

Quinn glanced at Nicole, who'd linked arms with Lillian the moment they'd ascended the grand house's sweeping front porch and refused to leave the frail girl's side.
While Lillian gaped in unconcealed wonder at the soaring library shelves stuffed with books, Nicole frowned at
Patrick's pained, pale countenance.

The boy would have to be seen by the doctor. His leg
wound clearly hadn't healed properly.

As if sensing the direction of his thoughts, Lucian motioned to the plush sofa and chairs situated before the fireplace. "Why don't we have a seat for a moment? Mrs.

Calhoun, our cook, has prepared a special treat in prep-
aration for your arrival." He moved to the wide, arched
doorway. "Megan, care to lend me a hand?"

Megan took his outstretched hand and accompanied
him down the hall.

Patrick sank into the nearest cushioned chair, white
lines bracketing his mouth. Quinn prayed the brave young
man would be able to find relief. He'd be sure to discuss
the matter with Lucian.

Sensing Nicole's worried gaze, Quinn intercepted it and
offered what he hoped was a smile of encouragement. That
was the extent of what he could offer her. Touching her,
even briefly, carried immense risk. Those tense moments
on her porch last night proved it.

Thankfully he'd reined in his foolish longings.

Going to stand at the window, he propped a shoulder
against the frame and watched as she and Lillian whispered together on the sofa.

"Mr. Darling?"

"Yes, Lillian?"

Toying with the ends of her long, wavy blond ponytail,
cheeks bright pink, she said, "Thank you again for the
clothing and supplies."

"It was very generous of you," Nicole said. Hands folded
primly in her lap, she made a striking picture. Clad completely in black—anti-summer and in opposition of the
happy events of this day—the look should've been severe.
It wasn't. The hue, which matched her carefully styled
curls, added luster to her pearl-like skin.

"Glad I could help."

Patrick stuck out his chin. "We'll pay you back someday."

Quinn's first instinct was to insist it was a gift. But he

recognized the boy's need to contribute, to repay perceived debts, when he'd been the recipient of charity for so long.

"Perhaps you could help me in the store after Nicole leaves."

Brow furrowing, he snapped his attention to Nicole. "You're leaving?"

Lillian looked stricken. "Where are you going? You're coming back, right?"

Uh-oh. Mouthing *I'm sorry* to a flustered Nicole, he wished he'd kept his mouth shut. He'd assumed she'd told them.

Sadness stealing over her face, she took the other girl's hands in hers. "I've tried to think of an easy way to tell you both."

When she'd revealed her plans, the siblings sat there looking stunned. And guilty, which was exactly why she hadn't told them, Quinn realized.

"I promise to come and visit you as often as I can. And once I'm settled, you can come and visit me."

Patrick kneaded his forehead. "I wish you'd told us in the beginning. We could've moved on—"

"No. The truth is, I needed you as much as you needed me."

"I don't understand."

"Before you came along, I had never experienced true friendship. Trusting others isn't something that comes naturally to me. But with you and Lillian, I felt free to be myself."

Again, Nicole looked at him, and he got the feeling he was included in the handful of people who'd seen the real woman beneath the icy facade.

Lillian clung to her. "I'm going to miss you so much!"

From this angle, he could see Nicole's battle to keep

her emotions at bay. Leaving Gatlinburg wasn't going to be without cost.

Quinn wouldn't allow himself to imagine what daily life would be like without her, how strange the mercantile would feel. Why imagine when he'd experience the reality soon enough?

"We don't know what's going to happen to us or where we'll end up," Patrick said gruffly. "We can't take advantage of your family's kindness indefinitely."

"What if Sheriff Timmons believes Carl's account of what happened?" Lillian pulled back, worry pulling at her mouth. "What if he makes us go with him?"

"Shane's not going to do that." Pushing away from the wall, Quinn went to sit on her other side. "He and his deputy are going to your stepfather's homestead today. They won't reveal your whereabouts just yet."

Lucian and Megan walked in bearing trays of lemonade and an assortment of sweets. While Megan played hostess, Quinn caught Nicole's attention and motioned to the door.

"Please excuse us for a few moments," she announced to the room in general, rising and smoothing her full skirts.

In the hallway, he gestured to the rear of the house. "Care to take a quick stroll about the gardens? Lucian insisted I see them before I go. Seems to think I'll be impressed."

"This is hardly the time." Her dark brows collided.

"I will not keep you long," he promised.

"Fine."

She preceded him out the door and onto the wide porch. The heat hit them like a wave, and Quinn immediately removed his coat jacket and looped it over the railing. Nicole removed a fan from her reticule and lazily fanned herself.

They strolled along stone pathways beside lush flower beds lined with meticulously pruned bushes. Bright yellow golden asters mixed with delicate purple Southern harebells and Turk's Cap lilies. Azaleas in varying shades formed the outer row.

"I owe you an apology." He stopped to face her. "It wasn't my intention to put you in a tight spot."

"I should've told them." Perching on a stone bench, fan discarded on her lap, she observed a pair of butterflies. "I'm worried what will happen to them, Quinn. Their stepfather strikes me as a determined, ruthless man."

Unable to resist comforting her, he sat and took her hand in his. "I care about their well-being, too, and you have my word I'll do whatever necessary to protect them."

"You're a kind man."

He laughed outright. "You don't have to act so surprised."

"Well, I couldn't fathom making such an observation the first night we met."

Their intertwined hands resting on the cool, gritty stone between them, his chuckles rumbled in his chest.

"Seriously, Quinn, you've been a huge help in this situation. It means a lot to them. And to me."

Suddenly her soft-as-velvet lips were grazing his cheek, shocking him into silence.

He could so easily turn this into a real kiss. All he had to do was twist his head to the right a few inches. They were alone in this romantic, orderly maze of flowers and trees, shielded from the house. No one would see them.

Quinn squeezed his eyes tight, battling this yearning for her that, should he give in to it, would confuse their friendship.

He dropped her hand and shot to his feet.

"We should rejoin the others."

"It appears I'm not the only one who finds it difficult to accept compliments."

Nicole brushed past him. Flouncing down the pathway, her hem swiped at the fragile stems edging it. Quinn sighed. She was irritated with him again. Or had his reaction to her unexpected overture embarrassed her?

Either emotion was better than hurt feelings.

At least he could face her at work Monday morning with a clear conscience. She didn't have to know his heart was a little bruised.

Chapter Seventeen

"It was kind of Quinn to give you the day off. Saturdays must be the busiest shopping day of all."

Lounging on the quilt beside her mother and making a clover chain, Nicole observed the twins wading calf-deep in the river.

"He can be nice when he puts his mind to it."

He'd delayed opening in order to help with Patrick and Lillian's move. After their walk in the flower gardens, he'd told her to take the rest of the day off. She hadn't argued. Not after her silly kiss and his abrupt reaction.

She needed space from him and all the turmoil he was stirring to life inside her.

"I wish you would've felt comfortable confiding in me. I would've helped you, you know. And those poor kids."

At the underlying hurt in her mother's voice, Nicole shifted her gaze. Butter-yellow sunshine highlighted the age spots on her cheeks and glinted off her spectacles.

"I'm sorry. It's just that…if I'd told you, I would've been breaking my promise."

Her mother cupped her cheek. "I love you, sweet daughter. I wish your father could see you now. He'd be incredibly proud."

Nicole blinked against an onslaught of emotion. Her mother wasn't normally a demonstrative person. And she rarely spoke of her deceased husband.

"You think so?"

"You're a lot like him, you know. Quiet. Private. He wasn't one to share his thoughts."

Bittersweet pleasure spread through her chest, and she dashed away rogue tears. She *hated* crying in front of others, no matter who it was.

Nicole had been small when he'd died suddenly of heart failure. As her mother's observations sank in, she couldn't help but wonder if things might've been different had he lived.

"Will you tell me more about him?"

Her smile wistful and full of sadness, Alice shared tidbits and stories Nicole couldn't recall hearing. All too soon, Jessica and Jane interrupted, laughing and dripping on the quilt, bits of grass dirtying their feet.

Eager for time alone to process the revelations about her father, Nicole decided to stay behind and soak up another hour of sunshine.

"Don't linger too long," Alice advised, hefting the basket containing their leftover food. "It's nearing four o'clock, and we'll be having supper in a couple of hours."

"All right, Mama."

Alice and the twins left, but she was hardly alone. Other families were enjoying this mid-July Saturday, blankets spread out in the rolling, clover-dotted fields and fishing or swimming in the river. Untying her bonnet, she lay back and tilted it so that her face was shielded from the light. The scent of grass and baked earth filled her nostrils. The longer she lay there, the more the tension she'd been carrying around these past months melted away.

Patrick and Lillian's well-being wasn't solely her responsibility anymore. Shane, Quinn, Lucian and Megan were all willing and able to do their part. She hadn't realized until this moment what a toll their predicament, and her part in caring for them, had taken.

If not for her confusing feelings for Quinn, she could be almost content.

She drifted to sleep replaying their earlier conversation and the feel of his smooth, firm jaw beneath her sensitive lips.

Masculine laughter startled her awake.

Struggling to clear the fog from her mind, she blinked, frowned at the unfamiliar plaid shirt filling her vision. Where was she? The hard ground beneath her clued her in. She'd fallen asleep, but for how long?

A sharp yank on her hair had her gasping.

"Hurry up."

Timothy? What was he—

The glint of a knife blade flashed near her nose, and fear cascaded into her bloodstream. She shoved at the broad chest hovering over her. "Get off me!"

The chest didn't budge. "Hold her down. And make sure she doesn't scream."

That was Kenneth's voice. Was Pete with them? Where was everyone? Why wasn't anyone helping her?

"Hel—"

A rough, sweat-dampened hand smashed her lips together, stifling her plea. Kenneth's face appeared above her. His callous sneer filled her throat with bile. Someone pulled on her hair again until her eyes smarted with the pain.

When large hands clapped onto her legs to still her squirming, Nicole knew true terror. Obviously she'd slept longer than she'd realized and the other folks had already left. Otherwise, someone would've intervened.

She was alone with a man whose wounded pride had obliterated common decency and his cohorts, who didn't think to question him. Up until this moment, she hadn't believed them capable of violence.

Please, God. Thoughts failed her. Passing seconds stretched into an eternity as the men's raucous laughter assaulted her ears.

Kenneth was making a sawing motion with the knife. She braced herself for pain that didn't come.

Suddenly, he leaped off her, a victory whoop filling the air. He was waving something above his head. Her legs were abruptly released. The hand imprisoning her mouth fell away.

Heart shuddering like a frightened rabbit beneath her rib cage, she couldn't seem to force her muscles to move. She lay there on the quilt, frozen. Confused. Dread coated her mouth.

"I cut off the witch's hair," Kenneth chortled. Beside him, Pete and Timothy laughed so hard they bent over, hands on their bellies.

Arms like jelly, she pushed herself into a sitting position. Kenneth noticed. Lunged at her.

"You always did think you were better than everyone else, you little witch," he spit, tossing the black thing on her lap.

She yelped, batted at the thing until she recognized the ribbon attached. The ribbon she'd tied her hair back with that morning.

"My hair!" Hands flying up, she whimpered when she encountered the short, uneven ends. "What have you done?"

Kenneth roughly seized her jaw in his hand, bringing his face near. "You're lucky we didn't scalp you," he growled. "If you breathe our names to another soul, you won't be so lucky next time."

Pete grabbed his arm. "Let's go."

They left her then.

Sick to her stomach, tears streaming down her cheeks, Nicole curled in on herself, comforted by one fact—soon she would leave this town, and she was never coming back.

Emerging onto the boardwalk, Quinn locked the front door with a weary but satisfied sigh. The afternoon had passed in a blur. Without Nicole there to help, the customers had had no option but to deal with him. For the most part, they'd been patient and civil. Perhaps the news of his land purchase had already traveled the town's grapevine and they'd accepted he wasn't going anywhere.

Offering up a silent prayer of gratitude, he set his feet toward Plum's, mouth watering at the thought of Mrs. Greene's yeast rolls slick with melted butter. He was ravenous.

Traversing the dusty street, a bark of laughter from the vicinity of the post office caught his attention. Kenneth and his buddies stood in a circle of about half-a-dozen young men, talking and gesturing wildly. Whatever they were saying evoked a mixture of disbelief and reluctant amusement.

Appetite forgotten, Quinn had the overwhelming urge to see Nicole.

Pivoting sharply, he dodged a horse and rider and strode in the opposite direction, regretting his decision to delay purchasing a horse of his own. He was out of breath by the time he reached her cabin.

It's probably nothing. Better prepare a sound reason for your unannounced visit, he told himself.

Alice opened the door, and the smell of roasted beef

and fried onions hit him, reawakening his hunger. Maybe he could finagle a dinner invitation out of this. Enjoying a meal with his assistant and her family was preferable to a meal alone in the café.

"Mrs. O'Malley." He tipped his head in greeting. "I apologize for dropping by unannounced, but would it be possible to speak with Nicole?"

Behind the spectacles, her eyes crinkled with concern and she eyed the whitewashed sky beyond his shoulder. "She hasn't yet returned from our picnic. I was expecting her an hour ago."

Lassoing his imagination, he forced a calm he didn't feel. "If you point me in the right direction, I'll go and check on her."

"Oh, would you? I was going to send one of the girls once we'd finished in the kitchen."

"Can I borrow one of your horses?"

"Certainly. And once you've brought her home, I'd love for you to have supper with us."

"Thank you."

But satiating his hunger no longer dominated his thoughts. All he could think about was her tormentors, gleefully gloating on the boardwalk.

After fifteen minutes of slow progress through the woodland trail, he reached the clearing. With the faint sound of trickling water riding the gentle breeze, he scanned the verdant landscape. The green fields stood empty. Portions of the riverbank were dotted with willow trees. Drawing closer to investigate, he spotted a hunched, black-clad figure seated at the water's edge.

He breathed a sigh of relief. *See? All that worrying for nothing. She's fine.*

Dismounting, he led his borrowed mount through the

high grass, calling out to her when he drew near. She didn't respond, however, and the bonnet's brim hid her face.

"Nicole?" He stopped directly beside her, unease slithering through him. Surely she wasn't still irritated with him?

He dropped onto the grass, and she shifted slightly away from him.

"What's the matter? Are you upset with me?"

He'd never known her to completely ignore him. Annoyance sharpened his voice.

"Your mother is worried about you."

A small sniffle caught him off guard. She was crying. Sad…not angry. Trying to hide her tears from him.

"Hey." He settled a hand on her shoulder, and she jerked as if prodded with a branding iron. "Okay, you're starting to scare me," he exclaimed. "Why won't you speak to me?"

Gently taking her chin, he urged her head around and received a shock. Her face was ravaged with tears, skin red and splotchy, lips trembling, violet eyes awash in misery.

His heart stopped. "What happened?"

Throat working, Nicole untied her bonnet ribbons with trembling fingers. Then she slowly lifted it from her unbound curls. Curls that had been shorn off to about an inch below her ears.

Without thinking, Quinn reached out and fingered a lock of hair. This hadn't been done using scissors, but with a blunt instrument.

"Kenneth was here." A shudder racked her shoulders. "I fell asleep, and when I woke up he and his friends were holding me down. For a minute, I—I thought they were going to—" She pressed her lips tightly together as more tears seeped out.

Rage, searing and white-hot, seeped into his gut as he pictured the ugly scene.

"Tell me exactly what they did," he managed, fingers shaky as they trailed her cheek.

The account came tumbling out, her terror at finding herself at their mercy tormenting him. He would make sure they paid for their crime. He may not be the law in this town, but he had a different sort of power at his disposal.

Justice was going to have to wait, though. Right now, Nicole needed comforting. And Quinn desperately needed to be the one to give it to her.

With effort, he bottled the burning drive for retribution and worked to gentle his words and touch.

He fished out his handkerchief and wiped the moisture from her cheeks. Her luminous gaze clung to his as he worked, her hitched breaths settling into a more natural rhythm, the trusting nature of her regard nearly felling him. Her trust didn't come easily. That he'd somehow won it humbled him.

When he'd dried her tears, he gingerly fluffed her shiny locks. He gave in to the temptation to explore the silky texture. She watched him with wide, barely blinking eyes.

"This length suits you, you know," he murmured. "It draws attention to your eyes, not to mention the elegant line of your jaw."

A line appeared between her brows. "You're just saying that to make me feel better."

"I have always been honest with you, Duchess. And right now, I can honestly say you take my breath away."

She sucked in air, pink lips parting. "Quinn."

Fingers grazing her cool cheek, he leaned in close and brushed his lips against hers in a light, barely there kiss. Her warm breath mingled with his. A bruising, sweet ache built in his chest. Instead of deepening the kiss as he yearned to do, he wrapped his arms about her, tucking her head beneath his chin, holding her as he'd done in the springhouse. Warming her. Cradling her. Protecting her from his own foolish wishes.

This woman had plans. Plans that had nothing to do with marriage and family. Plans for a new life far from Gatlinburg. And him.

They remained locked in each other's arms until pink streaked the sky and lightning bugs blinked on and off on the opposite side of the river.

She pulled away first. Grabbing her bonnet, she said, "I shouldn't put off going home any longer."

Quinn hurried to his feet, dusting off his pants before extending a hand to her. "I'll take you home, seeing as I have your horse in my possession."

Avoiding his gaze, she nodded, springy ringlets caressing her jaw. He hadn't lied. While short hair wasn't the fashion, it did suit her.

They rode together in silence. Quinn took guilty pleasure in holding her close, his arms looped about her waist as she rested against his chest.

Inside her barn, she repeated her mother's invitation to supper. He declined.

She laid a hand on his arm to forestall his departure. "Don't try and avenge me, Quinn. It'll grow back."

"It goes against my upbringing to allow this type of behavior to go unchecked. They are a danger to you, Nicole. Next time might not be so innocent."

The fury was boiling up again.

"Before you act, think of the store and the possible consequences."

Unable to resist, he stroked her cheek, mesmerized when her lids drifted closed and she wove toward him. When he'd first met Nicole, he couldn't have imagined she'd one day welcome his touch.

"Do not worry about me," he whispered. "Let me handle this my way."

Her expression grew troubled. "Easier said than done."

Chapter Eighteen

He confronted Kenneth first.

Having ridden directly from Nicole's to the jail, he'd told Shane everything and requested his company during the formal visits. The lawman had grimly agreed. Now they stood inside the doorway of the Joneses' home, explaining the evening's events to his dismayed parents.

Kenneth lounged defiantly in the bedroom doorway, arms crossed and a scowl on his face. "That conceited witch deserved it and more," he drawled.

Fists balling, Quinn lunged.

Shane barely caught his arms in time. "Don't. He's not worth it," he growled.

"Go to the barn," Mr. Jones ordered his son.

Clearly unrepentant, he slunk past and slammed the door behind him. Only then did Shane release Quinn.

He plunged a shaky hand in his hair. "I shouldn't have let my emotions get the better of me," he told the couple in a formal tone. "I didn't come here to fight with your son. I came to inform you that he is no longer welcome to do business at my store."

The farmer appeared flustered.

"I understand what the boys did was wrong, but to bar them completely is taking it too far."

"Kenneth and his friends aren't boys," Quinn said "They're grown men who ganged up on a young woman and terrorized her with their actions. What they did wasn't only wrong, Mr. Jones, it was cruel."

"Will he ever be allowed to come back?" the farmer's wife asked.

"Once Nicole has left town, I will reconsider my decision."

The couple didn't attempt to argue the point, but they clearly weren't happy. Shane bid them good night and, no doubt alert to potential problems, stuck close to Quinn as they passed the barn where Kenneth waited.

Mounted on their horses, they headed for Timothy's place.

Though Shane's expression was indiscernible in the lamplight, the warning in his voice came through loud and clear. "You're aware there will be repercussions, right?"

"I refuse to stand by and do nothing."

While Alice had leaned toward asking Shane to bring charges against the trio, Nicole had refused outright. She was convinced Kenneth's bitterness would only grow, perhaps spill over to the twins.

"Look, I understand your motivation. But you're a newcomer. Not everyone has accepted your presence here." Shane bent his head to avoid getting swiped by a low branch. "We still haven't discovered who trashed your springhouse supplies. Barring these young men just might stir up a hornet's nest of trouble."

Gripping the reins with one hand, Quinn lifted the lamp a little higher. "I knew what the consequences might be going into this." Recalling Nicole's tearstained face, his conviction strengthened further. "She's my assistant, and it's my duty to protect her and provide a safe workplace for her."

The lawman was silent for a minute. "You care about her."

"Yeah." He blew out a breath. "Probably more than I should."

"I did tell you there was more to her than what was on the surface."

Quinn had grown to care for her, deeply. He fervently hoped that's all it was. Caring, as for a friend. Not love.

He came here to find a new life. It'd be the height of foolishness to fall for the one girl set on having the life he'd left behind.

Everyone was staring.

Why wouldn't they? She was the only female in attendance with cropped hair.

Of course, her family's pew would be situated in the front of the church, within spitting distance of the reverend's podium. Throughout the service, her exposed neck burned with unseen stares of parishioners behind her. Quinn was back there somewhere.

Quinn, who'd wiped away her tears and held her until her fear melted away. She'd lain awake for hours after he'd gone, reliving those tender moments and yet too cowardly to examine her heart.

In Nicole's arms Victoria stirred. Gnawing on her chubby fist, her lids struggled to remain open as she fought sleep. During those times when Nicole was too busy to visit Kate during the week, she looked forward to services so she could hold the baby. Seated beside her, Caleb reached out and ran a finger along the baby's cheek, a smile of affection easing the sternness of his features. He shot a look of such wistfulness at Rebecca that Nicole fought the wetness springing to her eyes.

For a long time, she'd wondered if her cousin would ever find peace. And here he was, married to a wonderful woman and about to become a father.

When the closing prayer had been said, she reluctantly returned Victoria to Josh's arms.

"Join us for lunch." He cradled his daughter close to his chest. "You can cuddle with this little girl once she's been fed."

Caleb and Rebecca added that they were going to be there, as well. Rebecca looked hopeful. "It's been weeks. I'm dying to hear more about your young friends."

Nicole's attention shot to the rear of the church, to where Lucian and Megan were introducing the siblings to folks. They'd arrived late and so hadn't seen Nicole's chopped locks. Dread soured her stomach.

She hated to think of poor Lillian's reaction. While she was thrilled about their change in situation, a tiny part of her was reluctant to expose them to her "real" life.

"I'll come," she told Rebecca.

"Well, if it isn't the most stylish lady in Tennessee."

A shiver of awareness whispered down her spine and, spinning, she met Quinn's shining eyes. "Hi."

Caleb and Josh took turns shaking Quinn's hand. "Can't thank you enough for what you did for Nicole," Josh said.

Before he could respond, the other male members of her family surrounded them in order to echo the gratitude. Others joined the circle to offer their pledges of support. Not everyone in attendance agreed with his decision, however. Some chose to take the young men's sides. Out of the corner of her eye, Nicole saw the angry glances and scowls directed his way.

When most everyone had trickled down the aisle, Rebecca invited Quinn to lunch.

"I wish I could," he said, "but Claude Jenkins and his wife asked me first."

"Another time, then," Josh said.

"I would enjoy that very much." Quinn addressed Nicole. "May I have a quick word before you go?"

Nodding, she accepted his proffered arm and allowed him to guide her out into the overcast day. They turned in the direction of the cemetery.

Once they were away from prying ears, he glanced at her. "How are you holding up?"

"I'm fine." Belatedly, embarrassed color suffused her cheeks. Focusing on the horizon instead of him, she said, "I apologize for blubbering all over you. I can't believe I overreacted like that."

Quinn halted, silent until she looked at him. Gone was the easy charm. His brown eyes were intent. "Don't apologize. You had every right to be upset."

His nearness proved too much of a temptation. She'd experienced the wonder of being in those arms and wanted to experience it again. She mustn't want or expect such things from him. More importantly, she would be saying goodbye in the not-so-distant future.

For much of her life, Nicole had relied on no one but herself. Whenever she'd been hurt or lonely, she'd escaped those feelings by losing herself in her work. She couldn't start relying on Quinn.

Pulling free, she walked a few steps away to rest her fingers on the cemetery gate, her attention on the procession of weathered headstones. A thick veil of whitish-gray clouds stretched across the sky. The air carried moisture that hinted of an impending rain shower.

"By defending my honor, you've put yourself in a terrible position. I wish you hadn't done that. I could've put up with their presence in the store a while longer."

He joined her at the gate. "My father taught me to stick to my decisions. He said that second-guessing them would foster distrust in my employees." Angling toward her, he gently tugged on a curl. "I did what I thought was right. I'm trusting God to work out the rest."

Quinn's solid faith was yet another quality she admired. Worrying wasn't going to solve anything. Plus, it surely didn't please God. She offered up a silent prayer for help in remembering to trust Him.

"I should go," he said, his reluctance plain as he gazed over his shoulder at the emptying churchyard.

Nicole had mixed feelings. While she would've liked his company at dinner, it really wasn't wise. His incredible gentleness held immense power over her, scattering her defenses like the wisps of a dandelion on the breeze.

Starting off toward the church, she said, "I'm glad folks are beginning to extend the hand of friendship to you. It's about time."

He fell into step beside her. "Your family has made me feel welcome from the very beginning. They're good people." His focus on his polished shoes traversing the trampled grass trail, he observed, "I have a suspicion you'll miss them more than you realize."

Before Quinn's arrival in Gatlinburg, Nicole would've refuted that statement with vehemence. Not now. Her relationship with the special women in her life had altered because she'd risked opening up to them. The move would interrupt that progress.

"You're probably right. However, distance from family and friends didn't stop you from pursuing your goals, did it? You're surviving."

"I am not trying to dissuade you. Simply warning you it's not easy, starting over in a new place all alone."

Her own doubts surging, she stopped midstride. "You don't think I can make it, do you?"

His soft laughter surprised her. "Quite the opposite, my dear. If anyone can make it in the business world, it's you. Not only do you have the mental tools—" he tapped his forehead "—you're passionate and driven. I have no doubt the ladies of Knoxville and beyond will be clamoring to model your clothes."

They parted then, and Quinn's words stayed with her the remainder of the day. As she sat in her living room and added inch-long ruffles to a skirt, she attempted to pinpoint why those words troubled her. While she wanted people to admire her creations and enjoy wearing them, her aim wasn't popularity. She didn't dream of nationwide renown.

What she wanted was to be a successful boutique owner, to consult clients and create fashions that would best suit their coloring and figures, kind of like what she'd done with Nathan's wife, Sophie. A tomboy growing up, the girl had had no one to guide her in the ways of feminine dress or grooming. Helping Sophie transform into a stylish young lady had been one of the most fun experiences of Nicole's life.

She would love to repeat it. To help others achieve their fullest potential.

Couldn't you do that here? a tiny voice prompted. *In Gatlinburg?*

Quinn's disturbing questions that night in the springhouse came rushing back.

Are you sure this desperation to leave isn't a simple case of you running from your family? Your reputation?

Lowering the material to her lap, Nicole stared unseeing at her surroundings. Could he be right?

Squeezing her eyes tight, she tried to will away the unease tightening her midsection. This was her lifelong dream. She couldn't allow petty doubts to derail her plans.

Or the memory of strong arms. Sturdy shoulders to cry on. Quinn calling her Duchess in that cultured accent of his.

"I'm going to Knoxville," she announced to the empty room. "I'm going to open my business. Make scores of interesting friends. And I'm going to enjoy every single minute of it!"

Business was slower than usual for a Monday. On edge and self-conscious about her hair, Nicole kept busy dusting shelves and sweeping the floor of debris. Some of the customers who came in were vocal in their support of Quinn and had gone so far as to express encouragement to her. Those opposed to his actions didn't openly voice their feelings, instead conducted their transactions with pinched expressions and obvious disdain. Through it all, Quinn remained pleasant and upbeat. He treated everyone with respect and civility.

She was going to miss him. A crazy thought considering she'd once dreaded the prospect of working with him day in and day out.

That morning, he'd informed her that her wage increase took effect today. And while she'd wrestled with accepting it, in the end she'd set aside her pride. The more time she spent with him, the more entangled her emotions became.

She'd just finished restocking the sewing needles when the bell above the door announced new arrivals. Looking up to offer a greeting, the words died in her mouth.

Her sister Megan and Lillian were coming down the

outside aisle toward her, goofy grins on their faces. Gone was Lillian's signature ponytail. Her beautiful blond hair had been cut off to match Nicole's length, and it fell in soft waves about her cheeks.

When the girls reached her, Nicole lifted a hand to gingerly touch the short ends. "What have you done?" she whispered.

Megan proceeded to pull off her bonnet, revealing her own haircut. Not as short as theirs, her curls brushed the tops of her shoulders.

Nicole promptly burst into tears.

Lillian's arms came around her, and Nicole rested her forehead on the slender but sturdy shoulder. Megan patted her back.

Then Quinn's distinctive footsteps neared. "Is she all right?"

The grave concern vibrating in his low voice only made her cry harder. More than any other time in memory, she felt deeply cared for.

Pulling herself together, she scooted back and found a handkerchief pressed into her hands. Quinn's, of course. Sniffling, she wiped her cheeks and shot the girls a tremulous smile.

"I can't believe you cut your hair for me."

"We love you." Megan's eyes grew misty.

Lillian waved a hand. "This is nothing compared to what you sacrificed for me. Besides, it takes a lot less time to dry."

Quinn stood watching them, the crease in his brow slowly smoothing. He looked impressed. Proud. And happy for her. Happy that she had friends and family who supported her.

"Lucian was okay with this?" she said, disbelieving.

Megan smiled. "When I explained my intentions, he encouraged me to do it." To Quinn, she said, "He would've liked to come with us, but he's taking Patrick to see Doc Owens."

"You'll let us know what he says, right?" Nicole said, worry mingling with hope the doctor could do something to alleviate Patrick's pain, as well as restore the full use of his leg.

Promising she would, Megan invited them to that Friday's story hour. "Lillian's going to read to the children this time."

"I wouldn't miss it for the world," Nicole said. "You'll be wonderful."

Her friend was blossoming in Lucian and Megan's care. Healthy color had been restored to her cheeks, and happy sparkles replaced the disquiet in her eyes. *Thank you, God, for providing for them. I shouldn't have tried to shoulder their care alone. Forgive me for not seeking Your guidance.*

Quinn slipped away to help a customer interested in the china collection.

Megan sidestepped Nicole to observe the row of fabric bolts on the shelves. "As you know, sis, Lillian could use new clothes. I'm planning to make most of them myself since your time is limited. However, I'd like to hire you to make several Sunday dresses. What do you say?"

Nicole tucked Quinn's now-damp handkerchief in her apron pocket and linked arms with Lillian. "I say that sounds like a fine plan to me."

The younger girl flushed with excitement. "Pink is my favorite color."

Megan dangled a fat ribbon in that color. Snatching the silky length, Nicole held it up to Lillian's hair. "Perfect."

"This is going to be such fun," the younger girl gushed, handling various ribbons.

By the time they'd chosen the necessary articles for Lillian's wardrobe, two hours had passed. Nicole couldn't remember feeling so relaxed around her sister. And she thrilled to see her young friend's excitement.

All those years she'd dreamed of a different life in Knoxville, she hadn't had connections to anchor her here. She would've thought strengthening ties to the people around her would be a positive thing. Only now did she understand how difficult they'd be to sever.

Chapter Nineteen

Quinn honored his promise to escort Nicole to the children's story hour Friday evening, despite the fact he'd rather be drawing out plans for his house. He was both physically and mentally exhausted. Maintaining an upbeat disposition for Nicole's sake, not to mention the constant effort of keeping his distance, had taken its toll. Craving space, he left her in the parlor with the other guests and found his way onto the back porch.

Deserted. Good.

He sagged against the railing and looked out over the rainbow-hued gardens. The rain clouds that had stuck around much of the day had finally dispersed, and water droplets clinging to the petals and blades of grass winked in the evening sun. The pungent smell of moist earth mixed with the sweet scent of the rosebushes hugging the porch.

Roses were his mother's favorite flower. More like obsession. Didn't take much to picture her in the estate gardens, on her knees in the dirt, babying her precious plants.

He missed his family. His mother's latest letter had been filled with nonessential tidbits about friends and business associates. Nothing substantial, like how Trevor was getting along and whether or not Tilly had been accepted in the ballet school she'd set her heart on. Frustrated, he'd penned an immediate response posing those questions and more and, on impulse, bragging about his efficient assistant and lamenting her impending departure. Only after he'd posted it did he realize his mother would likely seize on such information and assume there was more to what he'd shared. Like many mothers, his wanted him happily wed and producing grandchildren.

Instantly, the image of Nicole snuggling with baby Victoria filled his head.

He shook it away. *Nope. Can't go down that path.*

The door opened and closed, and Shane sauntered over, dainty china cup out of place in his big hand.

"Been looking for you," he said.

Turning so that his hip supported his weight, he folded his arms. "As a matter of fact, I've been waiting for you to find me. What did you learn about the stepfather?"

"Simmerly claims they stole from him, and that's why he has persisted in the search." Shane's fingers tightened on the cup until Quinn thought it might shatter. "The man's shifty. My gut says there's more to the story than he's telling."

Quinn had figured as much. "Did you question him about the mother's death?"

He shook his head. "Didn't wanna scare him into bolting."

"What's the next step?"

Glancing at the house, the people mingling beyond the windows, Quinn thought of the vast improvement in Lillian's appearance and overall demeanor in the short time she'd been here. And the doctor had given them hope Patrick's leg could be rehabilitated. Returning them to that monster was not an option.

"I've written to the sheriff and other local leaders near

Simmerly's homestead asking for information. I need to put together the entire picture before moving forward."

The door banged open then, and both men jerked.

Nicole's eyes were huge in her face. "Quinn! I need you. Please hurry."

Closing the distance between them, he took her hands. "What's the matter?"

"It's Carl. He's here, and he's demanding Patrick and Lillian go with him." Her grip tightened to an almost painful degree. "Quinn, you have to do something."

Shane was already striding through the door.

"I promise they aren't going anywhere with him," Quinn vowed.

She looked so distraught he couldn't resist pressing a kiss to her forehead. "Go. Stay close to Lillian. She'll need you nearby while we deal with Carl."

"All right."

Nicole trailed him inside. Although foolish sentiment, he couldn't help being pleased she'd come directly to him for help. Not the sheriff, who was the obvious choice to handle matters. *Him.*

Striding down the hall, he caught sight of Megan and her friends, Cole and Rachel Prescott, calmly shepherding the parents and children out the front door. Loud male voices reached him from the library up ahead on his right. He paused in the doorway to give Nicole a reassuring nod as she continued on to the parlor to where Lillian waited.

Carl's irate voice boomed through the arched opening. "You can't keep them from me. I'm their legal guardian."

Quinn surveyed the room's occupants. Carl stood in the middle, nasty boots dirtying the brilliantly hued rug. Lucian had taken up a post at the window. The New Orleans native looked displeased but surprisingly calm considering his home had been invaded and guests asked to leave.

Shane had parked his large form between the older man and Patrick, who was seated on the far end of the sofa.

Although his features lacked color, Patrick's eyes burned pale fire. "We don't belong to you," he cried, surging forward. "You killed our ma!"

Carl's face turned an ugly shade of puce. "That's an out-and-out lie." To Shane, he said, "Don't believe a word this boy says, Sheriff. He's hated me since the day his ma brought me home. He'll say anything to be rid of me."

Shane held up a hand, the other resting on his gun holster. "You've wasted your time coming here, Simmerly. These kids aren't going anywhere until I've completed my investigation."

Carl's hand sliced the air. "What is there to investigate? I told you they stole from me. Did you search their things?"

"The necklace belonged to my ma." Patrick gripped the cane propped across his knees. "She always said it would go to my sister one day."

"You're lying through your teeth," Carl snarled, took a step toward the boy until he caught himself, seeming to recall there were onlookers.

Quinn had no doubt that if the siblings were ever returned to his custody, they would be in grave danger. Shane obviously agreed. He edged sideways so that he blocked the older man's view of Patrick.

"It's your word against his, I'm afraid. Like I said, I'm sorting through the situation and will let you know what I decide."

"But—"

"In the meantime," he continued, blue eyes flinty, "Lucian Beaumont and his wife have agreed to be Patrick and Lillian's temporary guardians."

"I won't stand for this," he cried. "I'll involve my sheriff—"

"I've saved you the trouble."

Carl's head reared back. "You've contacted Sheriff Davis?"

Quinn's gut was telling him the man wasn't too happy about that bit of information.

"I have. Now, I suggest you start on home before it gets any later."

With a parting glare, Carl made for the exit.

"Oh, and Simmerly?" Shane called out.

"Yeah?"

"Don't attempt to come near these kids again until I've given you permission. Got it?"

He stomped past Quinn, mumbling beneath his breath.

Lucian strode after him. "I'll give him a proper escort off my property."

Shane headed for the door. "I'd better make sure there's no trouble. Lucian's unarmed."

When there were just the two of them, Quinn went and sank into the chair opposite the sofa. "You all right?"

Tension radiated from him. "I won't let my sister go back there. I don't care what I have to do."

Leaning forward, Quinn rested his elbows on his knees. "Did Carl ever hurt your sister?"

"No."

"You're certain?"

"I know her. She swore to me that he'd never laid a hand on her, and I believe her."

"Good." He looked around at the sumptuous furnishings. "You two comfortable here? Are you happy with Nicole's family?"

"They're nice folks."

"Why the hesitation?"

"I'm tired of accepting handouts. Being a burden. First to Nicole. Now Lucian and Megan."

"I'm not an expert, but the way I see it, you and your sister are fulfilling a need in that couple's life."

Patrick's brows crashed together. "What need?"

"They don't have children of their own. They want to share this home and the resources God has given them with others. You two being here has allowed them to do that. So, in a way, you're an answer to prayer."

He could see his words took Patrick by surprise.

Finger tracing the cushion stripes, he said, "I didn't think of it that way."

"Trust me, you're not a burden. Besides, you won't always be on the receiving end. You're still planning on helping me in the store, right?"

His chest puffed out. "Absolutely."

Slapping his knees, Quinn stood to his feet. "See? You'll soon be earning your own money. And ask Nicole. I'm sure she'll tell you I'm a patient and understanding boss."

"Among other things."

Turning, he saw Nicole beside the bookshelves, hands clasped behind her back.

"How long have you been standing there?"

"Long enough."

Patrick struggled to his feet. "I'm going to speak with Lillian."

Nicole's smile was tinged with compassion. "She's in the kitchen with Mrs. Calhoun, who's plying her with pastries. I'm sure they'll be willing to share."

His uneven gait echoed down the hall as he left.

Of their own accord, Quinn's feet carried him over to her. "Naughty girl." He wagged his finger. "It's not nice to eavesdrop."

She kicked up a shoulder. "Patrick saw me. Besides, you weren't divulging intimate secrets."

He chuckled. "Like you would've left if I had been."

"You're right," she cheekily agreed. "I would've stuck around."

Quinn fisted his hands to keep from reaching for her. He'd once asked himself who the real Nicole O'Malley was, confused by the cool composure she often hid behind. His question had been answered. Deep down, she was generous and brave, with a heart desperate to love and to be loved. He saw in her eyes the desire to be accepted for who and what she was.

You can't be the one to love her, he sternly reminded himself.

When she laid a hand on his bare forearm, he inwardly flinched. Her skin was warm and soft. He felt like a drowning man flailing about for a safety net that wasn't there.

"I heard what you said to him," she said softly. "You couldn't have said anything more perfect."

"I'm right, aren't I?" He strove for an even tone. "Your sister and Lucian needed someone to look after. Now they have two."

"Without your intervention, Patrick and Lillian would still be living in that shack. And I—" She worried her lower lip. "I'd still be an outsider looking in at my own family."

She was regarding him as if he was a hero in a storybook, as if he could fix the whole world's problems, and it was a 180-degree change from how she used to look at him. A heady thing, that.

"Nicole…" Her name was more of a groan than anything.

Her fingertips lightly caressed his arm. His gaze dropped to her mouth.

Quinn lowered his head a fraction. She sighed a sigh of surrender. Tilted her chin up.

The front door slamming at the end of the hallway stopped him cold. Footsteps neared.

He'd just stepped away when Lucian reached them. He took one look at their faces and smiled knowingly. "I don't mean to interrupt, but Megan is requesting your presence in the dining room. Seems everyone left before the refreshments were served, and she doesn't want them going to waste."

"We're right behind you," Quinn rushed to say, gesturing for Nicole to go ahead of him. Cheeks a bright pink hue, she followed her brother-in-law without a word.

Glad for the interruption, Quinn lagged behind. Strange, he'd never before suffered this sort of weakness where a woman was concerned. It shouldn't be this difficult to keep from kissing Nicole.

Lord, give me strength.

He was going to need it.

Two weeks later on a Sunday afternoon, Nicole left Megan's house in a daze.

Her first reaction was to find Quinn. How would he respond to her news?

He wasn't in his quarters. She paused on the stairs and surveyed the river and the woods beyond. There was no sign of him.

Determined to speak with him, she paid the Prescotts a visit. She'd seen his new horse following their wagon after services. Maybe he was still there.

Cole answered the door, his adorable little girl, Abby, in his arms. "You missed him. He left about half an hour ago. Is everything okay?"

"Everything's fine. Did he say where he was going?"

Frowning, he stroked his chin. "He did mention his property and plans for a house. You might look there."

"Thanks, Cole."

Hurrying on her way, she ignored the pinch in her toes. She was wearing her Sunday boots, and they weren't exactly meant for traipsing all over town.

The church's bell tower came into view. To reach Quinn's property, she bypassed the white clapboard building and proceeded along the lane leading away from Main Street. She walked slowly, scanning the woods for a sign of him. Unlike her homestead, there wasn't yet a trail leading to the clearing where he'd put up his home.

There. A flash of white. Rapid movement registered, but no sound.

Lifting her skirts, she wound her way past lichen-encrusted tree trunks, avoiding stepping on mushrooms and watching out for exposed roots. When she reached the edge of the clearing, she froze, taken in by what she was seeing.

Fencing foil in hand, Quinn thrust and whirled in a graceful choreography of movement, his expression focused as he battled an unseen adversary. His white fencer's breeches and jacket outlined his taut physique, muscular legs supporting his weight as he parried and swung his weapon. Perspiration glistened on his forehead. His black hair was mussed, strands falling forward into his eyes.

He was magnificent. If only she could watch him square off against a flesh-and-blood opponent.

She stepped into the clearing, and he faltered, head whipping in her direction as he lowered the foil to his side.

"Nicole." Dark brows crashing together, he didn't look particularly pleased to see her. "What are you doing here?"

Fascinated by this sweaty, messy version of her boss, she came nearer. He was winded. That broad chest heaved as he sucked in air.

She dared to touch the thick, white glove covering his hand. "Will you teach me to do that?"

His throat convulsed as he visibly swallowed. "I don't think that's a good idea."

Spinning on his heel, he crossed to a fallen log where he'd left his things and seized a towel, mopping his face with it. His hair stuck up at odd angles.

She really, really liked this version of Quinn. She frowned, not moving from her spot. Problem was, she liked the cleaned-up version of him, too. Her news pulsed in the back of her throat, begging to be shared. Once she told him what she'd learned, everything would change. She wasn't sure she was ready.

Watching him remove his gloves and place the foil in its box, she said, "Why won't you teach me? Because I'm a female?"

"No."

Irritation bubbled to the surface. Ever since their exchange in the library, when Lucian had forestalled their embrace, Quinn had treated her differently. Oh, he wasn't harsh or unkind. Yet there was a distance in his honey-colored eyes that hadn't been there before. A reserve in his conversation that cut her to the quick.

The hurt wouldn't be so deep if he acted that way with everyone. But no. It was just her he'd chosen to freeze out.

Stalking over to him, she poked his unyielding back. "I want to know why you're acting this way. Lately, you've hardly spoken a word to me. You act as if you can't stand to be in the same room with me."

Oh, no. Those weren't tears clogging her throat, were they? She couldn't cry in front of him again.

Twisting sideways, his expression was cool. He said tightly, "I've spoken to you. Of course I have."

"About business. That's it." Fists on her hips, she continued, "With everyone else but me, you smile that charming smile of yours and chat about the weather. You're the suave, too-slick Northerner you've always been. So tell me Quinn, *darling*, what exactly have I done to deserve your disdain this time?"

He matched her stare, posture stiff and hands fisted at his sides, clearly unhappy at being questioned. For long, tense moments, he didn't speak. Nicole struggled to maintain eye contact. Bewilderment, hurt and forbidden longing swirled inside her.

Then, in a move so fast she gasped, he grabbed her hand and placed it over his heart.

"Feel that?" he ground out.

Beneath her flattened palm, his heart thundered against muscle-cloaked ribs. "Y-you've been exercising."

"Your presence is the culprit."

Moving away from her touch, he stepped behind her and, close but not touching, brought his arm around and took hold of her hand. His hot breath stirred her short curls, sending shivers of delight along her skin. She never wanted to move from this spot. Shameful, but true.

"In order to teach you, I'd have to hold you like this." His voice was low. "Do you see the problem?"

Problem? There was a problem?

His jaw skimmed her ear. With a sigh, he released her. Nicole's heart fell. She hugged her middle against the yawning loneliness creeping in.

"I'm sorry," he said behind her. "The reason I've been distant is because I'm having an extraordinarily difficult time honoring my promise to you."

She whirled. "What promise?"

A muscle jumped in his jaw. "I gave you my word I'd provide a professional environment for you. You shouldn't have to worry whether or not you're safe from my advances."

Before she could form a coherent reply—and honestly, was begging him to break his word and take her in his arms the right thing to do?—he continued on.

"I'm drawn to you, Nicole. That's no surprise. It would be very wrong of me to kiss you again when we both know we're not meant for each other. My world is here. I'm convinced this is where God wants me." A glimmer of indefinable emotion shimmered in the brown depths. "And you're meant to follow your dream."

His words arrowed through her, sharp and honest and poignant.

He was a good, good man. Ever her protector, even from this invisible force pulling them together.

"I have to sit down."

He followed her to the log, where she sat and stared at his black boot tips amidst a smattering of blue, purple and orange wildflowers. The July air was sweltering, and yet her bones were brittle with cold.

"You won't have to endure my presence very much longer."

He waited, unspeaking, until she lifted her gaze. He'd gone very still.

"Shane dropped by Megan and Lucian's after lunch with some news. It appears the siblings' maternal grandfather has been searching for them. He'd lost contact with their mother in recent years and, when he learned of her passing, hired a detective to find them. The detective paid a visit to Carl's and let slip that they were due a substantial inheritance."

Brows rising, he dropped onto the knobby log next to her. "Their mother had money?"

"She kept it a secret. Patrick and Lillian were dumb-founded when they heard the news."

"That's why Carl was desperate to get them back. He planned to get his hands on the money."

"The grandfather also hired a lawyer, who contacted Carl and demanded to see the siblings before granting him access to it."

Quinn shook his head in disbelief. "Where is he now?"

"The sheriff there has him in custody while he investigates the murder. The grandfather is planning to travel to Gatlinburg. I'm not sure if he'll try and take them east with him or not."

She frowned, recalling Megan's troubled features. Her sister had grown close to the siblings in a short amount of time, as had Lucian. They would be devastated if they left.

"I hope he lets them decide their future. They've been through a lot." He studied her profile. "So what has this to do with your leaving?"

"Patrick and Lillian insisted they repay me for the supplies. They wouldn't be dissuaded, no matter how much I argued." She tilted her head to return his regard. "With that money, I'll have enough to go ahead with my plans."

He shoved his fingers through his unkempt hair, messing it further. "When?"

"Caleb offered to take me next week to scout out potential shop locations. Once I've decided on one, we'll return to pack up my things. I suppose the timing depends on when the shop becomes available."

Quinn's expression growing earnest, he said, "You've worked hard for this, Nicole. You deserve to get what you want. I'm happy for you."

She drummed up a smile. He was encouraging her to go. What did she expect? That he'd beg her to stay? She didn't want that…did she?

No, of course not. This was her much-thought-about future. The future she'd plotted and planned and coordinated in her mind for years. The one she'd slaved to be able to afford.

"I'm sorry I can't give you an exact date. If you need for me to go ahead and quit so that you can hire someone else, I will."

"That's not necessary." He casually brushed off her suggestion, standing to his feet and gathering his things. "I'll put the word out that I'll need a new assistant soon, but that the start date hasn't been determined. I've already promised Patrick he could come in on the days he feels up to it. He'll be my part-time help."

His nonchalant attitude stung. Her leaving didn't come as a shock to him. Still, expressing a bit of regret couldn't hurt, could it? Something like, *I'll miss you, Duchess.* Or, *I'm not sure how I'll ever find anyone to replace you.*

Don't be absurd. He's clearly fine with my imminent departure.

She'd promised herself she'd leave town with her whole heart intact. She had a sinking suspicion she'd failed to keep that promise.

Chapter Twenty

Thunder rumbled in the distance, and Alice frowned at the darkening sky outside the kitchen window. "Maybe you should stay home."

Nicole laid the sandwich in her lunch pail and covered it with a cloth. "I can't. Quinn needs me. If I hurry, I'm sure I can reach the mercantile before it starts raining."

"You're going to miss that young man, aren't you?"

"I'm going to miss a lot of people," she said over a lump in her throat, impulsively going and hugging her mother.

Last night, her mother had invited Nicole into her room, where she'd taken out a small wooden box containing tintypes of various family members. Nicole had lingered over the portraits of her father, especially, and his mother. Alice had smiled fondly. "You're the exact likeness of Grandmother O'Malley," she'd said.

The resemblance was undeniable. She'd died when Nicole was very young, so she didn't remember her. Alice had offered to let Nicole keep the tintype.

She eased out of the embrace, but not before she glimpsed her mother's concern.

"You don't seem as excited about this move as I thought you'd be. Is something bothering you?"

"Everything is happening really fast, that's all."

In a few short days, she'd be in Knoxville searching for the perfect spot to open her boutique, as well as a place to live. Once her choices had been made, she'd have to say goodbye to her family and friends. She wouldn't be around to see Patrick's progress or visit with Lillian. No more snuggling with Victoria.

"If you're going, you should scoot along," her mother said, interrupting her musings.

A strong gust buffeted the cabin. "I'll see you tonight."

"Be careful."

With the warning lingering in her ears, Nicole hooked an umbrella over her wrist and hurried to the lane. The air was damp and heavy with impending rain, the forest unnaturally devoid of animal life, birds and squirrels likely in hiding. She walked as quickly as she could and reached the short wooden bridge leading into town just as fat raindrops splattered on the ground.

Opening the umbrella, she picked up her pace. Bad weather meant not many customers would venture out. She wasn't looking forward to being cocooned in an empty mercantile with Quinn all day, not after his utter complacency regarding her news. She'd clearly overestimated her importance to him, both professionally and personally. The revelation stung far more than it should.

A crack of thunder rattled the living room windowpanes, and the ground vibrated with its intensity.

Quinn reluctantly tore his focus from the unfinished house plans spread across the kitchen table. Through the window overlooking the river, he could see entire trees swaying in the wind. That didn't bode well.

Tossing his pencil down, he strode into the hallway and threw open the rear door. The store was due to open in half an hour. The low, churning gray clouds made it appear more like dusk than early morning. As the first smattering of raindrops hit the stair landing, he glimpsed a bobbing pink-and-white umbrella in the vicinity of the bridge.

Nicole.

He almost wished she'd stayed home today. Yesterday's scene in the woods still had the power to make his ears burn. He'd been too blunt with her. While he'd spoken the truth, declaring his inner struggles—*showing* her how she affected him—it wasn't conduct becoming of a gentleman.

The wind whipped his hair in his eyes, flattened his pants against his legs.

Quinn wasn't sure if it was this place or the woman bringing about these changes in behavior. He certainly wouldn't enjoy his current pristine reputation if he'd treated the socialites in his circle in a similar manner.

Rain pinged against the landing and bounced up, splattering his boots.

Caught by the wind, Nicole's rose-colored skirts tangled with her legs. Her bonnet strings whipped about her neck. "Hurry up, Duchess," he murmured as the rain intensified.

She was going to be soaked from head to toe if she didn't.

Directly across from where he stood, the limbs of a massive maple tree bowed beneath the onslaught. The river pulsed and swirled between its banks. A wall-shaking rumble sounded directly overhead, and he flinched as a jagged lightning bolt split the purple sky.

Nicole stopped in the middle of the lane, tipped her umbrella and lifted her gaze to the tree.

"No." Quinn didn't attempt to raise his voice. She couldn't hear him above the rain and wind and rushing water. "Don't stop. Get inside." He stared hard at her as if he could will her to obey.

Light flickered in the gloom. Another thunderclap reverberated overhead, followed by an earsplitting crack.

Everything happened in slow motion after that.

The trunk groaned. Snapped. Branches twisted.

The centuries-old tree toppled straight for the mercantile. For him.

The last thing he saw was Nicole's face, frozen in abject terror.

It took several seconds to register what had happened.

One minute she was looking up at Quinn, framed in the doorway at the top of the landing, the next she was watching the tree smashing into the mercantile. The roof had given way. Walls buckled.

A large limb with numerous branches filled the hallway where Quinn had been standing. The section housing his quarters had been crushed. She couldn't even make out where the window had been.

The umbrella slipped from her fingers. Horror locked her muscles into place even as the rain pelted her like sharp stones, dripping off her bonnet's brim.

He hadn't had time to get out of the way.

Please, God, no.

Adrenaline dumped into her system. Screaming at the top of her lungs for help, she scrambled down the grassy bank leading to the river, circumventing the damaged tree base and slipping and falling up the incline to reach level ground. The stairs were no more, flattened beneath the barrel-like trunk. No matter. She would get to him, one way or the other.

He can't be dead. He can't be dead. The refrain poked and tore at her, inciting bone-numbing fear. *Stop it, Nicole. That's not helping.*

"Help! Someone help!"

Edging along the narrow ledge of earth along the building's rear wall, she batted away branches and stepped over thinner limbs to reach what had been the doorway. Glass crunched beneath her boots. Several times, her skirts snagged on jutting log fragments, hampering her progress.

"Quinn!" Unmindful of her hands, Nicole snapped off leafy branches one by one and tossed them aside. "Can you hear me? Quinn?"

Half climbing onto the tree, she squinted into the darkness, steeling herself for what she might find. Heart in her throat, she considered going in there.

"Miss Nicole?"

A small cry slipped through her lips. Startled, she twisted and, through the downpour, saw the bent outline of Mr. Walton from the barbershop. He stood near the building's corner, rivulets of water streaming from his hat. Successive lightning strikes lit up the sky.

"Quinn's trapped," she called. "I need help getting to him."

He nodded. "I'll fetch the sheriff!"

Turning back, she pulled herself entirely onto the trunk. Bark bit into her knees as she inched forward. Juts of wood scraped her palms. Frantic prayers tumbled from her trembling lips.

She eyed the remaining beams overhead. Rainwater leaked through the holes. Would they hold? And for how long?

"Quinn?" she tried again.

When there was no response, she pressed a fist to her mouth and blinked away useless tears. He was probably unconscious. Or unable to hear her over the storm.

The long interior walls looked to be intact, for the most part. There were gaps here and there. Through one she could make out his kitchen stove. Through another she glimpsed a flash of red and white. The checkered curtains.

When she had passed under the doorway, she gulped in air and, gathering her courage, scoured what parts of the floor were visible on either side of the tree trunk.

There was no sign of him.

He hadn't been crushed, then. He'd somehow managed to move out of the way.

Why then wasn't he answering her?

Suddenly, a powerful arm twined about her waist and lifted her clear. A muffled scream lodged in her throat as the unidentified male swung her around and set her on her feet.

"Quinn?"

But the hard blue eyes didn't belong to him.

"Shane." Fingers fisting in his shirt, she brought her face close, her bonnet brim slamming into his Stetson. "You have to find him. He's in there. Maybe hurt. Bleeding." *Dying.* Panic ratcheted up her pulse. "Please."

His hands on her shoulders steadied her. "Breathe, Nicole," he ordered. "Tell me what happened."

In the recesses of her mind, she acknowledged the fact she'd never dared come this close to the intimidating lawman.

"He was standing right here in the doorway when the tree fell. I—I don't see how he could've gotten to a safe spot." Her gaze bounced off the broken logs where his living room had been. "But I didn't see him in the hallway."

No articles of clothing. Nothing.

Shane surveyed the debris. "We need tools, mostly saws and axes. As many as you can get. You'll find what we need at the livery. Walton's already combing the streets for able-bodied men to assist in the search."

"I'm not sure—" She bit her lip. What if she left and

they found him? What if they wouldn't let her see him? What if—

Squeezing her eyes tight, shudders racked her as her imagination called forth disturbing images of Quinn's broken body.

Shane's fingers bit into her flesh, not bruising but enough to ground her thoughts. "Listen to me."

She forced her lids open. The lawman's eyes blazed, but his features held unanticipated gentleness.

"I need you to do this for me, Nicole. Without those tools, we can't get to him."

"I understand." *Help me, Father. I'm drowning in possibilities. Horrible, gut-wrenching possibilities.*

"Good." With a firm nod, he assisted her to the corner of the building before turning back.

Her boots squelched in the mud as she made her way through the driving rain to the livery. The clouds had stalled over Main Street. Thunder rolled through the town, sounding like boulders crashing into one another. Beyond the sound, she heard the faint calls of men sprinting to the mercantile.

The balding, built-like-an-ox blacksmith must've heard the news, for he was dumping tools into a wheelbarrow when she stumbled inside. Smells of horse and damp hay washed over her.

"Mr. Latham."

He didn't spare her a glance. "Give me five minutes."

Five minutes didn't sound like much in the grand scheme of things. But for Quinn, who was somewhere in that broken-down wreck of a store, five minutes could mean the difference between life and death.

Chapter Twenty-One

Something heavy and unmovable pinned him face-first to the floor.

His right shoulder ached clear through to the bone. Pain ricocheted against his skull, and he tried to blink away the misty haze marring his eyesight. His living space—what was left of it—was cloaked in watery shadows. Bits of leaves and bark and spilled coffee grounds littered the wet floorboards. Broken mugs and dishes, too.

By the grace of God, he'd managed to get inside this room, out of the way of the larger tree section. All he had to do now was wait and hope the roof didn't give way.

That final image of Nicole shimmered in his mind's eye, intensifying his discomfort. Not knowing where she was, whether or not she was unhurt, was far worse than any physical pain he had to endure. *Please Lord, let her be okay.*

Shifting his lower body, he tried to dislodge the object holding him down. The bad news? It didn't budge an inch. The good news? He didn't seem to have suffered any major injuries in his legs or back.

Stars danced in his vision. His temples throbbing, Quinn rested his cheek once more against the floor and focused on steadying his breathing. The weight made it tough to fully expand his lungs. As he lay there, he began to make out repetitive sounds above the noise of the rain splattering through the ceiling.

He couldn't identify the source for long minutes. The hammering in his head made it difficult to string thoughts together. *That's it. Hammers.*

Or were they saws?

A male voice called out, followed by a series of replies.

People were out there, trying to get to him.

Was Nicole out there? Or was she lying unconscious on a bed at Doc's?

He had to get free. Had to find her. *Now.*

Gritting his teeth, he braced his palms beneath him and pushed upward with all his might. His shoulder screamed in protest. Beads of sweat popped out on his forehead. Frustration swept over him as the futility of his actions registered.

A familiar voice pierced the fog clouding his brain.

"Shane?" he pushed out, wincing at the breathy weakness of his voice. No way was the lawman gonna hear that.

The minutes crawled by. Quinn wasn't certain how much time passed. The rain lessened to a pitter-patter, and the peals of thunder echoed from miles away. He fought against the need to sleep, no matter that it would bring relief.

"I see him." Shane's excited shout dimly registered.

Rest. That's all he craved…a couple of blessed minutes in the encroaching blackness.

There came a shuffling sound. Boots scuffing against the boards.

"We're gonna get you out of here, friend." A hand skimmed his back.

"Where—" He gulped in air. "Nicole?"

"She's fine. Actually, that's not entirely true. She's making my job nigh impossible."

If Nicole was giving the lawman fits, she really was fine.

Quinn let go of the fear and worry he'd been holding on to. Then he slept.

"Something's going on." Slipping her arm free of Jane's, Nicole craned her neck in an effort to see past the dirt-and-sweat-streaked men sorting through the debris. From her position near the side wall, she couldn't make sense of the increase in activity.

The earth was a muddy morass, the skies a gray, undulating cauldron. Word of the accident had spread like wildfire through the town. A large crowd of onlookers—mostly women, children and the elderly, who weren't directly involved with the search—filled the street and the area beside the mercantile, where she and her mother and sisters waited anxiously.

They'd tried to convince her to go home and change out of her torn and sodden clothes, but she'd refused. She'd also refused to seek treatment for her bloodied, splintered hands. She wasn't leaving this spot until Quinn was located.

Rain-scented wind tugged at her damp hair. "I'm going over there."

Jane protested. "Maybe you should wait—"

"I'm done waiting!"

Weaving around the workers, she reached the place where Caleb had been sawing through the logs. He'd moved to the doorway, attention on someone inside.

"What's happening?" she demanded.

His mouth flattened. Neither he nor the lawman were happy with her almost constant requests for updates. That was okay, because she wasn't too happy with them for not letting her help.

Beneath the irritation, sympathy swirled in the brown depths. "Shane found him."

The world tilted, and she shot out a hand to balance herself against the building, oblivious to the stinging sensations crawling up her arm. "How is he?"

"A little banged up, but he's going to be all right. We just have to free him first."

Something in his voice sounded an alarm.

Free him? Nausea roiled. "I want in there."

"Absolutely not."

"If it were Rebecca in there, would you be content to remain an onlooker?" She glared at him.

Surprise flitted across his face. "Are you saying...you and Quinn—"

"N-no," she sputtered, heat climbing into her cheeks. "I didn't intend to make it sound like— Look, he's more than my boss. He's my friend. I care about him." With deliberate, careful steps, she closed the space between them, looking up at him beseechingly. "I know without a doubt that if our positions were reversed, Quinn would do everything in his power to help me."

He'd already put his community standing on the line for her. She'd no doubt he'd risk his very life for her.

"The building isn't stable, Nicki. I understand how you feel—"

"If you don't let me in, I'll simply find another way."

There were men working to clear the broken glass and logs at the front of the store. She could try there.

One black brow arched. "Or I could throw you over my shoulder and take you home this instant."

Desperation burned in her veins. "Caleb, please," she

whispered, her voice raw. "If you've ever cared about me, you'll let me do this."

Eyes narrowing, his jaw worked.

Claude Jenkins appeared in the hallway. "Sheriff wants you to fetch Doc right away."

"Got it. He headed up front a few minutes ago." Caleb sighed and balanced his saw against the wall. "Try to stay out of trouble, will you?"

"I promise."

Addressing the banker, he said, "Help her inside."

Claude hesitated for an instant before extending his hand. Her legs suddenly like jelly, she concentrated on where to place her feet.

Nicole wasn't prepared for the sight of Quinn's still, prone form facedown on the floor.

Ignoring Shane, whose frown deepened at the sight of her, she fell to her knees beside him and lightly stroked his cheek. "Quinn?"

Behind her, Claude resumed his attempts to saw through the spot where the limb on top of Quinn connected to the larger, thicker trunk.

"He was awake when I found him," Shane said, gloved hands clamped around the limb and lifting up, trying to relieve the pressure on Quinn's back. "He asked about you."

She blinked away tears. Blood matted his hair. The sight of it, along with his torn shirt and more of the sticky red substance soaking through the material, left her insides numb.

"Should I put a compress on that?" She pointed to his shoulder wound.

Strain tightening his features, Shane jerked a nod. "Go easy. He's having trouble getting enough air in his lungs."

With trembling fingers, she peeled the cotton away. The gash didn't appear too deep.

Scanning the kitchen area, she located a stack of cloths scattered across the work surface. She grabbed the one on top. When she dropped down to place the makeshift compress on his shoulder, she noticed his lids fluttering. A groan escaped.

Gingerly smoothing the hair from his forehead, she leaned close. "We're going to get you out soon."

He blinked. Confusion and discomfort lent his eyes a glassy look. "Duchess?"

"I'm right here."

"You wouldn't happen to have a peppermint in your pocket, would you?"

His question elicited a surprised laugh. "Only you would be thinking about such things right this minute."

He licked his lips. "Dry mouth."

"We'll get you water."

An overhead beam creaked and bits of dirt rained down. Shane, who'd been observing them with open interest, eyed the ceiling with concern.

Quinn speared her with an imperious look that no doubt had had his employees back in Boston scrambling. "You should go."

"I'm not leaving."

"I'm your boss."

She gestured to the ruined quarters. "Not anymore," she said gently.

He closed his eyes. "How bad is it, Shane?"

"The building's a total loss. Should be able to salvage some of the merchandise, though."

"What wasn't damaged in the initial accident was probably ruined by the rain," he said, and sighed, eyes still closed.

Claude paused to swipe his sleeve across his forehead.

His cheeks were red from exertion. "I'm about to sever the limb. Be ready."

On his knees facing her, Shane nodded and braced his body. Nicole scrambled to assist. Her hands would pay for this later.

Within moments, they had it rolled off him. Quinn started to push himself up.

"Whoa, there," Shane hurried over. "Maybe you should wait until Doc takes a look at you."

"I'm fine," he panted, easing into a sitting position. "Just light-headed."

His skin was pulled tight across his cheekbones, his lips colorless. Her heart pinched in the face of his pain. *At least he's awake and coherent. His injuries could've been worse. Much worse.*

Offering up a prayer of heartfelt gratitude, she was about to go to him when Caleb appeared in the doorway. He shot Nicole a searching look and, apparently satisfied she was unharmed, sidestepped to allow Doc Owens room to pass.

The cursory examination didn't take long.

"You're a fortunate man, Mr. Darling. I detect no broken bones." To the other men, he said, "Help him to my office so I can stitch up those gashes."

Caleb and Shane assisted Quinn to his feet. Claude waited by the door.

"Come with us," Caleb told her. "Doc will need to tend your hands."

All heads swiveled to her.

Quinn's features sharpened and his brow creased. "What's wrong with your hands?"

"It's nothing."

"Let me see." Despite his weakened state, the command brooked no argument.

Acutely aware of their intent audience, she held them out, wincing at his quiet gasp.

"How?"

Nicole wasn't about to explain that, in her desperation to reach him, she'd paid no heed to the obstacles, had clawed at the branches and broken boards blocking her way. "Doesn't matter."

"I beg to disagree." He started forward, only to weave slightly and put a hand to his head.

"While I admit I'm fascinated by this conversation," Caleb drawled, a twinkle of amusement in his eyes, "I think we'd best concentrate on getting out of here."

Quinn's jaw went taut. "I'll let it drop. For now."

Progress to Doc's house was slow. The crowd cheered and clapped at the sight of him walking out of the wreckage. Disregarding his physical injuries, folks surged forward to offer a word of encouragement or to tell him not to worry about the store. Nicole lost count how many offers of assistance he received.

He patiently responded to each person, sincere in his appreciation. Was she the only one who noticed his increasing pallor? The deep grooves carved on either side of his mouth?

Just when she was about to stomp her feet in frustration, Shane shooed everyone away.

At Doc's, Nicole waited alone in the parlor while Quinn's injuries were tended. He'd sent the lawman and her cousin on their way. And she'd insisted she didn't need her mother and sisters hovering while she waited.

When the unflappable doctor motioned for her to enter the treatment room, she paused on the threshold. She hadn't expected to find Quinn still awake. His hair had been washed, and he wore a clean shirt that was several sizes too big. No doubt one of Doc's.

"I thought you'd be asleep," she said, going to sit in the chair Doc indicated.

"I don't particularly like taking medicine." He followed the older man's movements as he methodically gathered gauze, a jar of white paste and tweezers.

"Put your hands on the table," Doc ordered, lowering his bulk into the chair opposite.

Nicole did as instructed, averting her eyes to a waterfall painting in order to avoid Quinn's scrutiny. She did her best not to flinch. By the time he was finished, she was tempted to toss those hateful tweezers in the river.

Standing with her back to Quinn, she flexed her stinging, gauze-encased hands and wondered how she was supposed to complete her sewing projects on time. Or pack.

When Doc left them to rejoin the cleanup efforts, she trudged to the bed Quinn occupied. Her uncomfortable clothes were finally getting to her. She longed for a hot, steaming bath and her favorite nightgown.

"How's your shoulder?" Nicole said.

"Bruised."

"And your head?"

"Doc sewed up the gash."

Taking hold of her wrist, he tugged her close until her legs nudged the mattress. Against the crisp white linens and mountain of pillows propping him up, his raven hair gleamed and his brown eyes were shadowed. "I'd like an explanation now, please."

In her mind's eye, she pictured him as he'd looked seconds before that tree collapsed. The exhaustion and jumbled emotions she'd been holding at bay rushed in, buckling her knees. It was either take refuge on the bed or land on the floor. She sat down on the edge, the mattress dipping beneath her weight.

Residual fear muddied her throat. "I wasn't thinking clearly. I...needed to find you."

His fingers traced lazy circles on the skin above the gauze. "You were worried about me, Duchess?"

"Yes."

"I was worried about you, too." His expression darkened. "I don't like that you hurt yourself on account of me."

Her gaze freely roamed his face, his dear and familiar countenance, and she wondered how on earth she was going to function without encountering it on a daily basis. Those eyes full of life and humor, the languid, too-confident smile that did crazy things to her equilibrium.

I can't love him, can I? I don't even know what that feels like.

"My reaction would've been the same no matter who was trapped in the store."

That's not entirely true, though, is it?

His fingers stopped their motion. He folded his hands atop the blanket, and she hid hers behind her back, missing the reassurance of his touch.

"Speaking of the store—" she pushed herself up, relieved when her legs held her weight "—I'm so sorry."

His temporary home, along with his business, had been utterly destroyed.

"I can rebuild. Restock the supplies. What matters is that no one was killed."

"I know you're right. Still..." His dream was in ruins. Her heart ached for his loss. "Tell me something. Have you ever regretted embarking on this crazy adventure of yours?"

"Not once."

She gaped at him. "Not even when we were locked in the springhouse?"

"I don't deny there have been obstacles along the way.

This is the biggest one of all. But I'm confident this is where God wants me."

Was she confident Knoxville was where God wanted her? Had she even prayed for His direction?

I can't alter my plans now. What reason could I possibly have for giving up my dream?

"I'll miss you, Quinn Darling," she blurted.

He blinked, dark brows lifting.

Something sorrowful flitted across his face. Surely she'd imagined it.

"Would you like for me to come and visit you? Knoxville isn't that far away, after all."

Quinn visit her? "You would visit an ex-employee?"

"No. But I would visit a friend."

"I would like that very much."

Had he noticed the hitch in her voice? She hoped not. Averting her face, she attempted to gain control of her unruly emotions.

He hadn't said he'd miss her.

He hadn't asked her to stay.

Chapter Twenty-Two

Quinn felt numb inside.

Her admission had rocked him. He'd had to bite his tongue to keep from begging her to stay.

He sternly reminded himself not to be selfish. If his family had tried to talk him out of leaving Boston, he would've been torn, confused and, more likely than not, resentful. He would've left home with mixed feelings and regrets. Thankfully, they hadn't burdened him with that. While they'd expressed their sadness at his leaving, they'd ultimately freed him to pursue his dream.

Asking Nicole to give up her dream wouldn't be fair. And what, exactly, would he be asking? Not only had she made her views on marriage plain, he didn't know how deep her feelings for him went.

She deserved his support and encouragement, and he would give them no matter how much it cost him.

Settling into the pillows, he soaked in her bedraggled appearance, his gaze lingering on her wrapped hands. She must've been terribly upset, and he hated that he'd inadvertently caused her distress. Remaining in this bed while Doc had dug bits of wood out of her tender skin had gone against every instinct. He'd wanted to hold her, comfort her, absorb her pain.

Watching her now, his heart twisted with acute regret. It wasn't difficult to imagine spending the remainder of his days with her, loving her and any children God blessed them with. He disagreed with her summation of her maternal instincts. All a person had to do was watch her interact with her cousins' children to know that she'd be a kind and nurturing mother.

You are not a part of her plan, Darling. And neither is a future in Gatlinburg.

Funny, he'd initially deemed her unsuitable for the role of his wife. He'd had this preconceived notion of a sweet, biddable woman. Someone like his mother, who catered to his father's wishes. Only now did he understand how skewed his thinking had been. He wasn't his father. He wouldn't be content with a relationship like theirs.

Nicole kept him on his toes. He certainly couldn't fathom ever being bored with her. She brought sunlight and joy to his days. Her reaction to his teasing charmed him, and he found himself searching for new and innovative ways to do it. From the beginning, her work ethic had impressed him, and the depth of her generosity was something he hadn't encountered before.

All solid reasons for wanting to marry her, but not the chief one. Plain and simple, he yearned to be the man who poured love into her life, who made her feel special and wanted and needed.

It was a new and unexpected dream, one he hadn't anticipated, one destined to go unfulfilled. Something told him the loss of it would stick with him the rest of his life.

She stopped in her pacing. "I think I should postpone my trip to Knoxville."

"What? Why?"

"You're going to need help rebuilding." At the sight of his expression, she said, "I don't mind waiting a little longer."

Although he hadn't thought it possible, his love for her grew in that moment, making it difficult to speak. "You are not postponing your move. I refuse to be the cause of another delay. It's time you thought about yourself for a change."

The look in Quinn's eyes nearly caused her heart to stop.

No one had ever looked at her with that degree of earnestness before. Having warmth and approval directed her way was a heady thing. Disconcerting, too. Because, as the knowledge of what might've befallen him hit home, she'd accepted how precious he'd become. The idea of him hurting hurt her.

It was a novel experience. For years she'd lived a selfish existence. Afraid of rejection, of not measuring up, she'd closed everyone out and focused on her own wants and desires. For whatever reason, Patrick and Lillian had breached that self-absorbed bubble, and she'd let herself care without reservation. But that was a friendship type of love. Things were different with Quinn.

He'd waltzed into her life, breezing past her barriers and thawing her heart with barely any effort. He'd teased her, pushed her to try new things, comforted her. For the first time ever, she desired someone else's good above her own. She would sacrifice everything if it meant he'd be safe and happy.

Why was she surprised he wouldn't let her?

Quinn Darling was an honorable man. Noble and good.

"That's the thing. I've spent most of my life thinking about myself. It feels good putting others' needs first."

She shook her head. "I'm not sure I can leave with your store in ruins."

"Pray tell me, how could you possibly assist me?" He gestured to her injuries. "I appreciate the sentiment, but there's nothing you can do."

He hadn't said it with the intent to wound her. She knew that. "I understand." Sliding errant curls behind her ears, she edged to the door. "I'll let you get some rest."

He lifted a hand. "Nicole, wait—"

"No. I'm hungry and dirty and too tired to think straight. We'll talk later."

Hurrying outside, she took the long way home, skirting Main Street and the lingering crowds. She shouldn't have worried about Quinn. A determined man, he wouldn't let this setback derail his goals. He would rebuild, and the mercantile would be better than before.

He'd be fine.

He didn't need her anymore.

The following evening, bathed and clad in borrowed clothes, Quinn paid Nicole a visit. After her hasty departure, he'd remained in that bed at Doc's, too drained to deal with either well-meaning townspeople or the damages wrought by the storm. He'd half expected her to come back this morning. She hadn't. And when he'd gone to the site, he'd been disappointed over her absence and oddly disgruntled at having been forced to examine his store's demise alone when he'd have given his right arm to have her beside him. What would she say if he admitted that he'd come to value her practical outlook, her unwavering confidence in his abilities?

Rebuilding would take some doing—many hours of hard labor clearing the rubble, assessing what to scrap and what to keep, not to mention compiling inventory and reordering supplies. He thanked God he had the means available to start over. Not every man in his situation would be so fortunate.

He'd been stunned by the outpouring of concern and support from the townspeople. Claude had organized a cleanup crew, and Quinn had arrived to find men of all ages—including some who'd opposed his barring of Kenneth and his friends—clearing logs and sweeping up the debris. Shane had ordered him off the site the instant he spotted him, insistent he rest his shoulder, at which point Lucian had stepped forward and invited him to stay at his and Megan's house. With his quarters buried and his personal items beyond reach, Quinn had gratefully accepted.

He'd spent much of the day assuring Patrick and Lillian that Nicole was fine. Thinking it best they not witness the mercantile's destruction, Megan had assured the siblings they'd be able to visit her the following day after she'd had a chance to rest.

Strolling along the path to her cabin, he'd passed the vegetable garden when he noticed the barn doors standing open and soft light spilling into the night. He paused to peer inside. His mouth dried at the inviting picture she made. Her hair gleamed, skimming the elegant sweep of her neck. She was dressed more simply than he'd ever seen her in a serviceable black skirt and loose-fitting white blouse. In her arms, she cuddled an adorable rabbit.

Seated on a hay square, she looked up at the sound of his approach, raven brows sweeping upward.

"Quinn. What are you doing here?"

He gestured to the spot beside her. "May I?"

Scooting over to give him room, she eyed the proper sling Doc had bullied him into wearing. "Is your shoulder paining you?"

Constantly, as did the stitched laceration at the back of

his head. Aloud, he said, "It's not too troublesome. The sling is Doc's way of insuring I don't use my arm during cleanup." Reaching out, he petted the trembling creature in her arms. "Who's this?"

Head bent, her fingers—the tips that weren't swallowed up in gauze—followed the path his took. "Puffy. Isn't he sweet?"

He chuckled. "What kind of name is that?"

"Considering he's a puffball, an appropriate one." She lifted her head and smiled. The lavender rings around violet irises were more pronounced tonight, her inky lashes thick and lush.

"I wouldn't have guessed you were an animal person when I first met you."

Kicking up a shoulder, she looked at the horses in their stalls. "Animals don't judge as harshly as people do."

Quinn was silent, continuing to pet Puffy as he pondered her telling words. He hated that she'd felt isolated and unwanted growing up and worried she'd experience the same in a new city. Since his arrival, he'd seen Nicole blossom and flourish, growing closer to her family. A small part of him had hoped the new development would change her outlook on Gatlinburg and that she would reassess her reasons for leaving. A foolish hope, it turned out.

He rested his hand on his thigh. "Are you taking him with you?"

"I'll probably be staying in a boardinghouse for a while. He wouldn't be allowed. Besides, he'll be happier here. The twins will take good care of him."

Standing to her feet, she replaced the bunny in his hutch and faced him. "What I said earlier about staying…I—I don't think it's necessary. You're right. There's nothing I can do at this point to help you." Hands linked behind her back, she rubbed the toe of her boot across the straw-strewn floor. "And since you don't need me anymore, I'm leaving the day after tomorrow for my scouting trip."

He desperately wanted to tell her she was wrong, that he did need her. Instead, he stood and nodded in agreement. "You will come and say goodbye first, right?"

"Yes. Of course."

Moving to where she stood, he cupped her cheek, thumb caressing the satiny skin. Her breath caught. Her eyes were wide and luminous, beckoning him closer, tempting him to pour out all his wishes and regrets.

This would have to be their one and only private goodbye. While she'd planned to return for the bulk of her things and to attend a going-away party, he wasn't sure he'd be able to trust himself to keep his true feelings hidden once he'd experienced her absence. He'd have to keep his distance, no matter that it'd kill him to do so.

"It has been a pleasure knowing you, Duchess."

She blinked, and he thought he glimpsed a tear clinging to her lashes.

His throat grew muddy. "I wish you all the best."

Bending his head, he placed a kiss on her cheek. It wasn't the ending he'd envisioned for them. Dissatisfied, what-ifs pounding at his temples, he let her go.

Chapter Twenty-Three

"I know this is going to sound selfish, but I wish you weren't moving." Lillian removed another blouse from the wardrobe, a wistful air shimmering about her. "Couldn't you open a shop here?"

Nicole clumsily placed the folded skirt in the trunk at her feet. Her hands were sore, and the gauze made it difficult to control her movements.

"I don't think Gatlinburg is large enough to support something like that." She reached for another skirt.

"It's just that you are my first real friend."

Nicole stopped midmotion. "Truly?"

Lillian held the blouse against her chest. "Our closest neighbors were three miles away. We were rather secluded. Patrick and I were all each other had besides Ma."

Forgetting the packing, Nicole settled a hand on her shoulder. "You are my first real friend, too."

Lillian enveloped her in a hug. "I'm going to miss you so much!"

"I'd take you with me if I could," she said truthfully. Pulling back, she inspected the guileless face. "Are you happy at my sister's? You can be honest with me."

Her expression brightened. "Oh, yes! They've made us

feel very welcome. I have free run of the place, even Lucian's study. Not that there's anything of interest in there. I spend the majority of my time in the library."

"And Patrick?"

"He's content. I can tell he really likes and respects Lucian. And Lucian treats him like an adult, which Patrick needs right now. He's felt helpless for so long."

As it often had in the past twenty-four hours, emotion welled up and threatened to spill over in an ugly outburst. "I promise to come and visit you as often as I can. And we'll write letters. Lots and lots of them. You'll be sick of seeing my return address."

"I'll hold you to that."

Lillian's smile was tempered with sadness, eyes bright with unshed tears.

Nicole sniffled. "Back to packing." Waving a hand about the room, she said, "I've lots to do between now and tomorrow morning."

"Right. No more whining."

They set to work emptying her wardrobe. Since this was to be a short trip, Nicole would pack only a few changes of clothes and personal items. The rest of her things she'd take with her on her return trip. Jane came in to help them, conversing easily with Lillian and sharing her and Jessica's plans for the going-away party.

She wished she could stretch out these final moments. All too soon, the supper dishes were cleaned and put away and Megan arrived to escort Lillian home. It was impossible to hold back the tears as she bid her older sister goodbye. Silly, really, when this wouldn't be the last.

She slept fitfully that night, thoughts of the upcoming trip plaguing her. And thoughts of Quinn. He'd worn a look of resignation in the barn last night. For a split second, she'd believed he might ask her to reconsider, and when he hadn't, her capricious heart had actually mourned.

I'll feel better once I reach the city and see with my own eyes the endless adventures awaiting me.

The lack of proper rest did nothing to improve her mood the following morning. As Caleb pulled the wagon to a stop in front of what used to be the mercantile, he remarked on her silence.

"Something eating you?" Beneath the hat's brim, his dark eyes probed hers. "I figured I'd be hard put to keep you in your seat at this point."

"I'm simply fatigued from all the packing yesterday." She shrugged, averting her gaze to the rubble.

She was supposed to be excited. Over the moon. Today was the first day of her new life, after all. Gatlinburg would soon be nothing but a memory.

Instead, her heart felt heavy, weighted with sorrow.

Fiddling with her bonnet strings, she prayed. *Lord, I don't understand why I'm feeling this way. Help me to embrace change. Lead me to my new store.*

Caleb tipped his hat up. "Looks like they're making progress." He squinted at two figures working where the sales counter used to be, digging for salvageable items. "Is that Kenneth and his pa?"

"Surely not."

Caleb hopped off the wagon seat and came around to assist her down. He pointed to the spot where the checker game and stove used to be. "That's got to be Timothy. Can't miss the red hair."

She spotted Quinn the same moment he became aware of their presence. With a word to the man beside him, he quickly picked his way through the site, long strides carrying him across the street. He was still wearing the sling, she was glad to note. He'd heal faster that way.

When he'd reached them, he and Caleb shook hands. "You've got a lot of helpers."

Quinn ran his fingers through his windswept hair. His intense gaze locked onto her face, as if loath to look at anything else. "I was not expecting a turnout like this, that's for sure. I'm grateful for the support."

Nicole dragged air into her oxygen-starved lungs. She could hardly think, trying desperately to imprint everything about him into her memory.

"Is that Kenneth and Timothy?" she forced out.

"It is. All three families came to me yesterday. Your tormentors apologized for what they did to you. They wanted to apologize to you in person." He frowned. "I hope you don't mind that I suggested they write letters instead. I knew you were busy and...I wasn't sure how you would feel about conversing with them face-to-face."

Quinn was intent on protecting her to the very end, was he? How would her life suffer without such a man in it?

"That was thoughtful of you. You were right to suggest such a thing."

A little of the tension holding him rigid seemed to ease.

"And I'm glad you allowed them to assist you," she said. "Why hold a grudge, right?"

He didn't smile, but affection broke through the clouds in the honeyed depths of his eyes.

Caleb cleared his throat and pushed off from the wagon. "I'll be over there talking to Shane."

She and Quinn watched as he sauntered across the street. The ensuing silence bordered on awkward, and she hated the uncomfortable tension stretching between them.

Eyeing the sling, she said, "You're taking it easy, I hope?"

"Following doctor's orders to the letter."

Free hand fisted at his side, he was somber and still,

nothing like the lighthearted boss she'd come to know. But then, he was injured and dealing with the stress of rebuilding.

"They seem to be making fast progress," she said to fill the silence. "I'm eager to see what all is accomplished while I'm gone. Maybe I'll be around long enough to see your new store take shape. Who are you going to hire in my place?"

His gaze was hooded. "I've been talking to a few young men who've voiced interest in the position."

Nicole's relief that he wasn't hiring a female was short-lived. It didn't matter. Eventually, he'd turn his attention to finding a suitable wife. He'd made his wish for a wife and children plain.

What felt like a physical pain dug into her chest and wouldn't be displaced.

"Quinn," someone called. "We need your advice over here."

He twisted and lifted a hand in acknowledgment. Turning back, he clipped out, "I have to go. And you should, too. You've a long journey ahead of you."

Why was he being so distant and formal?

Where was the easy smile?

Swallowing the sudden thickness in her throat, she wrung her hands. "You're right. I'll, uh, see you in a few days?"

"Take care of yourself."

He was going to walk away.

On impulse, Nicole threw her arms around his neck and hugged him tight. He stiffened. Then, after a moment's hesitation, his free arm came around her and crushed her to him. Her entire being rejoiced.

Until he let go and, without another glance, spun on his heel and left her alone.

* * *

The trip was uneventful.

Nicole tamped down her emotions and concentrated on the changing scenery. Beside her, Caleb was quiet, thoughtful, as if in tune with her wish to remain locked in her own confusing world. They reached Knoxville around suppertime. The downtown area near the Tennessee River was bustling with people—young dock workers, professional gentlemen, well-dressed ladies walking arm in arm and peering into shop windows. Wagons and single riders clogged the dirt streets.

She'd forgotten how noisy the city could be. Covering her nose, she attempted to block out the overpowering scent of manure and animal sweat. Above the rooftops was nothing but endless sky. Already she missed the familiar mountain peaks.

Between the occasional jostle of passersby, Nicole gave herself a stern talking-to. This was the fulfillment of a lifelong dream—she was not going to allow minor irritations to detract from that. Besides, Caleb had taken time away from Rebecca to accompany her here. She owed it to him to at least act overjoyed.

He chose a moderate-size hotel that, while not upscale, was clean and respectable-looking. After he'd secured two rooms, they shared a hot meal in that establishment's dining room.

She sipped her lemonade, wondered if Quinn was sitting down to supper with Lucian, Megan and the siblings right then.

"For a small hotel, they provide a fine-tasting meal." She indicated the buttery roll and steak that was surprisingly tender.

Caleb washed down his food with a healthy swig of steaming coffee. His assessing gaze touched on the other diners quietly conversing. The clink of silverware against china provided background noise. "We chose well. Centrally located, affordable and safe. Listen, why don't you retire to your room. I'll inquire about a reputable lawyer who can point us to available properties."

She was tired and would love a chance to rid herself of trail grit. Laying aside her napkin, she dredged up a grateful smile. "Thank you, Caleb. I know you'd rather be at home right now. I appreciate your assistance in this matter."

Concern darkened his eyes, the scar fanning across his temple stretching. "If you've changed your mind, we can leave for Gatlinburg first thing in the morning."

She shook her head. "I owe it to myself to give this a shot."

He studied her a long moment, then dipped his head. "All right."

Leaving him to settle the bill, Nicole retreated upstairs to her room. While not spacious, it was tidy, and a colorful quilt covered the bed. The view from the water-spotted window was one of the wide, murky green river. Boats bobbed in the water and workers scurried about the docks.

She watched the activity for a while before seeking out the water pitcher in the corner. While preparing for bed, her mind was consumed with thoughts of home. What were the twins doing? She hoped they'd give Puffy ample attention. He liked to be held and scratched behind his ears. Lillian was likely tucked into the library chair, curled up with a book. And Mrs. Calhoun was no doubt plying Patrick with treats in an effort to fatten him up.

Perhaps the shop space she chose wouldn't be available for some time. She could return home and spend several more weeks with her loved ones. Maybe even a month or two. She'd be able to see Quinn's new store.

She was about to blow out the lamp when a knock sounded. Caleb filled the doorway, hat in hand, expression confident.

"I located a lawyer, a Mr. John Arthur. The hotel manager recommended him, and I have to say he strikes me as an honest sort. He's going to show us several properties tomorrow morning."

"Wonderful."

He tipped his head to indicate the room. "You all settled in? Need anything before I retire?"

"No. I was just about to turn in when you knocked."

"I'm right next door if you need me."

"Sleep well, Caleb."

"You, too, Nicki." With a wink, he continued along the dim hallway.

The next morning, after a sumptuous breakfast of sausage, bacon and eggs and a stack of johnnycakes, she and Caleb walked to the lawyer's office. Once again, the boardwalk was crowded, the street traffic more than she was accustomed to. After introductions, Mr. Arthur took them to the first shop not far from the hotel. Nicole studied the long, narrow room with a critical eye. It had been used as a barbershop, which made her think of Tom Leighton and Jane and home.

"Not this one."

Mr. Arthur graciously bowed his head and swept them off to a quieter location several streets away from the hotel. Nicole liked the space, but the price was higher than she'd planned to pay.

Caleb's expression was disapproving. "This is too far from the activity. You wouldn't get as many customers here."

The lawyer cocked his head. "I have one other location I think will better suit your needs."

Located close to the river yet a fair distance from the dock entrance, the former millenary shop occupied the corner lot. There was even a view of the water from the front window. Diagonal from her was a nice-looking café called Rose's.

Caleb joined her at the window. "The shops on this end appear to be more upscale. And the customers going in there—" he pointed to Rose's "—look like possible future customers of a boutique like yours."

Nicole turned to the older man. "When is this one available?"

"Actually, it's ready for occupation now. You could set up today, if you were so inclined."

"Today." That meant no waiting period.

Instantly, those final, heart-rending moments with Quinn filtered through her consciousness. Could she truly find the wherewithal to say goodbye to him a second time? Going back, knowing she was leaving again would be too much to bear, she realized.

"I'll take it."

"I'll draw up the paperwork."

Nicole grabbed Caleb's arm. "Can I talk to you for a moment?"

His black brows met over his nose. "Of course." To the lawyer, he said, "My cousin and I are going across the street for coffee. We'll meet you at your office in an hour."

While Mr. Arthur locked up, she and Caleb walked to the café, which surpassed her expectations. The interior was both sophisticated and airy, with embossed cream-and-rose wallpaper and crisp white linens on the tables. The wood floors gleamed. Scents of freshly roasted coffee and cinnamon lingered in the air.

When their coffee and sweet buns had been delivered,

Caleb leaned back in his chair and crossed his arms. "What's on your mind?"

"Since the shop is available immediately, I'd rather not return with you."

She held her breath, waiting for an explosion that didn't come. He blinked. Confusion furrowed his brow.

"I thought the twins were planning a big to-do in your honor."

"It's just in the planning stages and can be postponed for when I visit next." At this point, she couldn't imagine when that might be. It would destroy her to see Quinn moving on with his life, possibly with another woman.

"Don't you want to say proper goodbyes?"

Tears threatened. She crushed the cloth napkin in her lap. "I need for you to trust me on this."

Silence met her statement. Finally, he spoke. "This is your fresh start, Nicki. We'll do it however you want."

Blinking rapidly, she managed a watery smile, grateful he wasn't choosing to be stubborn and challenge her decision. "Thank you."

He picked up the sweet bun. "So, I wonder where we can find a good boardinghouse around here?"

Chapter Twenty-Four

Nicole had been gone a month.

Thirty-one days of battling misery every waking minute. The selfish part of Quinn clamored for control, demanding he go to Knoxville and beg her to come home. That wasn't the man he aspired to be, however. God's Word instructed him to put others' needs above his own. Authentic love didn't seek one's own good above another's.

While his conscience was clear, living without her was the most difficult thing he'd had to do.

Standing behind the wooden counter, Quinn surveyed his new store. Perhaps recreating the original one hadn't been his smartest idea. Everywhere he looked, he envisioned Nicole.

Nicole dusting shelves. Laughing with the old men in the corner. Wrapping up purchases.

A sigh escaped his downturned lips.

He turned to his new assistant, Donald. "I'll be in the office."

The hardworking twenty-year-old looked up from rearranging the jewelry case. "Okay, boss."

Stalking into the office, he slumped into the chair and

extracted the letter from his jacket pocket. The paper was thinning at the creases, a result of his constant handling.

He'd been floored when Caleb had returned without her. Deeply hurt, too. Did he mean so little to her, then? Oh, he knew they'd said their private goodbyes in her barn. And a not-so-private one here on Main Street.

Had she known beforehand? Was that why she'd surprised him with that fierce, almost desperate hug?

As the days had crawled past, he'd come to accept that her decision had saved him. Watching her leave for what he'd thought was a temporary trip had ripped his heart out. He wasn't so sure he'd have been able to retain his dignity if he'd had to do it all over again, knowing it was permanent.

He sniffed the paper. Already her sweetly feminine scent was fading.

At least she'd taken the time to send this letter along with her cousin, explaining her need to seize the opportunities presented.

"Mr. Darling?" Donald hovered in the doorway. "Mr. O'Malley is here to see you."

Hastily returning the letter to his breast pocket, he strode into the front area. Caleb was leaning against the counter.

"Is everything okay with Nicole?" Quinn pushed out. "Has she written to you?"

"Got a letter yesterday, as a matter of fact. She's fine. Business is picking up to the point she's contemplating hiring someone."

His unease evaporated, leaving behind a hollow sensation. "That's good news."

Apparently he didn't sound convincing, because Caleb arched a mocking brow.

"I want her venture to be a success," Quinn said with

more starch. "And I'm glad she's happy. That's what counts."

Caleb grinned.

Okay, time to stop talking.

"The thing is—" Caleb leaned over the counter, lowering his voice "—I'm not so sure she is happy."

"What do you mean?"

"She sounds lonely."

Propping an arm along the silver-and-crystal case, Quinn ignored the compassion squeezing his chest. He'd been afraid of this. *She doesn't need me to rescue her. I'm not her protector.*

"I'm speaking from experience when I say it will take time to adjust and make new friends. Has she found a church yet?"

"She's visited a couple but hasn't decided on one in particular."

"And her lodgings? Is she content there?"

Caleb shifted to let another customer view the contents of the jewelry case. "The proprietress is a kind Christian widow. She's a substitute mother figure for Nicole."

Another customer approached the counter needing help with the fabrics, and Donald was busy packaging vanilla extract. "I have to help my assistant."

With a nod, Caleb waved a small paper scrap. "And I have to gather supplies for my wife."

Quinn considered asking the other man to include his regards the next time he wrote Nicole, but decided against it. He didn't want her thinking he was pining away for her up here in the mountains. Even if that was exactly what he was doing.

With one final glance in the mirror to inspect her hair, which had blessedly grown out enough to brush her shoulders, Nicole went to the door to flip the open sign. Judging from the still, stagnant air inside her shop, it was going to be a scorcher. Her gaze snagged on a man and woman strolling along the boardwalk. With his jet-black hair and her fair good looks, they made a handsome couple. Behind them trailed two young boys, as neatly dressed as their parents, making faces at each other and giggling.

Regret wrapped its tentacles around her and squeezed every last drop of contentment she'd managed to grasp since her arrival. Not that she'd managed much. No matter how many self-directed speeches she made about focusing on her blessings, the distance from Quinn overshadowed everything.

A cold chill seizing up her insides, she rested her forehead against the glass.

I admit it, Lord Jesus. I was wrong. Prideful and foolish. I thought I had my life all figured out, that I didn't need Your direction. I got what I wanted, yet I'm miserable.

She missed her sisters and mother. She missed Patrick and Lillian. She missed her cousins—she wouldn't even mind hearing Caleb calling her Nicki. She missed home.

Oh, her landlady was nice, and she provided tasty meals. There was a charming flower garden behind the house where she could sit and sew in peace.

Business was steady. Already she was having trouble keeping up with the orders for new dresses, in addition to the alteration requests she'd received from both men and women.

Nicole had every reason to be happy. The fact that she couldn't escape this melancholy made her feel childish and ungrateful.

Missing Quinn was normal. He'd been an understanding boss, a wonderful, supportive friend, her protector and avenger. But after six weeks of not seeing him, shouldn't this aching hole in her chest have disappeared by now? Shouldn't the sadness, the desperation to be near him, have already faded?

Forgive me, Lord. I'll get over this soon, I hope. I really am grateful for Your provision, despite the fact I don't deserve it.

Frustrated, she retreated behind the counter to where her brand-new sewing machine was set up, along with an assortment of threads and needles and other supplies. She set aside the dress Mrs. Elizabeth Moore had ordered and reached for the pair of men's trousers that needed hemming. She was in the wrong frame of mind to create something out of nothing. Better to stick with mundane tasks.

Nicole had just finished when the door swished open. Hanging the trousers on the rack beside her machine, she ran her hands along her full skirts and turned to greet the customer.

The words died on her lips.

Quinn, *her* Quinn, was standing inside the door, hat in his hands and looking more handsome than she'd ever seen him. Glossy hair slicked off his forehead, cheekbones stark and pronounced, his hard jaw clean shaven and his light eyes steady on her.

Advancing on wooden feet, she almost pinched him to check if he was indeed real and not a figment of her imagination. "Quinn Darling, you are the last person I expected to walk through my door today."

"I did promise to visit you."

Mouth crooking up at the corner, his warm, soothing voice washed over her in waves of true bliss.

"You *are* real." And he was here, in her store, close enough to touch. Somehow, she restrained herself.

The smile didn't quite reach his eyes. "Did you think you were dreaming?"

Clasping her wayward hands behind her back, she laughed softly, unable to hide her joy. "I'm very glad I'm not."

Oh, the sight of his face was so dear. Precious. Her heart vibrated with unbridled happiness, and she nearly bounced on her toes in giddy excitement.

He nodded, assessing the space, inspecting the shelves on either wall and the two table displays in the middle. Walking past her, Quinn leisurely explored, touching a long finger to this fabric and that blouse. Nicole remained in the same spot, blatantly soaking up his every movement.

Finally, he pivoted and smiled that peculiar, not-quite-happy smile again. "You've done well for yourself. Caleb tells me business has been good."

"Yes. I've been blessed."

Nicole didn't wish to discuss business. She wanted… what? For him to whisk her into his arms and kiss her senseless? To fall on his knees and confess his undying love for her?

"Yes," she blurted aloud.

His brow lifted.

A flush worked its way up her neck even as the truth registered, solidified within her soul. Quinn proposing to her was exactly what she wanted. Looking into his eyes, breathing the same air after too many days apart, it all became clear…why she couldn't shake the sorrow, the jealousy over the mere idea of Quinn with someone else, the envy she'd experienced while observing the family on the boardwalk.

She was in love with him.

Marrying Quinn, building a life and raising a family together—that was her true dream.

Another customer chose that moment to enter her shop. Nicole uttered a distracted hello. A muscle in Quinn's jaw twitched as he dipped his head in acknowledgment of the lady, who made a beeline for the ribbon rack.

Striding over to Nicole, he spoke in lowered tones. "I'll let you get back to work."

"You're leaving?" she squeaked, panicked.

He couldn't leave. He'd just arrived. They'd barely spoken.

"Not yet. I've procured a room." He named the same hotel that she and Caleb had lodged in. His hesitation, indeed his entire reserved manner, was at odds with his usual easygoing attitude. "Would you like to have dinner with me?"

"I'd like nothing better." She gave him directions to the boardinghouse.

"I will pick you up at six o'clock."

Emotions in a jumble, Nicole watched his retreating figure until he turned a corner. Today was going to be the longest day of her life.

Back in her rented room that evening, Nicole chose her favorite outfit, a lilac dress with tiny bows adorning the short sleeves and delicate black lace overlaying the skirt. With it, she paired black lace gloves and a filmy shawl. She wore her curls loose save for a single, sparkly hair clip on one side. Silver earbobs adorned her ears.

Picking up her reticule from the bedside table, she slipped it over her wrist and offered up a silent prayer for calm. The day had dragged. However, she couldn't recall a single exchange. Hopefully she hadn't offended any of her customers with her utter distraction. *Or sewed on the wrong color buttons. Or taken too many inches off Mr. Corelli's trousers.*

Her legs didn't want to support her as she navigated the steep staircase to the lower level. The smell of Mrs.

Keene's pot roast permeated the entry hall. Instead of re-acting with hunger, her stomach rebelled.

How was she supposed to make it through the meal with Quinn studying her with his enigmatic, too-knowing re-gard? What if he guessed her feelings?

They'd both wind up embarrassed, that's what. He hadn't asked her to stay in Gatlinburg. Quite the oppo-site. He'd encouraged her to follow her dream.

He couldn't know her dream had changed. Quinn had affected the change, barreling into her life and challenging her to take risks, to let others see the real Nicole O'Malley.

At the heavy tread of boots to her right, she whipped her head around. The object of her turmoil appeared in the wide parlor archway, elegant and intimidating in his coal-black suit, his dark gaze doing a slow inspection of her.

He let out a soft whistle. "You are…well, words really wouldn't do you justice. Consider me speechless." Clos-ing the distance between them, he lifted her hand and placed a kiss on her knuckles, the heat of his mouth burn-ing through the lace.

At her swift intake, he released his hold and gestured to the wood-paneled door. "Shall we go?"

Passing onto the wide veranda, she chatted nervously about Rose's Café and their mouthwatering beef stew. "Un-fortunately they don't have chicken and dumplings on the menu," she said when they reached the boardwalk. "I know that's your favorite."

Quinn held his arm out to her, and she settled her hand in the crook of his elbow, hard put not to edge closer to his side. The enticing scent of peppermint wafted over.

"I get enough of that at Plum's."

Her gaze flashed to his profile. "You're not staying at my sister's?"

"I decided to rebuild the store pretty much the same

as before. I moved back into the private quarters until my home is complete. The men I hired from Gatlinburg and Pigeon Forge will start work next week."

Although he continued to stare straight ahead, she glimpsed his slight frown.

"Is something wrong?" she ventured. "Have you changed your mind about the property?"

"It's not that." Guiding her around an elderly man walking his dog, Quinn exhaled. "I'm simply wondering if my plans for a large home aren't excessive. After all, what do I need five bedrooms for?"

Nicole bit her lip. Quinn wasn't acting like himself. He seemed distracted and…sad.

Not about to mention his desire for a wife and children, she said, "You'll need them for when your family visits. Have they indicated when they might come?"

Curious about his family, she wondered if she might arrange a trip home at the same time. His sister, Tilly, sounded sweet, and she was curious whether his younger brother was anything like him.

"They are waiting for me to send word. I plan to see how construction progresses before I do."

"I can hear in your voice how much you miss them."

Quinn angled his head to look at her then, his probing gaze making her feel as if she were missing the key clue to a riddle. "Is that all you've deduced in my voice? That I miss my family?"

Mouth working, she stumbled over an uneven board. His free hand shot out to steady her.

"I'm fine," she insisted, cheeks pinking as a trio of younger girls heading in their direction giggled and gaped at Quinn as if they'd never seen a handsome man before.

Quinn didn't repeat his question, and Nicole couldn't help but feel relieved. She despised the strained energy enveloping them, the uncertainty where camaraderie used to exist. Fortunately, the café's pink awning came into view. Surely the delicious fare and relaxed atmosphere would put them at ease.

The hostess on duty recognized Nicole and, with a friendly greeting, led them to a window table in the corner. Quinn pulled out her chair and waited for her to be seated before taking the one across from her. His lean form dominated her vision.

For the second time that day, she was tempted to pinch him. It was still difficult to believe that Quinn Darling was here, close enough to touch yet off-limits.

Constance inquired if they wanted coffee. Out of habit, Quinn accepted for himself but declined for Nicole.

"Actually, I would love a cup," she inserted, laying her reticle on the chair beside her.

With a dip of her head, Constance set off for the kitchen.

Quinn's jaw sagged. "I thought coffee and tea stained your teeth?"

She grinned. "If the amount of hard candy you consume hasn't affected yours then I feel free to indulge now and again."

He tapped his chin, trademark grin bursting through. "About that, I think your boutique would benefit from penny candy. I'm speaking as your former employer and the owner of an extremely successful country store."

"Oh, do you now?"

"Definitely. Not only would jars of penny candy add a splash of color, it would set your shop apart. When a customer is in need of alterations and is deciding where to go, they'll say, 'Hey, that Nicole O'Malley, she has penny candy. I should go there. I'll indulge my love of lemon drops while I wait.'"

"I will keep your advice under consideration, Mr. Darling."

"You're gone for a month and a half and already you're defaulting to formal address?" He shook his head in mock incredulity. "I wouldn't have thought it of you, Duchess."

The coffee arrived then, and, concentrating on stirring in milk and sugar, she attempted to gather her scattering wits. This charming, teasing Quinn was the man she'd fallen in love with, the one she desperately wanted to keep with her forever.

Nicole made it through the meal by plying him with safe questions, anything to maintain light conversation. There were a few hiccups. Like the moments before their pie arrived and she caught him staring, his honey eyes soft.

"What?"

"Your hair," he said quietly, elegant fingers skimming the fork and knife handles against the pristine tablecloth. "It's grown out."

She touched a finger to the ends self-consciously. "More slowly than I'd like, but I no longer receive odd stares."

"Are you sure they weren't stares of envy? In my opinion, you could make most any hairstyle look stylish. I can't say the same for every female of my acquaintance."

"You are very good for my self-esteem."

The memories of Kenneth's prank crowded in, and she was in that field again, Quinn comforting her, making her feel safe and beautiful despite everything. He was the only person she could envision beside her for the remainder of her days, facing life's trials and sharing in life's blessings together.

Could she…*should she* confess her feelings?

And put Quinn in an awkward position? If he'd returned my feelings, he never would've let me go. No, it was better to keep her secret to herself. That way their future inter-actions wouldn't be marked with humiliation.

Heart in turmoil, Nicole struggled to project a casual attitude. Aware she was wasting her scant time with Quinn but unable to alter her feelings, she craved the sanctuary of her room where she'd be free to let the pain out.

She left half the pie uneaten on the plate. Subdued once more, Quinn didn't comment on it. He was quiet during their return stroll to the boardinghouse. Dusk cast a yellow haze over the river. A mourning dove cooed above them. With every step, her heart sank a little lower.

Quinn didn't accompany her to the veranda. Instead, he stopped beneath the leafy bower of a dogwood tree, where they had a modicum of privacy.

"I'm leaving first thing in the morning."

Nicole dug her fingers into her skirts, uncaring she was crumpling the delicate lace. "I understand."

"Donald is a trustworthy assistant," he went on, "but he's not…you."

"I see."

"I'm not comfortable leaving him in charge for very long."

"That makes sense." Her throat was closing up. How many more goodbyes could she take?

Stepping close enough that she could see the pulse point on his throat, which at the moment was quite erratic, Quinn's large hand curved around her nape. She tried to sort the emotions in his hooded gaze and failed. His generous mouth lowered to graze the outermost corner of her lips, evoking shivers of pent-up longing.

He abruptly pulled away, disappointment palpable. "I should go."

"Quinn?" Apparently she wasn't done tormenting her-self. "Will you stop by the boutique in the morning?"

Jaw working, he jerked a nod. Then he was gone.

She gingerly touched the spot where his lips had been. "I'd give all this up in an instant if only you'd ask."

Chapter Twenty-Five

Coming here had been a huge mistake. Massive. What had he been thinking?

Oh, that's right. He hadn't. He'd acted purely on impulse, anxious to see her after too many weeks apart.

Anger focused inward, Quinn didn't immediately return to the hotel. He kept walking until he found himself on the docks. At this time of night, when darkness crept across the sky and the sliver of the moon was already visible, the riverside was practically empty. Boats of all sizes bobbed in the murky water. A handful of late arrivals tied off their vessels and began unloading supplies.

The cool breeze coming off the river pushed his hair into his eyes. Not bothering to fix it, he walked without seeing or caring where he was going.

Dinner was a disaster. He'd had trouble containing his emotions, had been on the verge of pushing his own wishes on her despite what an untenable position that would've put her in. His own uncomfortable state had made her anxious. He'd seen the distress in her beautiful violet eyes and hated himself for it.

He could not come here a second time.

Whenever she visited Gatlinburg, he'd make a point to avoid her.

All he had to do was get through yet another farewell tomorrow morning. No extended speeches, and absolutely no touching allowed. Quick and to the point.

Turning his feet toward the hotel, he took his time returning to his room. The ticking of the clock, along with the dread weighing in his chest, kept him awake until the wee hours. He skipped breakfast. Settled for several cups of bracing coffee before heading to the boutique.

He parked his wagon directly in front, beneath the branches of a solitary tree. Even at this early hour, the streets bustled with activity, similar to those in Boston only on a smaller scale. Was Nicole truly happy here? Did she long for the slower pace of Gatlinburg?

They hadn't spoken of such substantial matters last night, and he wasn't about to bring them up now.

Leaving his hat on the wagon seat, he hurried inside, intent on keeping this meeting brief. Nicole rounded the counter and met him in the middle of the store, fragile looking in the same demure, snowy-white dress she'd worn the first night they met. While there'd been fire in her cheeks and retribution sparkling in her eyes then, today shadows dulled her vitality. Her skin was nearly translucent. Soft and delicate.

He thrust his hands in his pockets. "I came to say I'm proud of what you've accomplished here. It took an extraordinary amount of courage to do what you've done."

Teeth worrying her bottom lip, she nodded. "Thank you, Quinn. Your approval means more than you know."

"You don't need my approval. The success you've achieved through your hard work and determination, aided with God's strength and guidance, is what matters."

Worry lines marred her brow. Hands tightly clasped at her waist, she looked everywhere but at him.

Battling the need to soothe away her tension, to say or do something to evoke that sunshine smile of hers, he edged backward. "I'll write to you."

"I'll write back."

The doorknob dug into his hip. "Goodbye, Nicole."

"Take care," she whispered, arms hugging her middle. "Stay safe."

The bell jingled as he pushed outside, humid air closing in on him, choking him. *Don't look back. Put her needs first. Give her the freedom to follow her dreams.*

He'd reached the wagon when he heard her call his name.

Dense branches providing shade from the overbright sun, Quinn stared as Nicole burst through the door. Rushing to join him beneath the tree, she clutched his arms.

"Take me with you," she pleaded, her eyes wide and earnest.

Confusion roughened his voice. "What?"

"Being apart from you has been the worst kind of torture." Her face turned up to his, he noted the trembling of her full lips. "I miss coming to work and seeing you dip into the peppermint jar. I miss watching you slip an extra scoop of sugar into the widow Weber's sack when you think no one is looking. I miss your scowls at the old checker players when they get too rowdy and the way you inhale Mrs. Greene's biscuits and gravy. I daydream about watching you practice your fencing." Pink flooded her cheeks. "I could do that all day without complaint, actually. I miss so many things about you I'd never be able to list them all. Quinn, I'm miserable without you."

"What are you saying exactly?"

"I'm saying I love you."

Her confession rocked him to the core. He hadn't let himself picture her saying such things to him and was unprepared for the elation bubbling through his system, edging out reason and sensibility. Nicole *loved* him? Wanted to be with him? Images flared in his mind, clear and vibrant images of him and Nicole exchanging marriage vows, moving into their new home behind the church, hosting family dinners…welcoming a baby.

Caught up in the prospect of a future together, he couldn't speak for long moments.

But then the gold lettering of her store sign glittered in the light and the images scattered like dandelion wisps on a stiff breeze.

Gently dislodging her hold, Quinn crossed to the shop's entrance and opened the door, turning to look at her expectantly. Her raven brows crashed together. Unease tightening her features, she preceded him inside haltingly.

"What is it, Quinn?" Pivoting toward him, she held out her hands in appeal. "Is it that you don't want me—"

"Look around you," he bit out, anguish and frustration coursing through him. "I cannot be the one responsible for destroying what you've strived to achieve. Why do you think I didn't ask you to stay in the first place?"

Hope flickered in the luminous depths. "So you did want me to stay?"

"Of course I did." Her feelings for him didn't change anything. The situation was impossible.

"Do you love me, Quinn?"

Nicole held her breath. The courage that had spurred her to run after him and admit her feelings was waning.

Quinn stared at her incredulously. "All I can think about is making you my wife. Does that answer your question?"

Tears blurred her vision, and suddenly he was before

her, his touch featherlight on her shoulders. "My darling Nicole." Tenderness marked his words. "'I love you' hardly expresses what is truly in my heart. You've captivated me from the moment you hit me with that pan." He hooked a curl behind her ear. "You challenge me to be a better man, to look beyond the surface to the person beneath. You make me laugh. You make me want to pull my hair out sometimes, too."

The side of his mouth lifted in a rueful smile, and she matched it with one of her own.

"In short, you make my life richer, fuller, brighter. If you were to accept my hand in marriage, I'd be the happiest man on earth."

"Oh, Quinn." He was saying all the right things, but there was a guardedness in his eyes she didn't trust.

"What worries me more than anything is the possibility you'd resent me later on."

"That won't happen."

"Maybe not tomorrow or a week from now. But months, perhaps years from now, would you be happy with your choice? You wanted to leave Gatlinburg long before I showed up. I'm not convinced you'd be content."

"You're right. For many years, I dreamed of a different life far from there. I didn't seek God's guidance as you suggested earlier. I decided what I wanted, what I thought would make me happy, and pursued it without consulting Him. I've come to realize how foolish I've been." She gestured to the intricate dress she'd designed and created in the window, the colorful fabric bolts lining the walls, her sewing station behind the counter. "The thing about dreams is this—reality doesn't always measure up to your imagination. You of all people should understand that."

"I do. I also know that it's hardest in the beginning. You're just starting out. Until you feel more at home here…

find a church you like and make friends, it's bound to be lonely. That's not a sign that you should give up."

"I don't deny I'm lonely, but that's not what this is about." She had to make him understand. Their future depended on it. "Don't you see? Maybe if I'd never met you, I could be content with this life. But I did, and those weeks with you were the most frustrating, exhilarating, *liberating* weeks of my life. Thanks to you, I felt more at home in Gatlinburg than I did my whole life. I finally felt I fit in. Accepted for the person that I am, not because of my last name or for my sisters' sake." Resting her hand against his cheek, she looked deep into his eyes, letting him see every drop of love and devotion she had for him. "You changed me, Quinn."

The color of his eyes deepened, intensified to dark cara-mel. Reaching up, he cradled her face with both hands. "I want very much to believe you. To trust in us."

"Then do."

Disquiet flashed. "What about your business? You were born with a needle in your hand, Nicole. You can't waste your God-given talent."

"That's the beauty of what I do. I'm not required to have a building to fill orders. I can sew anywhere." She paused. "Remember that night in the springhouse?"

"Are you referring to the night I used the cold as an ex-cuse to hold you in my arms?"

"What? You didn't even like me then."

He hummed deep in his throat. "You just assumed I didn't."

Heady warmth fizzed in her middle. "I admit I reveled in your closeness. It was a new experience for me, lean-ing on someone else's strength."

The pad of his thumb grazing her lower lip, his voice

grew husky. "Get to the point before my good sense fails and I kiss you like I've been tempted to do since I arrived."

Blinking at his bluntness and wishing he'd do just that, Nicole rushed out, "That night, you questioned my reasons for this move. You asked if I was running from my reputation. My family. Oh, I was madder than a hornet at such an outrageous assumption."

Quinn's lips twitched. "Really? I couldn't tell."

"I've had a lot of time to think in recent weeks. You were absolutely right. All those years of planning…I wasn't running *to* something. I was running *from* something."

Slowly, like clouds drifting across the moon, the doubts in his eyes cleared. "And now there's nothing left to run from?"

"Nothing at all."

"This is a lot to take in," he said in mock seriousness. "I may need some convincing."

At the sight of his glorious, mischievous smile, happiness chased away all the anxiety and fear and sorrow she'd been carrying around the past weeks. Going up on tiptoe, Nicole brushed her lips against his.

A shudder rippled through him. "Greet me like that every morning for the rest of my life?"

She smiled, shyness kicking in.

Quinn winced. "I'm not doing this right, am I?"

Releasing her, he dug in his jacket pocket and fished out something small and yellow. A lemon drop.

"Um, that's not what I was after."

Nicole pressed her lips together to hold back a nervous laugh. This moment was a turning point, one that would alter her life. She literally shook from the high emotions humming through her.

Putting the sweet in his other pocket, he went searching again and extracted a silk handkerchief. "This is for you."

She stared at the neat square he pressed into her palm. "Is it a peppermint stick?"

"No."

"A chocolate-cream drop?"

"Not even close."

Gingerly unwrapping the material, she gasped at the intricate ring in the center.

Quinn's smile lit up her world. "It belonged to my grandmother. I've carried it on my person since the day I discovered you alone and upset in that field. That day, I knew you were the woman I wanted for my wife. I didn't know if I'd ever get the chance to give it to you, but I kept it with me just in case. Hoping against hope…"

Taking her hand, he dropped to one knee. "I love you, Nicole O'Malley. Please make me the happiest of men and say you'll marry me."

With a half laugh, half sob, tears of joy skimming her cheeks, she nodded. "Yes. Yes, I'll marry you."

Quinn quickly slipped the ring on her finger and, standing, pulled her close. Adoration glowed in his eyes. "If my proposal is bringing you to tears, we have a problem."

"Oh, do be quiet and kiss me."

He kissed her until the bell dinged and a customer walked in. Lifting his head, he said, "I apologize, madam, but we're closed."

Nicole laughed at the woman's scandalized expression and held up her hand so that her ring was clearly visible. "We're moving locations."

Epilogue

September 1882

"Seventeen years ago today, I welcomed not one but two precious daughters into the world." Standing behind a table where a scrumptious-looking cake and jars of tea and lemonade had been set up beneath the trees, Alice beamed at the crowd. Close friends and family had come out on this pleasant autumn afternoon to celebrate the twins' birthday. "Some people might assume a man would be disappointed at having two more girls added to our brood. Not your father. He fell in love the instant he set eyes on you. If he were here today, I know he'd be bursting with pride just as I am. Happy birthday, my dears."

Whistles and hearty clapping echoed through the yard. On one side of Alice, Jane blushed. On the other side, Jessica smiled boldly, unfazed by the attention. Nicole studied the white dresses she'd designed for them during her weeks in Knoxville, satisfied with the results. Similar in material and outline, Jane's skirt sported a panel of royal blue beneath white eyelet lace, complemented with a ribbon about her slender waist. For Jessica's dress, she'd used forest green. They looked elegant and beautiful.

"Hard to believe they're seventeen." Taking their seats once the noise quieted and Alice began slicing the cake, her older sister Juliana reached up to readjust the pins holding her heavy flame-colored hair. "They seem older than the last time I saw them. Mature young women."

Nicole glanced around at the guests, noting the number of young men watching the girls with undisguised interest. "I have a feeling Mama won't have them at home for much longer."

Juliana touched her hand, deep green eyes frank and approving. "Jane and Jessica aren't the only ones who've changed. I noticed something different about you as soon as we arrived. You're..."

"Less annoying than usual?" Amusement marked her words. "Not as self-absorbed?"

A wide smile softened Juliana's features. "I was going to say content. At peace with yourself."

Conversation filtered around them as people found their seats at the handful of makeshift tables or on thick logs her cousins had dragged in for the occasion. Near the cake table, Kate comforted a sleepy Victoria while chatting with Rebecca, whose large tummy had seemed to drop in recent days.

"It took a while to get to this point."

Too much of her life, she'd depended on others' opinions and treatment of her to dictate how she viewed herself. Now she knew the truth. What counted was how God, her Creator, saw her. According to the Scriptures, she was wonderfully and fearfully made. She was God's beloved child, with her own unique strengths and shortcomings— His prone-to-weakness vessel to be used for His glory.

"I like Quinn. Evan does, too. He's a perfect match for you."

On the far side of the yard, Caleb, Lucian and Quinn

lounged along the barn wall with Evan, Juliana's husband. Their son, James, a mini-version of dark-haired Evan, held tightly to his father's hand and sucked his thumb.

Of course, her attention was all for her fiancé. Watching his animated face, she said, "Quinn balances my serious side. He makes me laugh."

"He makes you happy."

"Yes."

Quinn glanced in her direction and winked, lazy smile and waggling brows promising stolen kisses later. Her heart melted. She could hardly wait until she officially became Mrs. Quinn Darling. Fourteen more days.

"You make him happy, too," Juliana mused, studying their interaction. "That much is obvious."

"I try."

"You don't have to try. You just have to be. Trust me on this. It's plain he adores you, little sis."

"I wish you could move back here."

Longing surged in her eyes even as her ginger brows creased. "Evan and I have discussed the subject. We're praying about it. I've made precious friends in Cades Cove, but it's not the same. I miss my family."

Grateful she'd figured out how important family was before it was too late, Nicole squeezed her sister's hand. "I'll pray about the matter, as well."

"At least we get to stay for your wedding."

"The day can't get here soon enough."

Jessica arrived, balancing three plates, and passed Nicole and Juliana pieces of cake before sitting across the table with her own. "I wish you'd let me at least peek at your wedding dress," she complained before scooping up a bite.

Jane delivered lemonades and headed back for more, stopping briefly to thank well-wishers.

Nicole picked up her fork and repeated the answer she'd given over the past weeks. "You'll see it once I'm finished."

Returning to her seat, Jane sipped her drink. "I've no doubt it will be the loveliest creation you've made to date."

Jessica swept her long ponytail behind her shoulder. Nicole had offered to arrange her hair, but she'd insisted on keeping it simple.

"Well, hurry up. You know I'm not the most patient person in the world."

Juliana laughed outright. "Oh, we know."

Across from her, Jane sighed and scanned the faces as if searching for someone specific. Her shoulders slumped in disappointment.

"What's the matter, Jane?" Nicole had a feeling she knew, but she asked, anyway.

Jessica rolled her eyes. "What do you think? She's pining away for her one true love."

"Who's that?" Juliana swiped a napkin across her mouth.

"Tom Leighton," Nicole said quietly. "He used to own the barbershop."

"Oh. I remember now. Megan mentioned him in her letters."

Silence descended, Tom's proposal to Megan hovering unspoken between them. While Megan had considered him a good friend, she hadn't loved him. Her heart belonged to Lucian. He sold his shop and left town after she turned down his proposal.

Setting aside her fork, Jane gave up all pretense of eating. Nicole's heart broke at the evidence of her sister's misery. Tom had been a friend to the entire family, but he'd had a soft spot for Jane.

"He hasn't written. Not one single letter to let us know he's safe. He knows how I worry!"

Jessica rubbed her twin's back. "I'm sure he's fine, sis."

Jane touched a hand to her elegant, upswept hair. "I thought he'd come home for my birthday. Surprise me, you know? What a fool I've been."

"He's been gone a long time," Jessica said quietly. "Maybe it's time to move on."

Tears glistening, Jane reluctantly nodded. "I think you're right. I've wasted enough time on Tom Leighton. It's time to forget him."

Nicole wondered if Jane truly meant what she said and, if so, how long it would take to get over him.

Nicole's wedding day arrived crisp yet sunny, not a single cloud in the brilliant blue sky. Her cabin had been invaded by every last female in her family. Her mother and Aunt Mary were in the kitchen admiring the two-layer cake, a vanilla-and-cream confection that Jane had topped with chopped peppermints as a nod to the groom's candy obsession. Everyone else was upstairs with her. As if she needed eight people to help her prepare.

Seated at the dressing table, Megan carefully tucked flowers into Nicole's upswept curls, and lighthearted chatter and giggles enveloped her. In the mirror's reflection, Nicole watched Rebecca give her younger sister, Amy, a hug. Sophie and Kate admired the wedding dress hanging in the corner. Jane was trying to convince Jessica to let her fix her hair into something more formal than a ponytail, and Juliana stood quietly by, eyes shiny as she observed all her sisters.

Contentment eclipsed the beginnings of nervous jitters. She was incredibly fortunate to be in this place, in this moment, with people who loved her. And whom she loved in return.

A flurry at the stairs caught everyone's attention. A

slender form with bright blond hair emerged from the opening in the floor.

"I'm so sorry I'm late!" Lillian strode across the spacious room, covering her mouth when she saw what Megan was doing to Nicole's hair. "Quinn is going to swallow his tongue when he gets a look at you."

That startled a laugh out of Megan. "I certainly hope not."

Nicole smiled. "You look gorgeous. Did you get that dress in New Orleans?"

Nodding, she twirled. "Megan picked it out."

Patrick and Lillian had accompanied the couple on their yearly summer trip to New Orleans to visit Lucian's father. All these weeks later, Lillian was still talking about everything she'd seen and experienced. While Carl was in jail awaiting trial, their guardianship had been officially transferred to Lucian and Megan. Sheriff Timmons had assured them that they'd never have to go back to Carl. Their grandfather planned to visit around Thanksgiving, and both were eager to meet him.

"Pink *is* your favorite color," Megan said, affection for the young girl sparkling in her eyes. "Good thing it complements your fair complexion."

Nicole listened quietly as the two spoke of the fashionable shops they'd visited. In a different time, she would've been envious of those shop owners. Not now. She didn't equate giving up her shop to giving up a dream. Instead, she saw it as exchanging it for a new and better one.

A life with the man she loved was what she truly desired, a life made rich with relationships. Quinn had surprised her with plans for an addition to the mercantile. Once they got settled in their new home, he was going to transform the store's private quarters into her very own seamstress shop. He'd also offered to help her design an advertisement for surrounding communities so that she could receive and ship orders and not rely solely on the people of Gatlinburg for business. It was the perfect solution.

"Nicole, are you listening?"

"Oh, sorry. My mind was wandering. What did you say?"

Megan's smile was knowing. "We're returning to New Orleans at the end of this week. I'm not sure how long we'll be gone. Would you mind checking in on Patrick? He decided to stay here and continue helping Quinn at the store."

"You were just there. Why so soon?"

Hope burned in her sister's eyes. "Lucian and I plan to revisit some of the orphanages. We prayed about it and feel God is leading us to go back. We'd appreciate your prayers."

Twisting in her seat, Nicole squeezed her hand. "You have them, sis."

Their mother's voice carried up the stairs. "We have to leave in twenty minutes, girls!"

A flurry of excitement engulfed the room. Nicole was urged into her dress, her sisters fussing over the delicate buttons marching up her back.

"Quinn is not going to like this feature," Juliana chuckled.

She wondered what he was doing right that moment, what his thoughts were, if he was nervous.

Her flaring skirts were fluffed and straightened and a wildflower bouquet was pressed into her hands. And then they were making their way to the awaiting wagon.

Caleb's jaw dropped. Coming around to the front steps, he braced his hands on his hips. "This can't be my little Nicki."

Nerves and anticipation zipping through her, she shot

him a mock glare. "Don't start with me, Caleb O'Malley. It isn't nice to tease the bride-to-be."

Taking her hand, he helped her down the stairs and lifted her onto the seat. "You're right. Besides, you don't look like Nicki today." He waved a hand to indicate her dress. "Quinn is going to have trouble speaking his vows."

"Have you seen him this morning?"

He grinned. "I have."

She gripped the flowers. "And?"

"He seemed calm and focused. And eager to hitch himself to you."

Smiling in relief, she closed her eyes and anticipated seeing her groom while Caleb helped the girls into the wagon bed, where hay squares had been set up and covered with quilts for makeshift seating.

Quinn was thrilled to have his parents and siblings in town. Her nervousness over meeting them had proved pointless. While Edward Darling was a tad intimidating, with his booming voice and authoritative manner, he possessed a kind heart, and Edith Darling had treated Nicole with warmth and affection from the moment of their arrival. Quinn had apparently written glowing letters to his mother, and she was thrilled her eldest son had found love at last. Eighteen-year-old Trevor was even more outrageous than Quinn. Jessica had taken one look at the brash, handsome young man and become instantly smitten. And Tilly was a sweetheart, if a tad superior in her outlook. Nicole couldn't really blame her. Not considering her lavish upbringing and well-to-do friends. Having two protective, doting brothers probably hadn't helped matters.

Lucian and Megan had generously allowed the Darlings to stay with them. The past several weeks, Nicole had been given a glimpse into Quinn's previous life. Much to his dismay, Edith had regaled her with all sorts of stories from his childhood. She was looking forward to visiting his Boston home at Christmastime.

The ride to the church passed quickly. Soon she was being ushered up the stairs and through the doors. The interior was packed, but all that mattered was Quinn.

The piano music swelled. Clasping her uncle Sam's outstretched arm, she took her first step toward her future, toward the man God had brought into her life at just the right time. The moment their eyes met, Quinn's went wide and his lips parted. Frank admiration replaced the initial shock. His honeyed eyes warmed with pride and love, and his mouth curved in a smile that made her feel as light as an air balloon.

When she'd reached the front and Sam joined his wife on the pew, Quinn took her hands in his and, in a swift and unexpected move, placed a quick but searing kiss on her lips.

Everyone in attendance laughed, including Reverend Monroe. "Try to have some patience, young man. We haven't gotten to that part yet."

"My apologies." The twinkle in his eyes belied his words.

Happiness bubbling up, Nicole's smile stretched from ear to ear. With her hands tucked safely in her groom's, they exchanged the sacred vows committing themselves to each other for the rest of their lives. When the reverend pronounced them husband and wife, he said, "*Now* you have leave to kiss your bride."

Soft laughter again carried through the lofty space as her husband pulled her close and kissed her with a tenderness that caught her off guard.

The time of congratulating and opening presents and partaking in refreshments passed in a happy blur. Quinn never left her side. The moment came a couple of hours later when the expression on his face warned he was done waiting to have her to himself.

Leaning close, she whispered, "Take me home now?"

"I thought you'd never ask," he whispered back.

Firmly taking her hand in his, he loudly thanked everyone and urged them to stay and enjoy the celebration. Amid much teasing and clapping, they made their getaway. Their new home, a two-story home built in the same Victorian style as Lucian's but painted a deep green instead of yellow, blended in with the surrounding forest. Her favorite feature was the wraparound porch. She was already envisioning relaxing evenings seated on the porch swing with her husband.

Setting the brake, he came around to her side to assist her. Only, he didn't set her down. Instead, he swept her into his arms and started for the door.

Arms going around his neck, she relished the feel of his strong shoulders and chest supporting her. "You don't have to carry me, you know."

"Yes, I do. The first time you enter our home, I want it to be in my arms."

Opening the door took some doing because he kept stopping to kiss her. Finally they made it inside. When he set her on her feet, she didn't release him, instead using her hold on his neck to pull him closer.

"Alone at last," she breathed, fingers playing in his hair.

Quinn's hands tightened on her waist. Smiling, he dipped his head and explored her mouth in a kiss that branded her as his forever.

"When I saw you today," he murmured, "I couldn't help thinking how fortunate I am. You are the woman of my dreams."

"I know a thing or two about dreams." She cupped his

smooth cheek. "And you're it for me. I love you, Quinn Darling."

He brushed another thrilling kiss across her lips. "I love you, Duchess."

* * * * *

Dear Reader,

If you've read the previous books in this series, you know Nicole hasn't always been typical heroine material. So when it came time to plan out her story, I was a little nervous. Thankfully, I quickly fell in love with the idea of a confident, easygoing hero like Quinn Darling who would delight in teasing Nicole out of her comfort zone. Their journey to love, as well as the topic of closely held dreams and how they can change over the course of time, has been fun to explore.

The twins, Jane and Jessica, will be featured in the next two books. If you'd like more information on my Smoky Mountain Matches series, please stop by my website, www.karenkirst.com. You can also find me on Facebook and Twitter, @KarenKirst.

May your dreams come true,

Karen Kirst

COMING NEXT MONTH FROM
Love Inspired® Historical

Available May 5, 2015

WAGON TRAIN SWEETHEART
Journey West
by Lacy Williams

The hazards of the wagon train frighten Emma Hewitt even *before* she's asked to nurse enigmatic Nathan Reed. Yet the loner hides a kind, protective nature she could learn to love... if not for the groom-to-be awaiting her in Oregon.

SECOND CHANCE HERO
Texas Grooms
by Winnie Griggs

When Nate Cooper saves a little girl from a runaway wagon, the child's single mother is beyond grateful. But can Nate ever let go of his troubled past to forge a future with Verity Leggett?

LOVE BY DESIGN
The Dressmaker's Daughters
by Christine Johnson

Former stunt pilot Dan Wagner has already taken Jen Fox's seat on a rare expedition, and—despite their mutual interest—she's not about to offer him a spot in her guarded heart.

A FAMILY FOUND
by Laura Abbot

As a single father, Tate Lockwood has his hands full with two inquisitive sons. But maybe their headstrong—and beautiful—tutor, Sophie Montgomery, can fill the missing piece in their motherless family...

LIHCNM0415

REQUEST YOUR FREE BOOKS!

2 FREE INSPIRATIONAL NOVELS
PLUS 2
FREE
MYSTERY GIFTS

Love Inspired
HISTORICAL
INSPIRATIONAL HISTORICAL ROMANCE

YES! Please send me 2 FREE Love Inspired® Historical novels and my 2 FREE mystery gifts (gifts are worth about $10). After receiving them, if I don't wish to receive any more books, I can return the shipping statement marked "cancel." If I don't cancel, I will receive 4 brand-new novels every month and be billed just $4.74 per book in the U.S. or $5.24 per book in Canada. That's a saving of at least 21% off the cover price. It's quite a bargain! Shipping and handling is just 50¢ per book in the U.S. and 75¢ per book in Canada.* I understand that accepting the 2 free books and gifts places me under no obligation to buy anything. I can always return a shipment and cancel at any time. Even if I never buy another book, the two free books and gifts are mine to keep forever.

102/302 IDN F5CN

Name	(PLEASE PRINT)	
Address		Apt. #
City	State/Prov.	Zip/Postal Code

Signature (if under 18, a parent or guardian must sign)

Mail to the Harlequin® Reader Service:
IN U.S.A.: P.O. Box 1867, Buffalo, NY 14240-1867
IN CANADA: P.O. Box 609, Fort Erie, Ontario L2A 5X3

Want to try two free books from another series?
Call 1-800-873-8635 or visit www.ReaderService.com.

* Terms and prices subject to change without notice. Prices do not include applicable taxes. Sales tax applicable in N.Y. Canadian residents will be charged applicable taxes. Offer not valid in Quebec. This offer is limited to one order per household. Not valid for current subscribers to Love Inspired Historical books. All orders subject to credit approval. Credit or debit balances in a customer's account(s) may be offset by any other outstanding balance owed by or to the customer. Please allow 4 to 6 weeks for delivery. Offer available while quantities last.

Your Privacy—The Harlequin® Reader Service is committed to protecting your privacy. Our Privacy Policy is available online at www.ReaderService.com or upon request from the Harlequin Reader Service.

We make a portion of our mailing list available to reputable third parties that offer products we believe may interest you. If you prefer that we not exchange your name with third parties, or if you wish to clarify or modify your communication preferences, please visit us at www.ReaderService.com/consumerchoice or write to us at Harlequin Reader Service Preference Service, P.O. Box 9062, Buffalo, NY 14269. Include your complete name and address.

LIH13R

Emma went looking for Nathan.

He stood in the shadows behind the wagon. Alone, just as he'd been since he'd come into their caravan to drive for the Binghams. He watched her approach without speaking.

But there was something in the expression on his face. A wish…

Maybe the same wish that was in her heart.

Stunned that he'd allowed her to see it, he who was usually so closed off, she swallowed hard.

"I need you, Nathan," she said softly, reaching out a hand for him.

He jolted, as if her words had physically touched him.

"The children are restless. Come and tell a story. Please. At least until supper."

And he came.

He settled near the fire, but far enough away to be out of her way. His surprise was evident in the vulnerable cast of his expression when Sam crawled into his lap and rested his back against Nathan's chest.

As she worked with Millie to cook the stew and some pan biscuits, he told of tracking a cougar on a weeklong hunt. Of the winter that another trapper had stolen furs out of Nathan's traps until he'd figured out what was happening. Of losing a favorite horse and having to pack out a season's worth of furs by himself.

"Your beau is so brave, going on so many adventures," Millie said softly at one point, as they began ladling the stew into bowls for the children. "And not bad to look at, either."

Emma looked up to find Nathan's eyes on her. Had he heard Millie? She couldn't tell.

She didn't think quite the same about Nathan's stories of life in the wilderness. Each adventure sounded...*lonely*. His stories reflected that he was alone most of the time.

The isolation would have driven her crazy, she was sure. Not having someone to talk to, to listen to her joys and sorrows...

She regretted the resentment she'd held for her siblings over the trip West. She'd been at fault for not expressing her fears and desire to stay back home. She was thankful she'd come, or she never would have faced her fears.

But more than that, she wanted to give that to Nathan. Family.

Would he let her? Would he let her in?

Don't miss
WAGON TRAIN SWEETHEART
by Lacy Williams,
available May 2015 wherever
Love Inspired® Historical books and ebooks are sold.

*When the truth comes to light about Oregon Jeffries's
daughter, will Duke Martin ever be the same again?*

Read on for a sneak preview of
THE RANCHER TAKES A BRIDE,
the next book in
Brenda Minton's
miniseries **MARTIN'S CROSSING**.

"So, Oregon Jeffries. Tell me everything," Duke said.

"I think you know."

"Enlighten me."

"When I first came to Martin's Crossing, I thought you'd recognize me. But you didn't. I was just the mother of the girl who swept the porch of your diner. You didn't remember me." She shrugged, waiting for him to say something.

He shook his head. "I'm afraid to admit I have a few blank spots in my memory. You probably know that already."

"It's become clear since I got to town and you didn't recognize me."

"Or my daughter?"

His words froze her heart. Oregon trembled and she didn't want to be weak. Not today. Today she needed strength and the truth. Some people thought the truth could set her free. She worried it would only mean losing her daughter to this man who had already made himself a hero to Lilly.

"She's my daughter." He repeated it again, his voice soft with wonder.

"Yes, she's your daughter," she whispered.

"Why didn't you try to contact me?" He sat down, stretching his long legs in front of him. "Did you think I wouldn't want to know?"

"I heard from friends that you had an alcohol problem. And then I found out you joined the army. Duke, I was used to my mother hooking up with men who were abusive and alcoholic. I didn't want that for my daughter."

"You should have told me," Duke stormed in a quiet voice. Looks could be deceiving. He looked like Goliath. But beneath his large exterior, he was good and kind.

"You've been in town over a year. You should have told me sooner," he repeated.

"Maybe I should have, but I needed to know you, to be sure about you before I put you in my daughter's life."

"You kept her from me," he said in a quieter voice.

"I was eighteen and alone and making stupid decisions. And now I'm a mom who has to make sure her daughter isn't going to be hurt."

He studied her for a few seconds. "Why did you change your mind and decide to bring her to Martin's Crossing?"

"I knew she needed you."

Don't miss
THE RANCHER TAKES A BRIDE
by Brenda Minton,
available May 2015 wherever
Love Inspired® books and ebooks are sold.

Love the Love Inspired book you just read?

Your opinion matters.

Review this book on your favorite book site, review site, blog or your own social media properties and share your opinion with other readers!

Be sure to connect with us at:
Harlequin.com/Newsletters
Twitter.com/LoveInspiredBks
Facebook.com/LoveInspiredBooks